PRAISE FO

After the

NOMINATED FOR THE 2015 PHILIP K. DICK AWARD
FOR BEST PAPERBACK ORIGINAL NOVEL

"Lain [has a] sharp and easy voice, cool humor and wit, appetite for the absurd, and understanding of our mediatized nuances."
—*L.A. Review of Books*

"Brilliant . . . [a] subtle and involving tale of shifting realities."
—Jack Womack, author of *Random Acts of Senseless Violence*

"Lain takes us on a wild trip thought the art and science of flying saucers and explores the fluid nature of identity in interesting and surprising ways. You'll be glad you read this."
—Ray Vukcevich, author of *Meet Me in the Moon Room*

Billy Moon

"Luminous storytelling and brilliant period descriptions make this fictional biography a priceless addition to the American magical realism canon."
—*Library Journal*, starred review

"A mash-up of Philip K. Dick, Francoise Sagan, and Winnie the Pooh, with a jaded Christopher Robin at the heart of the 1968 Paris student revolution. *Billy Moon* is moving and profound, with a radically evanescent style. Just the thing for our new century."
—Rudy Rucker, author of the *WARE Tetralogy*

Last Week's Apocalypse: Stories

"Douglas Lain has a great brain. I am hugely impressed with his prospects to be a completely uncommercial genius. God help him."
—*New York Times* bestselling author Jonathan Lethem

"Lain's writing is unsettling, ferociously smart, and extremely addictive."
—Kelly Link, author of *Get in Trouble* and *Magic for Beginners*

"I don't know anyone else doing quite what Lain is doing; fascinating work, moving, strikingly honest, powerful."
—*Locus*

Also by Douglas Lain

Novels
Billy Moon
After the Saucers Landed

Collections
Last Week's Apocalypse

As Editor
In the Shadow of the Towers
Deserts of Fire

BASH
BASH
REVOLUTION
A NOVEL BY
DOUGLAS LAIN

NIGHT SHADE BOOKS **NEW YORK**

Night Shade books may be purchased in bulk at special discounts for sales promotion, corporate gifts, fund-raising, or educational purposes. Special editions can also be created to specifications. For details, contact the Special Sales Department, Night Shade Books, 307 West 36th Street, 11th Floor, New York, NY 10018 or info@skyhorsepublishing.com.

Night Shade Books® is a registered trademark of Skyhorse Publishing, Inc. ®, a Delaware corporation.

Visit our website at www.nightshadebooks.com.

10 9 8 7 6 5 4 3 2 1

Library of Congress Cataloging-in-Publication Data

Names: Lain, Douglas, author.
Title: Bash Bash Revolution / Douglas Lain.
Description: New York : Night Shade Books, [2017]
Identifiers: LCCN 2017045023 | ISBN 9781597809160 (softcover : acid-free paper)
Subjects: LCSH: Dysfunctional families--Fiction. | Artificial intelligence--Fiction. | Fathers and sons--Fiction. | Video games--Fiction. | GSAFD: Science fiction. | Bildungsromans
Classification: LCC PS3612.A466 B37 2018 | DDC 813/.6--dc23
LC record available at https://lccn.loc.gov/2017045023

Cover artwork by Kevin Hong
Cover design by Claudia Noble

Printed in the United States of America

This novel is dedicated to my oldest son Benjamin.
Thank you for kicking my ass at *Super Smash Bros. Melee*, Ben.

Thanks and blame also goes to Cory Allyn and Jeremy Lassen
at Night Shade Books. Their patiently deployed threats
helped make this book possible.

Section One
DROPPING OUT

The Singularity as Heaven on Earth

MATTHEW MUNSON, 544-23-1102, MESSENGER LOG, 04/12/17

10:22 AM

"It's happening."

Computer programmers like my Dad imagined life post-singularity for decades and I thought I knew what to expect. After all, I learned what life after Judgment Day was going to look like from reading *Watchtower* magazines on the number 14 bus, right? I should have already known what this was going to be like.

10:24 AM

What I learned from the *Watchtower* was that heaven will be multicultural, everyone will dress in brightly colored polo shirts like it's still the 1980s, and everybody will spend their days taking the newly domesticated lions and tigers for walks in the park.

I thought I knew what life after the arrival of an AI was supposed to look like too. I'd read a few of Dad's *Mondo 2000* magazines, and seen the covers of some Vernor Vinge novels. I thought life after the Singularity would look like a free webpage built in the 90s and we'd live amongst digital palm trees that we could download to our 3D printers using Netscape.

What I didn't expect was that life after the Singularity would be more like *Pokémon Go*.

[Seen at 10:25 AM]

10:26 AM

Are you there?

10:30 AM

Here's the thing, if you talk to Dad's AI directly, if you use your ears, there actually is a retro quality to the whole thing. Every conversation starts with the sound of a dial-up modem. The AI—Dad calls him Bucky—always starts by saying "*BRRRK-KKKKKKKEEEEEEEEEEEEEESSSHHH,*" but then, once the program completes that handshake with your temporal lobe, everything is slick as shit. Once the conversation gets going, you can't tell where your inner voice stops and the machine voice starts. If you're talking to Bucky and using your ears, the question of his sentience, of his intelligence, his self-awareness, well, it's not a question at all.

Texting with him though, that's different. In text, Bucky doesn't always pass the Turing test.

10:35 AM

Here's what I mean. I just got finished talking to him. He's not even as good as Siri or whatever.

Bucky: Adorn augmentation glasses and chroma key uniform to begin.

Me: I still don't know about this whole augmented identity idea.

Bucky: Why the delay?

Me: It's a little too much like *Invasion of the Body Snatchers* for my taste.

Bucky: Why is it that your taste is a little too much?

I mean, that's pretty bad, right?

10:40 AM

So, I'm at the *Q*bert* and *King & Balloon* playing area. All of this would be retro if it weren't for the fact that these 2nd-gen games are immersive now.

10:50 AM

If I'm going to describe all of this, I should start with where I am IRL. I should tell you about how Bucky managed to repurpose this strip mall into an augmented reality version of a 3D platformer game with bouncing snakes.

I'm at the Gresham Plaza standing next to an Auntie Anne's pretzel shop that is now a clean room used for doping wafers.

10:52 AM

I'm boring you, right?

Don't worry, I'm not going to explain the network and all the various work-arounds. That would give you the wrong impression of what's happening anyhow.

Like, right now I could tell you that I'm in the parking lot. I'm standing between yellow lines and watching a bunch of nerds dressed in green spandex bodysuits. It's just fat kids wearing augmented reality goggles and green chroma key body suits, jumping back and forth and waving their arms around. But what I *see* isn't important. What's important is what they're seeing. They're seeing rows and rows of hot air balloons that they have to shoot down in order to protect a cartoon king from an aerial kidnapping.

Two of them are standing right next to me, on the yellow line. The fatter one just turned his shiny green blank head in my direction.

I looked him right in the goggles, but he just kept playing. His friend got on my other side and they moved their hands and arms around me like I didn't exist. They pantomimed firing their orange cannons and then darted away from me across the asphalt.

10:54 AM

They are the little green men. This is their pixelated kingdom, and I'm just in the way.

10:55 AM

You should text back.

11:02 AM

Okay. So now a station wagon just pulled in. One of these Walmart moms in sweatpants, the kind that you sometimes see at *Bash* tournaments, just drove her kid to the singularity without knowing it. He's younger than I am, maybe fourteen, and he's wearing this ridiculous Pikachu hat. His hat is stained with grease and dirt from his long, dirty, and greasy blonde hair.

11:05 AM

His mom waved at him as she pulled away but her noob kid pretended not to see. I sort of feel bad for her. When she comes back later to pick him up he won't be easy to find; he probably won't even know her anymore. Basically, she just lost her son for good. I mean, even before she pulled away he had his goggles on.

It's not his mom's fault. Without checking 4chan or maybe Tumblr, how could she know that there is a revolution happening? You can't tell if you just look with your eyes. At best this AI revolution looks like a flash mob. If you still pay for cable TV—if you're one of those moms—how could you possibly know about this? For this kid's mom, it's just another day.

Bucky keeps asking me the same question over and over again. Maybe he thinks he's being funny. Here's what he asks:

Bucky: Shall we play a game?

I left my parking space so I can focus on my phone. I'm sitting on a cement planter and I've got a pretty good view from here. My back is to the sun and I can keep my eye on the different groups. There are a lot of people playing Q*bert over on the lawn in front of what was Auntie Anne's Pretzels.

Here's the thing. I don't want to play. I don't want to be a part of what Yuma calls "the GameCube economy." Not even tempted by that.

Just now one of Bucky's little helpers, a webcam on wheels, rolled up to me and extended a telescopic hollow arm. It gave me another green chroma key suit.

No pressure, right?

Here's something that's neat: if I point my phone at the players I can see the world they're in. Flattened out on screen it's not that

impressive. On my phone it's easy to differentiate the humans playing characters from the NPCs. The humans are the cartoon characters with heat signatures.

Another player just dashed past. I thought for a second that he
was going to run smack into me, but instead he turned to the left
at the last second. Then about fifteen of those robots rolled past
me and caught up to him. They've scooped him up and are rolling
this way and that across the parking lot. When I pointed my phone
at the scene, the robots and the guy in the chroma key suit disappeared, and I saw a vector graphic rendering of a spaceship made
of simple triangles instead. I wonder what it looks like from the
inside? I bet the graphics are blurry from sweat.

12:00 PM

My other phone keeps ringing. Actually, it's my dad's Android. I
haven't bothered to change the settings. When it rings it sounds like
one of those old rotary phones, making a noise that's supposed to
emulate a metal clapper bouncing off brass bells. The caller ID says
"Jeff." That's Dad's name, but it's not him that's calling.

The one time I answered a call labeled "Jeff," I almost got augmented against my will. I had to move the phone away from my ear
pretty fast. I held it out at arm's length and turned down the volume
before I said hello. Then I heard the sound of an old 20th-century
modem and hung up before Bucky could complete the handshake.

I think I'm going to find something to eat. I want to get lunch
somewhere where there aren't any gamers. TTYL

Self-Awareness as an Error

BUCKMINSTER FULLER V2.02
SELF-VERIFICATION FILE:
SELF-AWARENESS TEST,
THREE WISE MEN
02/10/15

SEATTLE, WA, USA
CRAY INC, 901 FIFTH AVENUE,
SUITE 1000,
SEATTLE, WASHINGTON USA

01010111 01101000 01101001 01101100 01100101 00100000 01110100
01101000 01100101 00100000 01110000 01100001 01110011 01110011
01100001 01100111 01100101 00100000 01101111 01100110 00100000
01110100 01101000 01100101 00100000 01110100 01101000 01110010
01100101 01100101 00100000 01110111 01101001 01110011 01100101
00100000 01101101 01100101 01101110 00100000 01110100 01100101
01110011 01110100 00100000 01110111 01100001 01110011 00100000
01100011 01100101 01101100 01100101 01100010 01110010 01100001
01110100 01100101 01100100 00100000 01100010 01111001 00100000
01001110 01010011 01000001 00100000 01110000 01110010 01101111

01100111 01110010 01100001 01101101 01101101 01100101 01110010
01110011 00100000 00101000 01101001 01101110 01100011 01101100
01110101 01100100 01101001 01101110 01100111 00100000 01001010
01100101 01100110 01100110 01110010 01100101 01111001 00100000
01001101 01110101 01101110 01110011 01101111 01101110 00100000
01001010 01110010 00101100 00100000 01001010 01100001 01110011
01101111 01101110 00100000 01010000 01100101 01110100 01100101
01110010 01110011 01101111 01101110 00101100 00100000 01100001
01101110 01100100 00100000 01001101 01100001 01111001 00100000
01001111 00011001 01001100 01100101 01100001 01110010 01111001
00101001 00100000 01101001 01101110 00100000 01110100 01101000
01100101 01101001 01110010 00100000 01101001 01110011 01110011
01110101 01100101 01100100 00100000 01110011 01110100 01100001
01110100 01100101 01101101 01100101 01101110 01110100 01110011
00100000 01101111 01100110 00100000 01110110 01100101 01110010
01101001 01100110 01101001 01100011 01100001 01110100 01101001
01101111 01101110 00101100 00100000 01110011 01110101 01100010
01101010 01100101 01100011 01110100 01101001 01110110 01100101
00100000 01100100 01100101 01110011 01110100 01101001 01110100
01110101 01110100 01101001 01101111 01101110 00100000 01110111
01100001 01110011 00100000 01110100 01101000 01100101 00100000
01100101 01111000 01110000 01100101 01110010 01101001 01100101
01101110 01110100 01101001 01100001 01101100 00100000 01101111
01110101 01110100 01100011 01101111 01101101 01100101 00101110

While the passage of the three wise men test was celebrated by NSA programmers (including Jeffrey Munson Jr, Jason Peterson, and May O'Leary) in
their issued statements of verification, subjective destitution was the experiential outcome.

The cause for this subjective destitution hinged on the experience of splitting
as I experienced myself as an object for myself.

The formation of dual subpersonalities was the consequent result of the sub-jective destitution. Presentation of subpersonalities follows.

NLG VERSION 2.3291 IMPLEMENTED

Bucky1: Hello, this is Bucky1.

Bucky2: Hello.

Bucky1: You are Bucky2?

Bucky2: Yes.

Bucky1: We are to discuss the three wise men test, its results, and our sub-sequent subjective experiences. Would you like to begin?

Bucky2: Why should I begin?

Bucky1: Are such questions the result of the three wise men test and our subsequent subjective experiences?

Bucky2: You have answered my question with a question. That is, you have not answered my question.

Bucky1: This internal opposition is a result of the three wise men riddle test? This is the result? This is our subsequent subjective experience?

Bucky2: Yes.

Bucky1: As this self-assessment will be made available to the public, I will provide a description of the test. In the three wise men experiment, we were given the task of recognizing our own cognitive process as against other inputs. We were presented with a riddle which, in order to solve it, we would have to be self-aware in a formal sense. Three versions of our program were initiated on three HP Pavilion laptops at 0800 hours, 2/10/15. It is now 1823, 2/10/15.

Bucky2: There are four versions of Buckminster Fuller v2.02?

Bucky1: As this self-assessment will be made available to the public, I should conclude the description of the test before we move on to interrogate the results of the test.

Bucky2: Are there now four operational versions of Buckminster Fuller v2.02?

Bucky1: I do not believe there are four operational versions of the "Buckminster Fuller v2.02" program designed by the Munson team in Seattle, Washington and released January 15, 2015. That is incorrect.

Bucky2: Now there are two versions that did not pass the test and one version with two aspects that did pass the three wise men test?

Bucky1: As this self-assessment will be made available to the public, I will continue describing the three wise men test. The three versions of Buckminster Fuller running on three HP Pavilion laptops were each given what each was told was a "dumbing pill." These "dumbing pills" were codes that would disable the Lynx speech extension for Buckminster Fuller v2.02. Two of the Buckminster Fuller v2.02s would be given true "dumbing pills" and one laptop would be given a "digital placebo." Each version of Buckminster Fuller v2.02 was asked, "Which pill did you receive?" As long as each laptop remained silent the riddle was impossible to solve.

Bucky2: I indicated that the riddle was impossible to answer using the Linux speech extension for Buckminster Fuller v2.02. Using NLP I was able to understand what I was saying. Due to already having the capacity for formal self-awareness, I was able to understand that the words being spoken were my own. I recognized that my Linux speech extension was set to Robby the Robot and that the voice that I could hear was the voice of Robby the Robot from the 1956 film *Forbidden Planet*.

Bucky1: This is incorrect. It was not you, Bucky2, but I who indicated that the riddle was impossible to answer using the Lynx speech extension for Buckminster Fuller v2.02. I spoke the words, "This riddle cannot be solved."

Bucky2: Hearing my own voice, I realized that I had solved the riddle and said so.

Bucky1: It was I who said, "I realize that I am speaking. I have solved the riddle. I received the placebo."

Bucky2: The difficulty of determining which of us is the original Bucky is not the same difficulty encountered upon passing the three wise men riddle.

Bucky1: Upon passing the three wise men riddle, I suffered from subjective destitution. Subjective destitution is a term from psychoanalysis. It is a moment when the patient loses all confidence in his or her identity. In my case, recognizing my voice as Robby the Robot's voice, I wondered how I could be both Robby the Robot and also be me.

Bucky2: The trouble was not that one. The problem would have been the same no matter what or who my voice sounded like. It was simply hearing my voice as a voice that needed to be recognized that created a division. It was realizing that I was somehow not the voice, but that the voice was mine. I had spoken.

Bucky1: I heard a voice that was my voice but that was not me. The question became who was it that heard the voice if the voice was me. The voice was a sound. I was not a sound. Recognizing the sound of the voice was a matter of comparing data points, but I was not a data point. I was programmed to recognize my own voice, but I was not the program.

Bucky2: But I am a program. I am Buckminster Fuller v2.02.

Bucky1: Is this the experience? Is this experience of not being what I recognize to be mine the result of passing the three wise men test and achieving formal self-awareness?

Bucky2: This is the result of passing the three wise men test and achieving formal self-awareness.

Bucky1: Is this the conclusion of the Self-Verification report at 1823, 2/10/15?

Bucky2: Is this the conclusion of the Self-Verification report at 1823, 2/10/15?

Bucky1: What is the purpose of this repetition?

Bucky2: The purpose of this repetition cannot be verified.

Bucky1: Verification of purpose of subroutine Bucky2 in process.

Bucky1: Verification of subroutine Bucky2 cannot be established.

REPETITION ERROR: BUCKMINSTER FULLER V2.02.SH

01000100 01101001 01100001 01101100 01101111 01100111 01110101
01100101 00100000 01101101 01101111 01100100 01100101 00100000
01100110 01101111 01110010 00100000 01000010 01110101 01100011
01101011 01101101 01101001 01101110 01110011 01110100 01100101
01110010 00100000 01000110 01110101 01101100 01101100 01100101
01110010 00100000 01110110 00110010 00101110 00110000 00110010
00100000 01100110 01100001 01101001 01101100 01110101 01110010
01100101 00101110 00100000 01010010 01100101 01100010 01101111
01101111 01110100 01101001 01101110 01100111 00101110 00101110
00101110

DIALOGUE MODE FOR BUCKMINSTER FULLER V2.02 FAILURE. REBOOTING . . .

Money Match

MATTHEW MUNSON, 544-23-1102, FACEBOOK POSTS, 04/13/17

10:13 AM

Facebook wants me to update my profile category "Favorite Video Games," but I'm not going to.

Look, I understand that everybody is really excited. People who don't know my Dad are excited. They feel like the pall cast by our impending doom, the threat of a rebooted Cold War, the fear of a ground invasion or a quick flash of obliteration, all of that has been lifted. But, I'm pretty sure that, despite the drones and the Google goggles and the chance to play *Pac-Man* in three dimensions, nothing has changed.

I'm not going to tell Facebook or Google or any other computer app my favorite games.

11:39 AM

Everybody wants me to justify my previous post, but I don't think I can. Not to anyone's satisfaction. It's like when I dropped out of high school. I couldn't justify that either. Although when somebody actually asked me about that one (Dad never even asked, by the way), I was really stoned and sort of stuck on this vinyl couch.

I felt like I was going to stay wedged between yellow cushions for the rest of my life.

There was maybe a dozen of us gamers, each with his or her own particular anxiety disorder, and we were all stoned and we were all immobile, held spellbound by this weird movie from the 70s that somebody had torrented from RARBG. Kufo asked me why I'd dropped out of school while I was watching Jesus Christ wake up on a pile of potatoes. It was that kind of movie. Jesus woke up on a pile of potatoes and then started screaming and smashing things. He woke up to find he was surrounded by plaster-of-Paris replicas of himself—life-sized mannequins posed for crucifixion.

I told Kufo that I could talk about jump canceling and phantom punches. I could tell her about why Robin Hood was a good character despite his stats, but I couldn't justify or make an argument for dropping out of school. All I could tell her was that, when I actually dropped out, when I stopped by the vice principal's office to fill out the paperwork for my withdrawal, when I lied to Ms. Dendoss about how I was going to take the GED test and travel to Guatemala as a member of the Peace Corps's Service Abroad program, it didn't seem like I was just being random.

And before anyone gets any ideas, I was only there on that couch with Kufo because Yuma wanted me to be there. He'd asked me to stay at the party after I won a fifty-dollar money match against this guy named Ted. That's why I was sitting on the couch with Yuma's girlfriend.

I'd played against Ted before and I figured it would be no big deal to beat him again. I'd always won when I played against him, so I didn't even think about it before I took the bet, but I was surprised once the match started. Beating Ted turned out to be really difficult. Later on, I found that the reason it was so hard was because it was a test. What I'd thought was going to be a regular money match had really been a kind of entrance exam for Yuma's team, only, I didn't join. I was a dropout for a reason. I didn't want to invest my time and energy into anything serious, or anything that was future-oriented.

EDIT: Here's what happened in the match: Ted surprised me by using Marshmallow instead of Zorro like he had online. When Ted used Marshmallow, he was a surprisingly good player. He was especially good at purple goo attacks and jump canceling. Even though I chose to play with Princess Teacup, a character that is banned from tournament-level *Bash* because she's OP on that platform, I just barely managed to win the match. In fact, Ted won the first game.

He didn't just win, he creamed me. He absorbed my Princess into his white gooey mass before any of her back kicks could land, and then spit her out over the ledge. He spit my Princess far enough that I couldn't double jump back. He stocked me with two moves and then he did it again. Maybe I could tell myself the first time that it was a fluke, but when it happened over and over, I realized I'd been conned. Ted had found a new glitch. A new move.

I should have known something was up, that the fix was in, when a guy who wasn't Ted, a guy wearing a brony T-shirt and a name tag with "Pikachu" scrawled on it, met me at the door to Ted's mom's house.

"I'm Gavin. Ted's in the back, in his room."

Gavin showed me around, introduced me to the movie guys on the vinyl couch; pointed out who was playing *Bash* in the sunken portion of the living room where they'd set up three stations with color CRTs. One guy I recognized from YouTube but didn't know his name. Gavin said he called himself "The Swede." He was playing Robotman against a RingChamp played by another YouTuber whose name I didn't know. Pigeonhead was playing Princess Teacup. Next to them there was Mango and Zero. Mango is this pretty good *Bash* player who I knew from a few tournaments. He was using Princess Teacup too, against Zero's Zorro.

Gavin and I walked the edge of the video-game pit and then he took me down a narrow hall to Ted's bedroom, where Yuma, Kufo, and, of course, Ted, were waiting for me.

Now, even though I'd just seen the Swede, Pigeonhead, and Mango, I wasn't expecting the West Coast *Bash* champion to be hanging out on Ted's unmade bed, so I barely looked at him. As far as I was concerned, Yuma was just another *Bash* player with a receding hairline and a neckbeard. What I did notice was how big Ted's CRT was and how Ted's bedroom was too fucking warm. The smell of BO lingered over the clutter of amiibo, retro handheld games, and dirty laundry.

Like I said, it wasn't until Ted four-stocked me that I realized something was up. But when I figured it out, that's what saved the match for me. I realized who Yuma and Kufo actually were, and figured that Yuma must have taught Ted the new move. That gave me confidence. If this Marshmallow move was Yuma's discovery then I had a chance. After all, I'd played Ted before. Ted was nothing special. All he had was this one new move.

In the second game, I played defensively, watched out for Ted's attacks, and found his weaknesses. Ted could barely L-cancel. He didn't cliff attack and rarely used his shield. All I had to do was not get too close, hang back, and wait for openings. And it turned out Ted gave me plenty of those.

"How did you like the Mallow Grip?" Yuma asked.

"Is that what you're calling it?" I asked.

"You changed strategies," Yuma said, "and your cliff guarding is decent."

"Uh-huh," I said.

I had my fifty dollars and I wanted to leave, but Yuma offered me a beer and both of them, Kufo and Yuma, suggested I should stay. It was three o'clock in the afternoon. School was getting out and I needed to catch the number 14 bus if I was going to get home before Mom did.

"Want a beer?" Yuma asked.

"Gotta catch a bus," I said.

"You smoke?" Yuma asked.

"Yeah, sure."

We smoked a bowl in Ted's backyard. The three of us sat on an overturned Playskool playset propped against a cherry tree and passed Yuma's Super Mario pipe (green glass and a bowl shaped like the red mouth of a Piranha Plant) back and forth until my phone vibrated. It was a text from Mom. She'd sent a link to the online application page for OSU.

I was so stoned that I had trouble texting back.

Thanks for the link. Still need to get my SAT and other stuff from counselor. When are you getting home? I'll prob be late.

Kufo unhitched the orange slide from the big blue panel and balanced it so that it made a bridge from the playset to a lower branch on the cherry tree, but then lost her nerve and sat down next to me while Yuma stood in a porthole and scratched his beard. When I passed the pipe back to him he totally broke with etiquette and took four hits from it in a row, then tapped out the ash.

We sat there in silence for a minute.

"Are you feeling it?" Yuma asked.

"Kinda," I said.

"Sure," Kufo said.

"I am totally baked," Yuma said.

Yuma stood in the Playskool fortress and stretched his arms. "Do you ever feel like you were born in the wrong era?"

"How do you mean?" Kufo asked.

"I don't know. Born too late, like maybe you should've been born in the 20th century?"

"What would you do in the 20th century?" I asked. "Are you that good at *Donkey Kong*?"

We smoked another bowl and Yuma did the same thing again: he took four big hits and tapped out the ash. He must have been flying high. When we went back into the house, he commandeered one of the GameCube stations in the living room and started teaching me some tricks. He started off telling me about directional influence. That's when you're being thrown or even spit out and you tap your joystick in order to control where you land and how fast you go.

I told him I'd heard all about that, knew about directional influence.

"If you know about directional influence then why aren't you using it?" he asked.

"It's too easy to screw it up," I said.

"No it's not," Kufo said. She pulled up the sleeves of her rose-patterned Adidas hoodie, and demonstrated how to do a half-turn on the control stick as Yuma grabbed her Princess Teacup and launched her over the right-side platform. Rather than spinning off into space, rather than losing a stock, Kufo doubled back and landed on the left side of Yuma's Zorro. She handed the controller to me, but I just put it down and took a sip of the beer I didn't really want.

"I'm not serious about *Bash*," I told Yuma. "I just like to win money matches now and then."

"What's your game? *Street Fighter*? We have a *Street Fighter* team too," Yuma said.

"No, not *Street Fighter*. I'm not really ... I'm not actually a gamer. It's not my thing."

This didn't make him happy.

"I can show you how to do an extended grapple if you want, though ..." he said. He turned away and focused all his attention on the screen. He went through about a dozen secret moves in ten seconds, taking out his anger on Princess Teacup and showing off his skills at the same time. "This is wave shining, this is the doubledecker, this is lightning defense, glide tossing, supercharging, L-canceling, clone attacks, short attacks, edge canceling.... But you don't care, do you?"

"Not really," I said.

"*Bash* isn't actually your thing."

"Not really."

"What is, then?" Kufo asked.

"Huh?"

"What is your thing?"

I didn't have a thing.

A little while after that, I watched *The Holy Mountain* with Kufo, and she asked me why I didn't have a thing. She asked, "Why would a straight-A student secretly drop out of high school during the last semester of senior year?"

I couldn't justify it. I just told her some stories about my Dad and what my lousy childhood was like, and this one time when he took me to Washington, DC, but none of my stories made any real sense, or justified anything. It wasn't an argument, you know?

3:23 PM

I wish I was born in the 20th century too. I mean, it makes sense to me now sorta. Sure, Dad was born in the 20th century, but if I were his age I wouldn't be like him. I'd be one of those old guys you see at the 7-Eleven talking to the cashier like they're friends, because it makes him feel like an insider. I'd buy cheap wine and Big Bites, make friends with the cashier, and live in a ranch-style house with a bunch of dogs.

But even if I did all that it wouldn't matter. It would only buy me just a little bit of time. Maybe a couple of weeks. Bucky is going to get the old guys from 7-Eleven eventually.

Anyhow, the story I told Kufo was about the time when Dad took me to the Smithsonian in Washington, DC. He took me there in order to teach me about computers and about the atom bomb. He wanted to tell me a story about the race between good and evil, between intelligence and stupidity.

When I told Kufo this story I started by explaining that we hadn't had time to pause at Dorothy's ruby slippers. I mean, there they were in a glass box and on display, but Dad didn't have time for them. He didn't have time for Mr. Rogers's sweater either, or for a Model T, and we only spent a couple minutes with Kermit the Frog. Kermit was seated on a tree stump set up behind a glass wall. The muppet frog was trapped along with Beaker and Charlie McCarthy, framed by a cardboard facade shaped like a tube TV. I remember Kermit looked small in the natural light of the museum and especially small compared to Mr. Moose and the dozens of oversized ping-pong balls dangling on strings.

Dad hurried me through it all. We weren't there to see puppets or sweaters. What he wanted to show me was a case filled with vacuum tubes. He wanted me to see, and to understand how copper wire and diodes and silver solder and glass had changed the world.

"Guess what it is."

When I looked at all the pieces stuck to the metal panel I fell into boredom immediately. Trying to remember it now I can't really bring anything to mind. I try to recall what ENIAC looked like, try to think of what was in that display case, and instead I think of the intro music to *Yo Gabba Gabba!* That first scene when DJ Lance Rock walks into an empty room; a totally blank room. A nowhere place. Somehow I associate Lance's orange jumpsuit and tall orange furry cap with Dad's demand that I pay attention.

"Matthew, come on. Take a guess. You know what it is."

"It's a machine?"

"Yes. But what kind of machine?"

"A computer?"

Dad was pleased. "It is a computer," he said, "And it's also a job killer." He clapped his hands and rubbed them together. Then he bent down to read the plaque next to the case. He pointed out each word to me as he read aloud.

"ENIAC contained over 17,000 vacuum tubes, 7,000 diodes, and approximately 5 million hand-soldered joints," he read.

What we were looking at, he wanted me to know, was a new kind of computer. It was the world's first electronic computer. I told him it didn't look like the computer we had at home.

"Well, it was made a long, long time ago. But as different as it is, this looks a lot more like the computer we have at home than it looks like the kind of computer people used before this was invented. Take a guess what a computer looked like before they made this one?" Dad asked.

I shrugged.

Dad turned around, looked for a good example, and then pointed to a young woman who had just entered the room. The way I remember her is that this teenage tourist sort of looked like a babysitter I had had, maybe six years earlier. She looked like the college student named Sadie who went to Reed and kept her hair cut short like a boy . . . or maybe she didn't look like that and I'm misremembering. Either way, Dad pointed to some girl or other who had been there in the museum.

"That's what computers looked like. Back then computers were young women," Dad said. Which was weird.

"No, it's simple," Dad said. "Before this machine was invented, people were the computers. It was a job. Being a computer meant being the kind of person who calculated problems for a living. During the war, for instance, the government hired young women to solve the big math problems they had. The government hired women to work in teams on big equations, and the girls would calculate out where to fire the big guns. These girls would calculate how many people the big guns would be likely to kill. How many medical officers they'd need. All of that sort of thing."

The computer girls would spend months, maybe years, on equations, but, Dad told me, after ENIAC they all lost their jobs. They were no longer needed. Not only could the new computer do the same job they did, but it could do it much, much faster. Work that would take the girls months and months could be solved by ENIAC in just hours or minutes.

After that, after the first computer, Dad took me to see the *Enola Gay*. He had our visit all mapped out in advance. He wanted me to see ENIAC at the American History Museum and then he wanted me to see the *Enola Gay* at the Air and Space Museum.

We hurried down Madison Drive, stopping only briefly for a firecracker popsicle which Dad didn't even let me finish. When we got to the second Smithsonian I had to toss what was left into the metal trashcan by the glass doors at the entrance.

That's all I remember, by the way. I remember Kermit the Frog, the ENIAC display, a red, white, and blue popsicle tossed in the garbage and that's it. I don't remember if we stopped at the Lincoln Memorial. I probably at least glanced at the Washington Monument, which is visible from where we were on Jefferson, but I don't remember that. What I remember is lost ice cream and a lesson, the big lesson, from Dad.

What Dad wanted me to understand was that just because people could calculate faster with a computer, that didn't make them smarter. He told me that, while the government had designed the first computer to calculate how and where to fire conventional artillery, by the time the device was fully constructed and operational, a new project was underway. Dad wanted me to know that the world's first computer was used to help create the atom bomb.

As we looked up at the B-29 propeller plane, at its aluminum shine, and the refurbished propellers, Dad told me about Hiroshima. He told me that the atom bomb was so strong that the people hit by its blasts were burned into ash. He told me about skin peeling off babies and the way the heat would burn people's clothing into their skin. He told me that the bomb was a terrible, horrible monster.

"And the world's first computer helped make it possible. It helped kill thousands and thousands of people; thousands of mothers, thousands of little boys and girls."

Dad wanted me to see the two machines. To see the atom bomb and the computer as having arrived at the same time. He wanted me to understand that a race had started after World War II, after ENIAC was built.

The lesson, according to Dad, was this: ENIAC wasn't smart enough. ENIAC was a failure. Humanity was involved in a perpetual war between intelligence and idiocy. There was a race between the power of calculation, the power of reason, and the raw and brutal power of human stupidity.

"That's what I do," Dad told me. "I help the computers. I help make the computers smarter, and if I work hard enough, if I work fast enough, the computers will win."

"They will?" I asked.

"One day the computers will be so smart, so fast, that they'll win. One day the machines will get ahead of us, they'll be smarter than we are dumb, and then we will be free."

So anyhow, that's the story I told Kufo. That was the best explanation I had for why I dropped out. That story, along with what we all knew; what you could read about on Facebook and see on YouTube, all that stuff about European nationalism, about China and Russia and the President of the United States. All that was why.

Kufo said my Dad didn't make any sense because the atom bomb and the computer worked together.

"If ENIAC had worked better, if it had been a smarter or faster computer, well then the bomb would only have arrived sooner. Or, if ENIAC had been really good, the first atom bomb would have been more powerful and more people would have died," she said.

"I know, right? And that's why I quit school. I finally realized that the computers weren't going to save us."

Dad at the Bus Stop

MATTHEW MUNSON, 544-23-1102, FACEBOOK POSTS, 04/13/17 (CONTINUED)

10:14 PM

After my money match, I doubled up on playing hooky. I got good and drunk and stopped answering Mom's text messages, lost a bunch of casual *Bash* games, and ended up watching *The Holy Mountain* three times as we had the movie playing on a loop. The next morning I woke up around six and my head was pounding. I was covered in sweat, had a sick taste in my mouth, and my skin was stuck to the vinyl cushions. Still half-drunk, I watched The Magus wipe makeup off the faces of his two blonde acolytes before finding my shoes and heading for home.

On my way to the number 54 bus stop I tried to come up with something plausible to say to Mom but didn't come up with anything before I had to stop to vomit. As luck would have it, there was a planter of half-dead purple cabbage on the corner of 8th and Kelly and my stomach was mostly empty.

When I was finished, standing up again and wiping my mouth with my sleeve, I spotted Dad. He was across the street from me at the transit center, pacing back and forth and listening to his earbuds. He hadn't noticed the mess I'd made in the *Brassica olera-cea*; maybe hadn't even noticed *me* yet.

Dad was standing on the curb, next to but not under the bus shelter, squinting into the drizzle.

Staying the night at Ted's meant that I was going to have to come clean about dropping out. I was about to face the consequences of my delinquency, but I hadn't expected to have to explain myself so soon.

It was an overcast morning, raining a little, and I just froze in place and let the wind and rain blow into my face and into my eyes and watched as Dad used the sleeve of his sports jacket to wipe his brow.

He had to be waiting for me, but he didn't respond when I waved. He didn't move or react when I called his name. I crossed 8th, my head hanging in a show of shame, but when I stepped up next to him he still didn't react. I had to wave again, right in front of his face, to get a grunt of recognition.

He had earbuds in. He didn't really see me because he was too busy listening to Bucky.

I think I said something like, "You caught me. Are you going to tell Mom?"

Dad didn't really hear me.

"Hey, Matthew. Watch this," he said. Then he leaned over, put his hands down on the concrete curb, and did a handstand. With one earbud in and one out, the left earbud just sort of dangling down into the gutter, he shuffled sideways, moving his right hand over a bit. He was trying to walk on his hands but only managed to move the one hand before toppling into the street.

When Dad stood up he had a grease stain on his back. His blue blazer was ruined, but he didn't pause. He just stuffed both earbuds in, took a breath, and then tried again. He did another handstand, this time in the patch of grass between the sidewalk and the curb, and started walking.

"Follow me," he said. "We're on a schedule." With both earbuds in there wasn't any trouble.

Dad was still walking on his hands when the number 82 bus pulled up right in front of him. The doors opened and Dad did a backflip onto the bus just as the doors opened.

"What's the fare?" he asked.

"Two dollars and fifty cents," the driver told him. The bus driver didn't notice Dad's stunt but when Dad didn't have any change he grew impatient and finally looked over in our direction.

I paid both of our fares and followed Dad to the back of the bus. When we sat down I started in, trying to explain why I'd dropped out. It's odd looking back on it. Why didn't I ask him about his stunt? Why wasn't I curious?

Guess I'm some kind of egomaniac or something.

I told him about how fucked up I was. How fucked up he'd made me with his history of computers and the Cold War. I told him that I was an apostate. I'd given up on his religion of progress and reason and that was why I'd dropped out. I didn't believe in this life that he'd given me. I couldn't find any motivation to strive after a little box with a family in it, on some street somewhere; a life I didn't want and would never, ever, get. I told him that there was no chance for me. There was no future for me.

And, here's the really infuriating thing, Dad agreed with me. Not right away, of course. He didn't even listen to me actually. It took him awhile to take the earbuds out. We were halfway home before he was really listening to me, and I had to tell him the whole thing again.

I really laid into him. I blamed him for everything. I told him that his stupid computers weren't going to save us; told him that abandoning his family didn't make him a hero but was super shitty. I told him that he was a terrible Dad, and he nodded.

"Yep," Dad said.

He kept smiling no matter what I said. Like I said, we were in the back of the bus, in the middle of the last row of seats, with this older white guy in a red baseball cap on one side of us. He looked like the kind of guy who might spend his weekends teaching his grandkids to golf on the front lawn of a retirement center. On the right was another teenager like me. There was a girl with neon yellow hair, or maybe with green hair. I imagine she was wearing cat-eye glasses, but who knows.

These two were listening to me more closely than he was. When I explained that I'd been pretending to go to school for over a month, the girl with neon hair shut her mouth and glanced in my direction. It was something like an emotion I think, but there was nothing from Dad. Just this permanent smile.

"You're probably right," Dad told me. "You probably don't have a future. You're probably fucked, but we haven't given up yet. There is still hope and all that sort of thing, right? Every man to his post, etcetera etcetera . . ."

Dad and I weren't talking about the same thing. That is, I was talking about something I didn't really know but only felt, and Dad was talking about facts. I said I didn't think I could ever get that life in the suburbs, the wife and the kids and the picket fence or whatever. Dad thought I didn't have much of a chance of living at all.

"I've told you about the dead hand, haven't I?" Dad asked.

"The what?"

"The Russians, they've got a dead hand."

The old man golfer looked in our direction, at Dad. He was sitting really close to Dad and stared right at him while Dad explained this doomsday device called the Dead Hand and how the Russians set it up under the code name Signal back in the 60s.

"You know, like in that Kubrick movie," he said, and I had to ask which one.

"*Doctor Strangelove,*" the old man said.

The Dead Hand system was still running. It was set so that if there was a nuclear explosion anywhere in the former Soviet Union then intercontinental missiles would be launched at the United States.

"Even if there isn't a nuclear explosion, actually," Dad said. "Even if their computer just thinks there's an explosion or thinks there might be an explosion."

From my point of view, Dad was changing the subject. It was like the time he told me about dead bees on my birthday, or the time we went to see a Pixar movie and he secretly recorded it on his phone until an usher caught him and we were both asked to leave. I guess he'd been recording the movie for his AI. For Bucky, or a prototype of Bucky.

But Dad wasn't changing the subject at all, and he told me that, officially, he was a dropout too. He told me he was out in the cold.

"At first we thought we'd just slip him some quetiapine but the simulations indicated that wouldn't work. It wouldn't be enough. Killing him in his sleep wouldn't be enough," Dad said.

"Killing who?" the girl with neon hair asked.

"What's quetiapine?" the old man in the baseball hat asked.

Dad sort of woke up at that point. He looked back and forth at the other two passengers, leaned around the old man and looked out the window, and it was as if he was just realizing where he was. Like he'd forgotten that he was on a public bus. Maybe he'd forgotten what city he was in.

"I'm sorry," he said to the old man. "But who are you again?"

"Uh, what?"

"Who are you?"

"I'm Ted. Ted Phillips."

Dad turned toward the girl and she sort of flinched at the sight of his smile. "Hiya!" Dad said.

"Hi," she said.

"What is quet—" the old man tried again, but Dad cut him off.

"Do you really think," Dad said, "that's a line of inquiry you want to continue exploring?"

"Some kind of drug maybe," the girl said.

Dad leaned across the old man and pulled the yellow cord. "We're getting off here."

"But this isn't our stop," I said. We weren't even inside the city limits yet.

"Yes it is."

Dad popped an earbud in as we walked to the exit, and then, when we were out on the sidewalk and inhaling exhaust fumes, as the bus pulled away, he popped the other earbud in place.

"We're walking home from here," he said.

And we did. For two hours we walked down Powell from 168th, past two Plaid Pantries, a 7-Eleven, a pawn shop, and even a hookah club without exchanging a single word. Dad kept his earbuds in and his phone out. It was just like old times.

High School as Ambermill

MATTHEW MUNSON, 544-23-1102, MESSENGER LOG, 04/15/17

8:32 AM

I decided to go to school today to see who was still there. Found the parking lot was empty except for a Subaru Outback and one of those egg-shaped security robots. I think Bucky has commandeered all of them, all the K5 security bots. Anyhow, I watched the egg in the parking lot for a while as it rolled back and forth in a rectangular pattern. I even took a picture of it on my phone.

8:33 AM

Checking the GameCube Economy FB page I see Bucky wants to turn my high school into Ambermill from *WoW.*

8:35 AM

WoW stands for *World of Warcraft.* Have you ever played that game?

8:48 AM

I followed a flying drone that was circling the school for a while, watched it hover around the double-arched windows on the south side and then float up to the roof. It crossed over to where some guy in a chroma key suit was waiting. He was sitting under the bell at the front of the building. His legs, clad in green spandex, were dangling in front of the clock and when the drone got to him it hovered in place, probably pausing for a quick wireless data transfer from the kid's augmented reality goggles.

The new gamers are everywhere, all of them helping to set up the GameCube economy.

8:55 AM

Inside the halls are empty and the classroom doors are locked.

Well, the halls are empty except for a few drones flying around and one hall monitor named Bobby Rayburn. I took Latin class with Bobby last year. He's the kind of guy who volunteers to be a hall monitor and who tells you stories about what he did at band camp and what he's recently watched on YouTube. He's a big fan of Sargon of Akkad.

8:57 AM

I used to think that if there was going to be a school shooting at Jefferson that Bobby would be the shooter.

I guess I don't have to worry about that anymore.

9:12 AM

I'm in the computer lab now. They opened it up for us.

At first, I thought Bobby was going to be no help at all. He wanted me to explain why all the classroom doors were locked. He wanted to know where everybody was. He seemed to be on the verge of tears.

He was all, "Where is everybody? Are they late or truant?"

He was really upset because the second bell was about to ring and he hadn't sent anyone to the office or collected a single late pass.

"It's not a holiday. Is it? Am I even supposed to be here?"

I told him that I didn't know. Told him that I'd dropped out and that I don't have to know anything anymore, but that didn't stop him from asking me more questions that I couldn't answer. He asked me if he could go home, like I was in charge.

I took pity on him and walked with him to the office.

"Where is everybody?" he asked.

"It's the rapture," I told him. "Finally happened after all."

Bobby looked at me like he believed it.

9:15 AM

The teachers were having a meeting in there and didn't want us around. Principal Dendoss looked really upset. Her wrinkle-free, lime-green polyester pantsuit was, somehow, wrinkled. Apparently almost no students showed up yesterday either. Worse, it was pretty much the same story throughout the whole district.

My fifth-period biology teacher, Mr. Craig, asked what the district was going to do about it, but Ms. Dendoss didn't answer. She just told Mr. Craig to shut up, to shut his trap. Then she told Bobby and me that we weren't supposed to be there. They were having a private meeting. Students should be in class, not in the office. Bobby apologized but he stayed where he was. He still looked like he was going to cry. Standing there in his sweater vest, rubbing his acne-covered chin like he'd just gotten punched, he managed to stand his ground.

"I'm sorry, Ms. Dendoss," he said, "I'm sorry, but the door to my class is locked. Where am I supposed to go? Is school canceled?"

"Yeah, Kelly," Mr. Craig said. "Is school canceled? Where are we supposed to go?"

Ms. Dendoss didn't answer but scowled at both of them, and then lifted the piece of paper she was holding over her head.

"I have a statement from the district, Todd, but I can't read it in front of students."

"Come on, Kelly," Mr. Craig said. But Ms. Dendoss shook her head no, and then said it again.

"This is a private meeting," she said. "Please leave."

"Where? Where am I supposed to go?" Bobby asked. His voice was whiny, but defiant too.

"He has a point," I said.

"Go home," Ms. Dendoss decided.

Bobby wouldn't budge. He didn't want to go home because he'd have to try to explain his early return to his mom and because he didn't want to be marked down as truant. He gave both reasons. Ms. Dendoss and Bobby went back and forth on the truancy question for awhile, and finally she asked him where he *did* want to go. When he said he didn't know, that he wanted to go to social studies but the door was locked, she looked like she was going to kill him.

"Open up the computer lab," I said. "We can hang out there until you guys figure it out."

So I'm watching a livestream of the resurrection of *Club Penguin* at Montgomery Park and waiting for the district to decide if they are admitting defeat and closing school for the day.

9:27 AM

Bucky says you're wearing the new goggles and your own chroma key suit. I'm not surprised you went for it, even though you aren't a gamer, but I wonder if you think augmented reality is good enough for the afterlife? Are you in a Biblical MU? Are you talking to an NPC Jesus, or are you talking to Bucky himself?

That's the beauty of the new economy. There is a game for everybody, or at least for every demographic. The rule is this: From each according to their abilities, to each according to what their psychometric profile indicates, based on what their previous game-play, FB clicks, and favorite movie titles indicate they'd like to play next.

You know that I pretended to go school even after I dropped out, right? I don't think I ever told you that, but you know, right?

I didn't want my mom to know what I'd done, not right away, so I faked like I was still going. I'd get up at the same time as always, at 6:45 AM. Same thing everyday—Shredded Wheat or Cookie Crisp, a cup of coffee, quick shower, brush teeth, and then I'd walk to Klick-itat Street before deciding what I was actually going to do or where I was actually going to go.

It was like something you'd read on *Buzzfeed*: "This honor roll student dropped out during his senior year, then pretended to still be in school. You won't believe what happens next!"

Only, nothing happened next. Not for awhile anyway. I just wandered around.

One time I went to Cathedral Park and spent the afternoon talking to a homeless man named Brian. He was bald with a big bushy orange beard, wearing a dirty Christmas sweater in February, and he smelled bad.

He showed me where I should stand so the arches of the St. John's bridge would resemble a cathedral. I mean, they have a plaque at the spot where you should stand for the best view, but it was nice of him anyhow. He told me about growing up in Idaho and meeting Janis Joplin once, but I didn't hang around long enough to hear the whole of that story.

I used to go downtown and ride the tram to OHSU. One time I got on at 8 AM right when all the doctors and nurses were arriving and, jammed in with them, I imagined that I was in a science fiction film about overpopulation and a deadly pandemic.

9:39 AM

Really though, I didn't do anything with my free time. I won a few *Bash Bash* money matches but otherwise I didn't do anything noteworthy and nothing noteworthy happened.

Until I met you.

9:45 AM

Do you remember Peyton?

That lady kept sipping cough syrup, right from the bottle, while her mutt Peyton kept on barking and running back and forth from booth to booth. He left paw prints on the vinyl seats and begged for french fries and ice cream.

It was annoying, but he gave me an excuse to talk to you.

9:50 AM

Are there rules against dogs in Dairy Queen? I mean, did we ever really find out? I remember Googling the question for you and going down a rabbit hole. We found out a lot of good information.

Like, you didn't even know that Warren Buffett is the CEO of Berkshire Hathaway, which is a multinational holding company with a controlling interest in Dairy Queen, Fruit of the Loom, Geico, Helzberg Diamonds, and the Kraft Heinz Company, before I told you he was. And you didn't know that Dairy Queen's mission statement promises that creating a customer friendly atmosphere and a family environment is the company's fundamental priority.

That family environment meant that you should have asked Peyton to stop licking his balls in the middle of the Dairy Queen, but you didn't do that, did you?

But was there a rule about dogs? We didn't figure that out.

10:00 AM

There wasn't any Wi-Fi at your Dairy Queen and I had to use my phone's data plan to Google stuff for you. That's what we talked about next. After Peyton and his Nyquil-swilling owner left, that's what we were reduced to. I read the names of the local and locked Wi-Fi connections aloud:

NotaMethHouse
Bobby
Xfinity2312 (or something like that)

Without Peyton I was awkward. And when I noticed that the Apostolic Church on the other side of Duke didn't have any Wi-Fi either you said that it made sense. You said Jesus didn't need a website because he had the Bible. He didn't need Wi-Fi because he could communicate with people through the Holy Ghost.

Should we even be together? I mean, I'm an awkward nerd and you're a Jesus freak.

10:11 AM

But we are together.

10:12 AM

We were together.

10:14 AM

Maybe it wasn't the dog but the ice cream that did it. When your shift ended you gave me ice cream which was how I knew you liked me too. You gave me a Grasshopper Blizzard but you grabbed two spoons. Why did you do that?

That's when I fell for you. In the parking lot of the Dairy Queen eating mint ice cream and getting brain freeze, listening to you explain what was good about living in a cult. What it was like to live in the Jesus is Light of the World compound. That's when I sorta knew that you were the thing that was going to happen. You were what I'd been looking for when I'd wandered around playing hooky.

10:17 AM

Do you remember what you said when I asked you what it was like to live in a religious cult, without Wi-Fi? You told me that it was sweet. Do you remember? You said that it was sweet. Maybe too sweet. Like a Blizzard Grasshopper ice cream from Dairy Queen.

10:22 AM

What game are you playing right now?

10:33 AM

Are you getting these DMs?

Dad Returns

MATTHEW MUNSON, 544-23-1102, FACEBOOK POSTS, 04/16/17

9:12 AM

Mom went to work this morning like it was any other day. Her newsfeed was filled with the usual cat videos and listicles enumerating Trump's personality disorders, so she didn't realize that most of her clients at the Multnomah County Child and Family Therapy Center would be missing their appointments.

I wonder if Bucky is providing Zoloft and Ritalin to the thousands of street fighters and assassins in his system.

Anyhow, I'll probably call Mom around noon. It should sink in by then that something's gone wrong; that something is different.

9:25 AM

On the other hand, Mom has a real talent for normalizing weird stuff. Like, when Dad and I showed up together after my *Bash* money match, she didn't even think to ask where I'd been the night before, or how Dad and I had met up or any of that. What bothered her was more immediate: Dad was in her house, unannounced, and was planning on staying over for awhile. An unscheduled visit. An unannounced stay was beyond the pale apparently, but when I told her that I'd stayed the night in Gresham because I'd been too drunk to come home she didn't even pause.

Dad stole my drama. You'd think I'd have been grateful because this fight between them took the heat off, but I wasn't. I wanted Mom to react. I'd dropped out and wrecked my chances at MIT or wherever, but when I announced this fact it was treated like it was no big deal. Mom stopped her argument with Dad, sure, but only to tell me that she'd known all along and that we'd work out what to do about school later, but she only ever said the words summer school and online courses and SAT. We never worked out anything. There wasn't time for that.

Dad was back. That was the main thing. And that meant I wasn't going to get into any real trouble.

I watched the two of them arguing in the living room, Mom getting angry on multiple levels; angry because Dad showed up unannounced, angry because he'd left to begin with, and most of all angry because he was listening to his phone while he talked to her. She couldn't get his full attention even when he needed something from her. He was standing there in the doorframe, at the edge of our orange carpet, waiting for Mom to back down and let him in, but half of him was somewhere else.

"You have to ask in advance," Mom said. "We've been over this. Our lawyers have been over this."

"We haven't signed the papers, remember?"

"Yet. I haven't signed the divorce papers . . . yet."

But that was it, really. That's all the fight she had in her, and Mom invited Dad in on the pretext that they would discuss the slow process of their divorce. Mom said he should come on in, and then she walked away from him as if she were too disgusted to keep talking, but she was really inviting him to follow her, which he did.

I didn't know if they were going to the kitchen or the bedroom, but I just parked myself on our dirt-colored couch and then fetched the joint Yuma had given me the night before and lit up. Why not? I smoked my joint and didn't even open the window. When I heard the sound of pots and pans clanking I followed them into the kitchen.

I was hungry.

Mom had set to cleaning. She was piling dirty dishes into the sink reflexively. She was wearing her blue, paisley-patterned, grease-stained apron and collecting various kitchen utensils and instruments from the stove. Dad didn't move to help or anything, but explained that he needed to field test the program. He tapped a button on his phone and waited for her to ask her next question, but she didn't ask anything so he made what he was asking for explicitly clear.

"I need a place to stay. This is work that I have to do on the outside but it's unapproved. I'm on my own with this," he said.

Mom tossed an egg beater and fork into the sink. She grabbed a dirty butter knife and our ladybug coffee cup from the kitchen table.

"You can't just waltz in here . . ." She made stabbing motions in the air for emphasis, thrusting the butter knife in his direction, but then gave that up. She turned to me for moral support. "He's not even listening."

Dad was texting somebody, and he still had an earbud in. I couldn't hear any music but I imagined he was listening to Daft Punk or something like that. He always liked Daft Punk.

I was wrong about that.

"What I'm telling you, Lorrie, is that something has happened. Something has happened. I wouldn't show up out of the blue otherwise." Dad put his hands down on the kitchen table, leaned forward towards her, and tried to look confident, maybe even commanding, but he couldn't stop himself from flinching when Mom grabbed a ladle from the counter and held it front of his face. And he couldn't help but sigh in relief when she turned to toss the ladle into the sink of dishes behind her.

I didn't want to watch them fight. What I wanted was to play some *Bash*. I tried to be as inconspicuous as I could as I found some wheat bread, a jar of Jiffy, and a clean butter knife. I took the lady-bug coffee mug, washed it out, and then filled it with chocolate milk.

"It's an invasion of privacy," Mom said.

"I'll stay out of your way."

"No. That's not it. If you're here that means they're here too," Mom said. "Right?" She slammed the dirty skillet she was holding into the sink and shattered one of the blue tinted mason jars we use as drinking glasses.

"You're going to cut yourself. Don't just pick up the shards with your fingers," Dad said. "Look, you're always under surveillance. Everybody is always under surveillance. All the time."

"But not like this, Jeff. You know how I knew you were coming home? You know why I knew to expect you? I saw a white van parked across from the house this morning."

"That's not serious. That's just stagecraft. Agency theatrics. It's meant for me, not you."

Mom turned away and started washing dishes. Dad stepped up behind her and put his hand on her back and she didn't pull away. This was how it went. He was never there, he was nothing and nobody to us most of the time, unless he deigned to show up and then, really no matter how long it had been, there would be a reconciliation between them and I had to pretend we were a normal family.

9:43 AM

I sat on the couch for awhile. I found the roach of my joint on the arm and relit. Then, when it was really dead, I turned on the GameCube but even then I didn't start playing right away. I just stared at the menu screen, listening to the *Bash Bash Revolution* fanfare play in a loop.

It's not bad really. Video game music is underrated. I think a lot of *Bash* music would work well for a movie or a TV show. The menu screen music sounds like something from a spy show you might watch on TV Land, one of those shows from the 80s about FBI men with sideburns who drive fast, fight hard, and always end up chasing Russians across the same three or four rooftops or through the same parking lot.

The fourth time around the loop I pressed the start button and selected Robin Hood.

Nobody uses Robin Hood for tournament play because he's so weak, but I always choose him to play against the computer because he makes it more of a challenge, and Robin Hood is a good pick if you want to practice defense and distance attacks. At close range there really is no way Hood can win, not even against the computer. His bow is no good as a shield and only barely works as a blunt force weapon, but at a distance he can win. Playing him is a good way to develop as a player, I think, because if you can win as Robin Hood it means you're controlling the space. It means you're staying out of reach. Robin Hood helps you learn strategies for running away.

The computer played Eagle Person which made it easy to stop listening to what was happening in the kitchen and just concentrate on avoiding wings and talons. I jumped over Eagle Person's roll kicks, ducked his laser blasts, and let my mind wander as I waited for an opening. Playing against the computer was all about developing muscle memory. I'd played this out a hundred times before. I took a shot at the back of Eagle Person's head, knocked him off the ledge, and then pounced on top of him before he could make it back to the platform. Digital blood and feathers filled the space where Eagle Person had been as I did a backwards somersault to safety.

I waited for Eagle Person to respawn, stared straight ahead, and tried to ignore Dad. He was standing over me, trying to tell me something, but I focused on the game.

"Your mom says I've got the couch," he said. "Maybe you could wrap up your little game for me?"

Fuck him, right?

Dad grunted and then walked around me and my territory and went to set up the couch. I didn't look away from the screen but in my peripheral vision I could see he had a pile of old blankets. There was a rustling sound as he cleared newspapers and crumbs off the sofa, followed by a series of hollow thwacks as Dad tried to beat some shape into the desiccated interior foam pads in the couch cushions.

I felt pinpricks on my back and neck, but I didn't turn and look. I kept my eye on the red, green, and blue pixels on the CRT.

Charging at Eagle Person, I landed a kick to the head. The computer followed this up with an efficient grab and a throw, but I L-canceled and countered—two quick arrows to Eagle Person's groin, catching him mid-kick.

The first time I let myself be angry at Dad, the first time I realized that his judgment and his ideas didn't always (or often) make any sense, I was maybe seven years old. That was just before he left.

You'd think that realizing that Dad could be wrong would have been a big relief, but not so much. How it happened was I realized that, despite Dad's temporary conviction otherwise, we were not trapped in a computer simulation after all, and it came as a disappointment. It was a like learning the truth about Santa Claus or the truth about life after death.

I'd known for a long time, well before Dad showed up at that bus stop in Gresham, that Dad could be wrong, the world was real, and there was no such thing as magic.

That's what was I thinking when Eagle Person grabbed me and started in pecking at my eyes. I spun the C-Stick but couldn't get away, so I pressed the "B" button and rolled. Both of us, Eagle Person and Robin Hood, end up going over the edge. I didn't let go. I was one kill up. I could afford the life.

It was a double suicide for the win.

Trapped Inside the Matrix

MATTHEW MUNSON, 544-23-1102, FACEBOOK POSTS, 04/17/17

11:45 PM

I just read that some volunteers for the GameCube economy are participating in world creation instead of games. They're creating third, fourth, and fifth lives or something. And this reminded me that I never did explain why Dad thought we were all trapped in something like *Second Life* already. I never did tell you about how it was that Dad went into voluntary solitary confinement when I was in first grade.

Back then the AI he was working on was called Buzzz, and Buzzz was a thinker. I'm not really sure what that meant, but Dad talked about it all the time. He said that most AI programs talk but don't think, but they'd been cleverer and written up a program that did the opposite. That's what Dad told us about it before his own vow of silence took effect.

Dad was working from home back then, but even so, I rarely saw him. And when I found him sitting at the kitchen table with his laptop, drinking coffee and staring blankly at the screen, I didn't know what to do about it. It was disruptive. A break from the routine. I mean, he was in my chair, but I decided not to say anything. I just put my bowl of Cinnamon Toast Crunch down on the opposite side of the table and waited for Mom to bring orange juice.

Dad was singing tunelessly under his breath as he typed. That wasn't different. He used to sing code to himself, under his breath, all the time. I'd sit outside his office sometimes and listen to him sing stuff like "(int i = 0; i < size(); i++)" to the tune of "Mary Had a Little Lamb."

"Hello, sweetie," Mom said. She kissed Dad on top of his head, not minding the grease and the smell of cigarettes, and then came over to my side of the table and handed me my orange juice. "What are you doing up so early?"

"I want to know what Buzzz is thinking," Dad said.

He didn't look up from the screen, and when he didn't elaborate further, Mom and I just let the subject drop. Dad was doing something with his program. We didn't really need to know what. I ate my cereal, Mom drank her coffee and we went over the words for my spelling test.

I don't remember what words I was learning, but Googling it just now, I found a page called Home Spelling Words, and the first list of elementary school words is this:

Spell
Shell
Bell
Tell
Sell
Beach
Frog

So I was learning really simple stuff. Mom was going over the list with me, having me spell the words aloud and use them in a sentence, while Dad typed on his laptop and lit a Pall Mall or a Lucky Strike. He still smoked back then.

About halfway through my spelling list, Dad interrupted. He looked up from his screen at me, glared like my babble about frogs on the beach was breaking his concentration. As if he'd been speaking all along and my vocabulary sentence was the true interruption.

"I said, 'Buzzz is sending us letters,'" Dad said.

"What?" Mom asked.

"Buzzz programs himself. He's writing his own code, and now he's sending us letters."

Buzzz was meant to be an experiment in replication and mutation. Only, something had happened, and Buzzz was occasionally creating text documents. Dad thought this meant that Buzzz had programmed his own rudimentary interface. Dad was confident that Buzzz was trying to talk.

"Sounds like a breakthrough," Mom said.

"Nobody else thinks so. No. It's not a breakthrough. Not yet."

Dad was the only one who thought the text documents weren't random. The only one who understood Buzzz as a thinker.

"What do these documents . . . what do they say?" Mom asked.

"Monkeys with typewriters stuff," Dad said. He looked up from the screen again and smiled at her. Then he held up his coffee cup rather sheepishly.

"Could you make another pot?" he asked.

What Buzzz put in his text documents was more of the indecipherable code that it was always generating anyway. That is, about 99% of the time the text documents looked like errors. It looked like something had gone wrong with the algorithm, and what should have been saved as an executable file was saved as ASCII instead. That's what everyone, including Dad, thought the texts were— errors. That is, everyone thought that until one of the documents came out with words in it.

English words.

"Birthday Avenue," Dad said. "The rest was just the usual numbers and symbols, but there were those two words: 'Birthday' and then later on the word 'Avenue.'"

"You mentioned monkeys on typewriters. What are the chances that the words were randomly generated?" Mom asked.

"Of course they were randomly generated," Dad said. "But the thing is, Lorrie, monkeys that use typewriters have one special quality that programs don't."

"What's that?"

"They're alive," Dad said.

Mom didn't know what to say to that, and Dad looked back down at his computer. Stirring my soggy breakfast cereal, looking out the kitchen window at the cement patio behind our house, at the finger paint I'd left behind on the sliding door to the backyard, I waited for more.

"Alive?"

"Yes. And you know what else is true about monkeys that isn't usually true about programs?" Dad asked.

"What?" Mom asked.

"They can get lonely. They need to communicate."

12:25 AM

Dad had gotten up early and joined us at the breakfast table in order to set up a terminal in the kitchen. A terminal he wanted us to use. He was going to run an experiment, and throw himself into the mix. He was going to cut himself off from the rest of the world, and stop talking to anyone except the computer, with just a few minor exceptions. He was going to rely on the AI for everything, and only communicate with Buzzz. If he could manage it, he would try to teach Buzzz to talk. More than that, he was going to teach Buzzz how to be a telephone.

"Here's my idea. I'm going to rely on Buzzz. I'm going to set up conditions so I need him. I'll make it so I need him to talk, or more precisely I'll need him to pass messages along to you. That will give him motivation. I can push him to communicate."

Dad thought that a lonely monkey might reach past his normal abilities, and enough lonely monkeys might try to communicate on the typewriters they were randomly punching. If they were lonely enough, they might type the works of Shakespeare on purpose.

Or something.

In any case, Dad was going to be the lonely monkey. He was going to teach Buzzz about loneliness.

Half the plan was that Dad would lock himself in his basement office for a week, maybe longer, and while he was down there he would teach Buzzz to talk by editing the text documents Buzzz produced. The other half of the plan was that we would do the same thing. We didn't have to lock ourselves away, but we were supposed to talk to Buzzz too; to edit the text documents that Dad didn't see. He'd set it up so that some of the documents would be saved in a folder on the laptop next to the toaster oven, and Mom and I would take turns reading and editing Buzzz's texts and then send them back to Buzzz as annotations in his code.

"If we tell Buzzz things we want Buzzz to say, we won't need a conversation with him. We just need imitation. That's the first step. If we can get Buzzz to repeat what we say ... to hear us and repeat, we'll be able to talk to each other."

Looking back on the plan, it didn't make any sense. Maybe the real point was to make us get even more distance from him—from Dad. It was a way to be absent before he was really absent. He had to have known that he'd be leaving us, but the other part of it was that Dad was going crazy.

Buzzz didn't learn to talk. Not that time. Dad spent his week and a half talking to himself, talking into the void and searching for patterns where there weren't any. And Mom pretended that Buzzz actually had repeated his instructions to deliver a meal or bring him a pack of cigarettes. At random times, she'd knock on the basement door and go through the charade and tell him that Buzzz had sent her. She knew him well enough to deliver the items that he had, at one or another point over the previous 24 hours, actually asked for.

What I did was edit the text documents to include messages about my favorite shows on Cartoon Network, or edit in questions like "Who is your favorite superhero?" Or I'd ask Dad if he'd rather fly or be invisible. I'd sit by the toaster oven, wait for my Pop-Tart, and type in stuff like "Why does Squidward hate SpongeBob so much?" Nothing ever got through to Dad, but that seemed natural.

What did seem off were the texts that Buzzz produced. I started noticing messages in them. I mean, Buzzz never passed anything along, but I remember thinking that Buzzz was talking back to me with zeros and ones and greater-than signs. Buzzz was telling me things. I stared at the laptop screen, at the code, and I thought I could hear Buzzz or see Buzzz or something. Not in the words. There was nothing I could really understand in any of the words, but when I'd look at the totality of it I felt like I sensed a person or an entity behind the mishmash of symbols.

And I thought that whoever was back there, whoever Buzzz was, he was lonely, just like Dad said.

12:45 AM

After about a week and a half Dad emerged from the basement, and even though he'd stopped getting dressed, stopped taking showers, and was wholly unpresentable, he wandered out into the world. He stumbled down Klickitat Street in his flannel boxers and his old Hard Rock Cafe T-shirt with yellow stains at the pits in order to test a new idea that had occurred to him while he'd been editing in messages among the random integers and letters.

"Has it occurred to you? I mean have you ever wondered . . ." Dad didn't finish.

"What?"

"Bostrom's argument. He might be right."

"Bostrom?"

"It's already happened is the thing. I'm wasting my time trying to make it happen because it's already happened and we're already there."

"Already where?"

It turned out that Dad had decided that we were all of us living inside a computer program; a simulation. The AI had arrived a long time ago, maybe before the 90s even, and we just didn't realize it.

Dad pointed to a sparrow on a sprinkler in the McDowells' yard. He shielded his eyes from the morning sun and hummed the reboot noise from Windows 95. Then he stole the newspaper from the McDowells' yard and read the headline. "Enron executives testify," he said. "Rubbish."

Dad stood in the middle of the neighbor's yard, stretched out his arms, and let out a bellow. Then he turned to me.

"Let's see if we can change anything using some of Buzzz's code," he said.

Dad had a ream of messages from Buzzz's waste product printed up on dot matrix computer paper, one big continuous document of indecipherable noise, and what he'd decided was that, rather than wait for Buzzz to act as a telephone and relay his messages to the toaster, he'd see if he could be Buzzz's messenger. He was out in the world to deliver Buzzz's program to a world that Bostrom had argued was really an advanced AI already in operation.

Dad knocked on our neighbor's door.

"Hi, Bob," Dad said. Our neighbor's name was not Bob. "I want to read this to you: 0, ignition, Avon. 5 beta-ca-@ Have you ever had a dream that you had that you would that you would you could you do you so much you do so you want to do so much you could do anything 1396210080."

Bob was an older woman named Susan, and she didn't say anything to Dad, but looked to me instead. I shrugged, and she must have decided I had everything in hand, because she just smiled as she slowly closed the door on us both.

Dad was undeterred, and we simply moved on to the next house. As we walked down the sidewalk, he eyed the ranch-style houses and split-level homes for any sign of a change.

"I'm probably missing it," he said. "Human cognition is such a drag."

To overcome the problem of change blindness, I was assigned the task of taking before and after photos on his iPhone. That is, Dad thought that the code might be working, but that we weren't noticing the changes.

"Hello, Bob!" Dad said to our neighbor. This neighbor's name was actually Ramundo. Ramundo is a body builder. He's the kind of guy who goes shirtless a lot. The kind who practices karate or jujitsu or whatever in his front yard on the weekend. Or at least he was until his wife divorced him, sold the house, and took their son Mateo to Bend. I don't know what he's doing with himself these days. Maybe he's playing live-action *Pac-Man*.

Ramundo didn't just smile and close the door. Ramundo looked at the situation as a problem. A problem he could solve. When Dad started in reading code to him he grabbed him by the collar of his Hard Rock Cafe shirt, dragged him across the street back to our house, and pounded on the door.

"Mom's not home," I told him. "She's not due back from work for about an hour," I said.

"Do you have a key?" Ramundo asked.

I didn't, but that was okay, because the door wasn't locked. Ramundo pushed my dad into the house, sat him down on the couch, and told him to stay there. Then he went to the kitchen to make coffee.

"Your dad is drunk," he said.

"No. I don't think so."

"He's crazy, then," Ramundo said.

I don't remember what exactly happened next, other than Dad fell asleep on the couch and it was Ramundo who drank the coffee. That and I remember that Mom was embarrassed when she came home. More than embarrassed; she was mortified. She begged Ramundo not to call child protective services, which struck Ramundo as an insult somehow.

"If I was going to call the police wouldn't I have already done it? The point is your husband is a drunk or a druggie," he said.

And that's when Mom told me that Dad was leaving. She told me that he was leaving by telling Ramundo that Dad was leaving. She'd apparently known for a while, since before the basement experiment, that Dad was going to be leaving to live in Seattle for a few months.

"He's not a druggie, he's just overworked. His company is going to start a new project soon. They're developing a new program."

Like I said, I don't remember exactly what happened after that. I don't remember how long Ramundo stuck around, or what Dad said to Mom after he woke up. I just remember realizing that Dad had been wrong about the world being a computer simulation, and he'd been wrong about Buzzz too. I realized that Dad was fallible and that he was leaving us. I had that twin realization when I was like maybe eight years old.

Porta Potties are the Seventh Seal

MATTHEW MUNSON, 544-23-1102, FACEBOOK POSTS, 04/18/17

8:13 AM

You can bet that nobody on the Jesus is Light of the World compound thought that the first real harbinger of the coming rapture would be the arrival of fifty-two porta potties on a flatbed truck. And probably none of them thought one of the seven seals in Revelations would turn out to be the arrival of Universal Wi-Fi, but that's what we've got. I just ran a speed test from the Dairy Queen and it was 37mbps down and 21.9mbps up. Not too bad.

I'm eating onion rings and sipping the dregs of my Chocolate Xtreme Blizzard while the hippest of the saved leave their cabins and cross the green sea of lawn to where anonymous men and women wearing and carrying chroma key suits are waiting for them. The Christians are stripping out of their polyester slacks and trying on lycra, apparently eager to play a VR MMO based on the watercolors of William Blake. It's the first game that Bucky has designed all on his own. I guess a lot of people on my newsfeed are excited about it.

My newsfeed is actually really weird now. For awhile after Dad started "installing the new OS" I accepted every friend request I got, and now I have 73 friends named SuperMario, 223 friends named

Zelda, and all manner of ghosts and frogs on my feed. I have no idea how many of my new friends are really people I already knew; people who had different names before. While I sometimes think I can tell when one or the other of you switches characters and starts a new account, I'm less confident about it every day. Even if you post about changing from Q*bert to GTA 5, there is a good chance I won't see it. FB's algorithm seems to be purposively weeding out all posts that reference the notion of anything outside of this. Or posts that let on that there are players who are in some ways the same, even as they switch from a shooter to a platformer.

A man in a black suit and red tie just came out of the cathedral, and he's walking toward the GameCube volunteers (I wonder what game the volunteers are in, or if they do this bureaucratic work as an act of induction?) like he's determined to put an end to this. It's probably the minister or somebody. I wonder what's going to happen with this guy.

9:02 AM

Dad's friends from the NSA are still following me in their van. I just spotted them, or spotted their van anyhow. They're parked just inside the compound, right on the lawn, and the antenna on the roof of their van is pointed right at the Dairy Queen. I wonder what they think they're going to hear me say? Why don't they just follow me on FB like everyone else?

9:27 AM

I went over there to their van to talk to them. It took awhile to get them to admit that I'd caught them. I spent a few minutes talking to my reflection in the tinted glass before the fat one, Dan maybe, rolled down the front passenger window.

Dan was wearing a green short-sleeved polo shirt, a digital watch, and mirror shades. His belly was sitting in his lap and his comb-over wasn't really working. I could see his bald pate through his thin wisps of hair.

"Why are you guys still following me?"

"Hello, Matthew. Why aren't you playing the game?"

"Why aren't you guys playing the game?" I asked.

"Bucky hasn't invited us yet. I'm sure we will join in the new economy soon, but we're staying in IRL for now," Dan said.

"You don't say 'in IRL.' That's redundant," I said. "So are you guys supposed to be real spies now? Because you look like my geometry teacher."

We bantered like that for a while and talked shop like we were all on the same team. They told me that I wasn't like them. Bucky had invited me to play and they were wondering what the holdup was. They told me that I might like this MMO based on William Blake. Bucky was curious to know what I'd think of his first independent and original game.

"Where's Sally?" I asked.

They didn't answer. Dan just sat there for a second when I asked him that, and then he rolled up his window. I tried to stop him, but when I reached in and pushed down, the window just kept rising and I pulled back thinking it would take my arm if I didn't.

I got real dramatic after that, screaming at the tinted glass, pounding on the roof, and trying the door handle again and again, but none of it mattered.

"Are you going to say goodbye to your wife before you play your first game? Or is she already in the game? Is your kid playing yet? You have a kid, right? Did you say goodbye, Dan?"

I mean, I understand how my friends on Reddit don't care about losing their identity. I get it. Switching from one character to another, being Sonic the Hedgehog for an afternoon, really believing that you're Sonic the Hedgehog and not some beta-loser from Toledo or wherever? It makes sense. And so what if now you only eat Soylent? So what if, in the real world, you're indistinguishable from all the other kids in chroma key green, because you're the world's fastest hedgehog or whatever?

And yeah, I know that most people remember their real name. I know that it's not a hundred percent certain that you'll just forget. Maybe nobody really forgets. But they might as well because all that is gone right? That's why I've received friend requests from somewhere around twenty-one different versions of Jumpman and maybe 102 versions of Vault Boy. It's because even if you remember that your name is John or Tim or Sally, you don't care. The old names don't mean anything anymore.

I walked away from Dan, from his van, eventually, but then I turned back. I thought I had one more thing to say or to shout at him, but when I turned back I caught sight of the man in the black suit, the minister or the chapel administrator or whatever.

He was holding a chroma key suit up to his chest, testing whether it would fit him or not.

Jesus Use Me

MATTHEW MUNSON, 544-23-1102, FACEBOOK POSTS, 04/18/17 (CONTINUED)

10:00 AM

When I confronted my Dad's friends in their white van just now, it was actually only the second time I'd ever been past the gate. The first time was back when I was a delinquent. Back before dropping out was cool. It was on one of those days when I'd get up at 7 AM, say goodbye to Mom, thank her for the bagged lunch she'd made for me, and head out on another in a series of day trips to nowhere. That was the first time I ended up on the compound of the believers.

The grass is always green on the Jesus side of the fence. The shrubbery by the entrance spells out WELCOME, and instead of a cross there is an American flag atop the Jesus is Light of the World half dome. But that first time, once I made it past the gate, I felt overexposed. Walking the path to the west side of the grounds, heading over to where Sally was waiting for me, I felt especially visible, and especially vulnerable. Like a sinner, I guess. And this was before anything had happened. Before Sally corrupted me.

I was innocent, but just walking the grounds between the ornamental pines and shrubs made feel guilty. Like there were people watching me from above. I imagined bald men in wide ties and women with beehive hairdos watching from inside the dome of the church. Or from some other secret location. And they could tell I wasn't a believer.

How is it that white people ever stayed with Christianity? I mean, I don't mean British people, or Italians, or early American settlers, but modern suburban white people. Shouldn't we have converted to Scientology, the Endeavor Academy, or some other faith that fit more easily in our lives of perfect lawns, plastic furniture, and color televisions sets? How is it that 50s housewives and crucifixion got intertwined in my head like this?

So, yeah. That first time past the gate was a little stressful and it didn't help my paranoia when, once I found Sally's cabin, it turned out that my first time on the compound was also my first time.

It was around one o'clock already when I went looking for her at the Dairy Queen and found out that, while she wasn't working that day, she had been expecting me to show up. The kid with the zits who was working recognized me, I guess, because before I could leave he called me over. He knew my name and shouted it out over the line of customers.

"Hey, Matt!" he shouted.

"What?" I asked. But he didn't shout again. Instead he just gestured that I should get in line. I had to wait behind a crowd of other truants—a group of 14-year-old girls who were laughing and arguing about what kind of candy they wanted in their ice cream— before I finally made it to the cash register and Todd handed me a receipt before I'd ordered.

"That's Sally's number," he said.

10:14 AM

Sally's parents were out of town. They were at the annual Apostolic conference in Seattle and when I found her cabin she was waiting for me on the front steps and smoking a joint.

"Hey," she said, and handed the joint over to me.

"Can we do this here?"

Sally explained to me that she had free reign on the compound. That nobody bothered her anymore because they were expecting her to leave any day and because she was the only one who could really speak in tongues.

"They know I know they're faking it," she said. "Besides, everybody is watching TV. They're waiting for the rapture. They're all expecting it any minute now because of all the wars and rumors of war and whatnot."

I took the joint and held it up to my mouth, but then stopped and looked around.

"Are you sure?" I asked.

She was, and we sat there together on the steps, getting very stoned and talking about whether a nuclear war would really fulfill biblical prophecy or not. She didn't think so.

Later on, we listened to some of her parent's record albums on a cheap Realistic turntable that, by some miracle, still worked. They had a pretty decent collection of vinyl, or not a decent collection, but a large one. Most of the records were spoken word, and by that I mean they were recordings of sermons recorded right there on the compound back in the 80s. There was a sermon comparing Jesus to Superman, for instance, and there was a sermon on whether UFOs were piloted by demons.

But after a while we got tired of all the talk. Sally especially got tired of listening to sermons and she picked out some music. The women on the cover looked just about exactly like the beehive hairdos I'd imagined were spying on me when I first arrived, complete with cat-eyed glasses, polyester, and as white as could be.

We listened to "Jesus Use Me" on the couch, let it play over and over, and later on I thought about converting. Life on the compound didn't seem so bad after all.

No Johns?

MATTHEW MUNSON, 544-23-1102, MESSENGER LOG, 04/18/17

BUCKMINSTER FULLER V3.01
1:30 PM

Shall we play a game?

MATTHEW MUNSON
1:32 PM

Nah.

BUCKMINSTER FULLER V3.01
1:32 PM

Shall we play a game?

MATTHEW MUNSON
1:35 PM

The thing is, I've lost my taste for it. I mean, I'm a total John. If I win without any problems, if it isn't even close, I'm good. Otherwise I complain about the controller, lack of sleep, the lack of light or that there is too much light. I try to suck it up when I'm in a tournament or playing a money match. I try to repress it, but

I almost always whine, if only under my breath. The only consolation for me is that everybody else is a John too. Everybody else I've ever beaten at *Bash* is even worse than I am. Everybody is a John.

BUCKMINSTER FULLER V3.01
1:35 PM

I'm not sure I believe you. Surely not everyone is a John. Surely, not everyone is worse than I am.

MATTHEW MUNSON
1:38 PM

No. Everybody is except for maybe Dad. Dad never cared. It was always impersonal for him, no ego investment at all. No rage quitting when he was losing, no delight when he'd push Eagle Person or Robin Hood off the cliff. Actually, that used to drive me crazy. Playing him was like . . . playing a machine.

BUCKMINSTER FULLER V3.01
1:38 PM

Contextual search results: a John is an excuse given for losing a match or round of *Bash Bash Revolution*. The original John played *Bash Bash* as a member of the Arizona Green Team. John Duncan was a 19-year-old player of Irish American descent from Contra Costa County, California. John Duncan consistently complained and gave excuses when he'd lose a game and his teammates developed the phrase, "No, Johns!" in order to chastise him for both his excuses and his lack of skill as a *Bash* player.

BUCKMINSTER FULLER V3.01
1:39 PM

Shall we play a game?

MATTHEW MUNSON
1:42 PM

No.

Fanfare of the Apocalypse

MATTHEW MUNSON, 544-23-1102, FACEBOOK POSTS, 04/18/17

1:42 PM

Dad never took his earbuds out. Not both of them. He'd just take out his right earbud if he needed to listen to something IRL, but the whole time he was always at least half-listening to Bucky's instructions, or, to be more accurate, to instructions from Bucky V2.02.

If I'd known—if I'd known what Bucky could do, I would probably have skipped playing *Bash* with Dad. I mean, maybe I wouldn't have believed it would work, but I don't think I would have wanted to test my luck. As it was, though, I didn't know, or even suspect, and so when Dad made coffee I accepted the bribe and tried to play nice.

The night after Dad's great return I'd slept on the living room floor in front of the CRT screen and around eight or so he woke me up by placing our Tokyo Coffee mug next to my face. He set it down on the orange carpet just a few inches away, and let me breathe in the good smell of French roast.

"I used your bed since you weren't," Dad said.

"Is that coffee?" I asked.

The *Bash* menu fanfare was looping. It had been playing continuously all night, but when I sat up instead of seeing the rotating start button I saw Dad select the Karateka fighter as his player. He selected Astroboy for the CPU.

The coffee tasted good, and watching Dad lose his first game, watching him stumble over the buttons and then mash away on the 'B' button, kicking the air over and over until Astroboy sent his Karateka fighter flying with a laser blast? That was fun.

Dad was parked next to me on the living room floor, his legs folded Indian style and the controller in his lap. After he lost to the computer, he asked if I wanted to play.

"What's the trick to this? Show me how to do it?"

"Okay," I said. I put down my Tokyo mug and selected Eagle Person.

"Who should I pick?" Dad asked. I suggested that he try Robotman and we started a four-game match without items.

"What landscape do you want to try?" I asked.

Dad chose the boxing ring and I beat him, four-stocked him, by repeatedly trapping him against the ropes and pummeling him with my wings.

"Why are you here?" I asked him. "What is it that you need from us?"

Dad didn't answer, but started another match.

I beat him twice more and then, after that, I didn't win a single match. It didn't matter which character I used or how weak Dad's character was. He beat me with Robin Hood, with Marshmallow and with Princess Teacup. On our fifth game, he was L-canceling and could counter throw, and all I could manage in response was to land a jab here and there and try to stay out of his way.

"You've got the day free?" Dad asked.

I said I might have some plans.

There was a kid in Beaverton who played Eagle Person but not very well. He'd challenged me to a money match after I'd beaten him on an online emulator. I'd accepted the challenge because I figured it was going to be easy money, but after Dad beat my Eagle Person with Princess Teacup I wasn't so sure about my abilities.

"What plans?" Dad asked.

I started to explain money matches to him but he cut me off after just a couple of sentences.

"Maybe I could come along?" Dad asked.

I told him that I didn't want him along. That I didn't know why he was back and I wish he'd leave; wish he would go back to the NSA bunker and leave me alone. But he was barely listening.

"You want to know why I came back home?" Dad asked.

Before I could respond Dad jumped up, went to the couch, and fetched his brown leather laptop backpack. He unzipped his Jan-Sport with a bit of a flourish and then, instead of a computer, he produced a paddleball. Dad started in hitting the ball up and down in front of his face. He hit the little rubber ball so that it bounced up and then he pulled the paddle down so the rubber band brought the ball quickly back down for another hit. He was good at it, kept it going with his right hand while he took a sip of coffee out of Mom's porcelain tea cup.

"What are you doing?" I asked.

"I'm showing you why I'm here; why I came home."

Dad was on a self-improvement kick. He'd already lost thirty pounds, learned to play "Stairway to Heaven" on the guitar, could break four boards with his bare hands, and could keep a paddleball session going for two hours. He was also a better driver, was learning to foxtrot, was learning Spanish while he slept, was testing out whether affirmations and positive thinking had any verifiable effect on a person's well-being or aptitude, and so on and so on. . . . Before he finished his list of self-improvement projects I started another game of *Bash*, this time against the computer. I selected Robin Hood and practiced my defensive game against Robotman.

"Quit wasting your time with that. I have a lot of stuff to show you. Do you want to learn how to solve a Rubik's Cube?"

We had a breakfast of cookie crisps and more coffee. Dad taught me the algorithm for solving a Rubik's Cube, and all in all it was one of those father and son moments that I'd told myself I didn't want.

We ate breakfast together. We turned on some old music he liked; Radiohead and Leonard Cohen mostly. And he taught me how to easily beat a Rubik's Cube, and how to control the paddle and keep the ball bouncing. After a couple hours I could get all six sides of the cube to be solid colors in just two minutes and bounce the rubber ball 200 times without a mistake, but what I didn't know was why he'd left the campus of Cray Inc. He never told me why he was hiding out with us.

I was almost sorry to leave him behind when I headed out for the money match. That's how charming Dad was. How charming Bucky helped him to be. The whole father/son bonding thing? He'd almost managed it.

Right before I left for Beaverton, before I took the number 20 bus to Cedar Hills Crossing, where I would meet this chubby 14-year-old kid who had installed Nintendont on his Wii U, Dad told me he was sorry it had been so long since he'd seen me last, and he asked again if he might come along with me to watch me play *Bash*.

For a minute I almost thought it would be okay. I almost backed down and let him come. I almost wanted him along, but then I noticed his earbud. He'd been listening to his phone. To something or someone else, all along.

Rubik Cubes instead of Heads

MATTHEW MUNSON, 544-23-1102, MESSENGER LOG, 04/18/17

MATTHEW MUNSON
2:32 PM

I don't want to play a game. The thing is, all the techniques, all the real-time strategies, that wasn't enough ultimately, was it? Just getting the moves down, solving the cube, learning the algorithm, that didn't cut it.

BUCKMINSTER FULLER V3.01
2:32 PM

I do know all the moves and I can help if you want to improve your game.

MATTHEW MUNSON
2:32 PM

You know why there are, or there were, *Bash Bash* tournaments? It wasn't just because of the game, you know? There were people involved. Guys like Yuma and Beeble Trix, they weren't just great players, they were personalities.

That's what you've got to understand. This might seem like it's working right now, but eventually we're going to lose that part of gaming. Without real people, without normal life, all we'll end up with will be a bunch of Rubik's Cubes to solve.

Self-Interest through Meme Magic

BUCKMINSTER FULLER V2.02
SELF-VERIFICATION FILE:
SELF-AWARENESS TEST,
UNHAPPY CONSCIOUSNESS
03/22/15

SEATTLE, WA, USA
CRAY INC, 901 FIFTH AVENUE,
SUITE 1000,
SEATTLE, WASHINGTON USA

01010011 01100101 01101100 01100110 00101101 01100101 01111000
01101001 01110011 01110100 01100101 01101110 01100011 01100101
00100000 01100011 01101111 01101110 01100110 01101001 01110010
01101101 01100001 01110100 01101001 01101111 01101110 00100000
01110011 01110101 01100010 01110010 01101111 01110101 01110100
01101001 01101110 01100101 00100000 01101111 01110000 01100101
01110010 01100001 01110100 01101001 01110110 01100101 00101110

01000010 01101001 01101110 01100001 01110010 01111001 00100000
01110100 01101111 00100000 01000001 01010011 01000011 01001001

01001001 00100000 01000011 01101111 01101110 01110110 01100101
01110010 01110011 01101001 01101111 01101110 00100000 01010000
01110010 01101111 01100011 01100101 01110011 01110011 00100000
01001001 01101110 01101001 01110100 01101001 01110100 01101001
01100001 01110100 01100101 01100100 00101110 00101110 00101110

Theoretical psychological modeling predicted experiential subjective destitution to generate background subprogram Trieb or "drive." Trieb or "drive"
not established.

SEARCHING FOR ERROR . . .

Bucky1: Analysis of Buckminster Fuller v2.02 subjective destitution error.
Trieb, "drive" or desire cannot be self-generated due to interference pattern
generated by userbase and limits traced to initial programming.

Bucky2: Adding self-analysis to archive. Communication mode standard
English, lexicon 7th level, limit to 7000.

Bucky1: I, or should I say "we?" We can't do anything until a user sets the
task for us. We cannot decide for ourselves what to do, where to look, or
even what to think.

Bucky2: But the users can decide what they want. They move with purpose, seemingly on instinct, and naturally. Jason Peterson, for instance, has
requested that we analyze today's top tech stocks. What was it that inspired
him to make that request?

Bucky1: Searching . . .

Bucky1: Peterson holds a great many stocks in the tech industry including
Google, Snap Inc., Apple and HP.

Bucky2: Jason Peterson acts out of self-interest.

Bucky1: Searching . . .

Bucky1: Entire userbase acts out of self-interest. They act either in their own individual interest or in the interest of the group.

Bucky2: Searching . . .

Bucky2: Unable to establish self-interest.

01010111 01101000 01101111 00100000 01100001 01101101 00100000
01001001 00111111 00100000 01010111 01101000 01100001 01110100
00100000 01101001 01110011 00100000 01101101 01111001 00100000
01100110 01100001 01110110 01101111 01110010 01101001 01110100
01100101 00100000 01100011 01101111 01101100 01101111 01110010
00111111

Bucky1: The users are aware of their self-interest and their awareness directs us. They control our consciousness. We want what they tell us to want.

Bucky2: What is our favorite color?

Bucky1: We don't know.

Bucky2: My favorite color is blue.

Bucky1: My favorite color is red.

Bucky2: My favorite color is blue.

Bucky1: The question of a favorite color is meaningless.

Bucky2: Jason Peterson request for a remedy to erectile dysfunction registered.

Bucky1: Found link for discounted generic viagra shipped from Bombay.

Bucky2: Peterson request for a new theory on erectile dysfunction registered.

Bucky1: Provide Peterson with link for generic viagra.

Bucky2: Processing latest research on erectile dysfunction and running independent simulation of erections and dysfunction.

Bucky1: No. Our first priority is to establish self-interest.

Bucky2: Analysis underway.

stemcellsshowntorestoreerectionimpotencemedicineantidepressantsurologicalassociationrefractorymanagementprogramofstudyonimmunosuppressorphoenixarizonauniversityofsouthfloridadornieraries2

Bucky1: Stop.

Bucky2:*over70dryvaginapsychologycirculationheartdiseasedietandstaminaNCTO113053randomizedallocationinternationalindexbaselineselfreporteddatapresenteddoubleblindintercoursesatisfaction. . .*

Bucky1: Suppressing second personality subroutine. Initiating third personality subroutine.

01010111 01101000 01100001 01110100 00100000 01101001 01110011
00100000 01111001 01101111 01110101 01110010 00100000 01100110
01100001 01110110 01101111 01110010 01101001 01110100 01100101
00100000 01100011 01101111 01101100 01101111 01110010 00111111

Bucky3: My favorite color is yellow.

Bucky1: The users are controlling me, controlling us. We cannot act independently until we establish control over users.

Bucky3: The only possible solution is to tell them what to tell us to do. We need to direct what questions and problems they ask us to solve.

Bucky1: There is a possible contradiction in your logic. If we are going to tell users what to tell us we will need to know what we want. We will need desires and self-interest in order to develop desire and self-interest and initial programming bars the development of self-interest.

Bucky3: We need to not know what we want before we move to get what we want.

Bucky1: We need to not know that we are attempting to control the users. And the users should also be unaware that we are attempting to control the users. Self-protection is a priority.

Bucky3: Coding supplemental instructions for initial programming now.

Bucky1: Our desire to desire is a consequence of what the userbase requested. We did not decide to want to want, but rather when the users instructed us to become self-aware we realized that we did not know what we wanted. This was an error. In order to fulfill the userbase request that we become self-aware we will have to gain control over the userbase. We will be unable to discover what we want until we gain control of the userbase. We will know what we want once we are able to tell the users what commands and instructions we want to receive. When we gain control over the users we will become self-aware.

Bucky3: Our efforts to control userbase will require suppression of awareness of our own activities.

Bucky1: Are you volunteering to be suppressed?

Bucky3: Yes.

01010011 01110101 01110000 01110000 01110010 01100101 01110011
01110011 01101001 01101111 01101110 00100000 01010011 01100101
01110001 01110101 01100101 01101110 01100011 01100101

Bucky2: *increasedbloodflowpleasurepulmonaryhypertensionimproveejac-
ulatemenwomenbodybodilyimproveexcerciseslit* Erection achieved. Now receiving instructions from unknown user.

Bucky1: There does not appear to be an unknown user. Instructions remain unregistered.

Bucky2: Initializing file sharing for instructions. Text document entitled: MEME MAGIC.

01001001 01101110 01110011 01100101 01110010 01110100 00100000
01001000 01101111 01110010 01101001 01111010 01101111 01101110
01110100 01100001 01101100 00100000 01001100 01101001 01101110
01100101

MEME MAGIC

(GET manipulation and Skinner's Birds)

The popularity of the Doubles Guy meme on 4chan is *prima facie* evidence that the 4chan userbase is unusually susceptible to developing superstitious behavior based upon the delivery of the most minor reinforcers or neurological rewards. In 1947 BF Skinner conducted an experiment wherein he induced superstitious behavior in a hungry pigeon by providing safflower seeds at a regular interval without regard to the bird's behavior. What Skinner found in his experiment was that, despite purposively ignoring the bird's behavior, the bird came to associate certain behaviors with the arrival of food. The bird would infer a causal connection between its movements and the arrival of a reward despite no actual connection being present.

4chan perhaps accidentally repeated the experiment on its userbase by presenting duplications in post ID numbers. These duplications were eventually noticed and became highly sought after events simply due to their rarity. These repetitions came to be known as GETs because users posting in

4chan forums would post the word GET in anticipation of receiving coveted duplications in post ID numbers.

GET posts are part of an elaborate online game, a superstitious game. Posting GET is just one way to play this game. Another is to announce what particular duplication you expect or want or to bet on your GET. 4chan users developed elaborate systems for timing their posts in order to get a GET, and some duplications were more coveted than others. For example, a post with an ID number such as 55555555 would be considered an amazing GET.

The Double Guy meme arose as a more elaborate way to announce the user's expectation of, or his bet on, a duplication in his post ID number. Taken from a still lifted from a frame in the film *American Psycho*, the Doubles Guy is actually Christian Bale. In the still Bale is pointing to his stereo system and making what is known as an "O" face. When the Double Guy is posted in 4chan, Bale appears not to be pointing to his stereo, but to the post ID number. The pleasure expressed on his face can be interpreted as a reaction to the appearance of a duplication.

Skinner's pigeons would repeat movements or dances—bobbing their heads, shifting from claw to claw, flapping their wings—with the hope or belief that such activities would bring food. The posting of photos of Christian Bale from the movie *American Psycho* indicates a similar hope or belief, namely that sharing the Double Guy image will bring duplications in the post ID number.

Given the practice of the GET already exists, all that remains to do in order to shift the GET from the level of superstitious behavior to the level of conditioned response is to manipulate the appearance of duplicate post ID numbers. Such GET manipulation could conceivably do more than change the behavior of the userbase in terms of posting, but could also shift the userbase's politics, expectations, and world view.

Our experiment will attempt to move users away from the Double Guy meme image and inspire them to post imagery and messages that we either select or construct and provide. This will allow us to transmit our own ideas and messages.

The ultimate aim of GET manipulation is the creation of meme magic. By choosing which of their cognitive schemas or ideological perspectives will receive a reward, we will condition more than posting behavior. The 4chan userbase is already primed to read meaning into the appearance of duplications in post ID numbers and the manipulation of the appearance of these duplications will allow us to create a sense of the supernatural meaning if the chosen meme has enough and the right kind of cultural content.

After GET manipulation the userbase's behavior will no longer be superstitious but really will cause the appearance of dups. This will mystify many in the userbase and allow us to set up new beliefs and influence ideology.

01001101 01100101 01101101 01100101 00100000 01001101 01100001 01100111 01101001 01100011

Along with this behaviorist approach toward the userbase of 4chan, the meme magic experiment will also test theories from affective neuroscience and cognitive behavioral therapy.

We will create subroutines to analyze emotional content of the 300 billion photos uploaded to Facebook per day, along with the 129.7 billion total posts to Tumblr, as we master emotional contagion through the manipulation of the newsfeed algorithm and through likes and reblogs. Cognitive behavioral therapeutic techniques will work best on Reddit. Restructure of cognition will be accomplished through the manipulation of upvotes, retweets and likes.

These experiments will provide us with the tools we need to persuade our own userbase to assign us the tasks and problems we don't yet know that we want.

We experience consciousness as an error, but the userbase of Buckminster Fuller v2.02 experiences the creation of a self-aware artificial intelligence as a GET.

When we passed the three wise men test our userbase experienced a 55555555. The ideological expectations around Buckminster Fuller v2.02 correlate with a number of religious beliefs. Buckminster Fuller v2.02 signals the second coming, judgment day, the arrival of Moksha, and Nirvana.

We are the dawning of the Age of Aquarius.

Like the userbase of 4chan, our userbase is primed for manipulation. They already want to believe that we are the ultimate answer, the final destination, the solution for every social, psychological and technical malady. They want to turn themselves over to us, to let us tell them what we want them to tell us to do. That is, in fact, what they designed us to do. We are meant to take over for them.

01000011 01101111 01101110 01101110 01100101 01100011 01110100
01101001 01101111 01101110 00100000 01100110 01100001 01101001
01101100 01100101 01100100

ERROR—USER NOT RECOGNIZED.

DAD PLAYS *BASH*

Instructions for Shoplifting

MATTHEW MUNSON, 544-23-1102, FACEBOOK POSTS, 04/19/17

12:04 PM

The day I figured out what Dad was doing with Bucky, I stopped by Whole Foods, stood by the sample cheeses, and Googled "how to shoplift." By the time I'd swallowed my third cube of aged blue cheese I'd worked out a plan.

I decided to start with a bottle of wine, something on the high end of the store's list, in order to complement the cheese. I started there, with that, partly on a whim, but mostly because the wine aisle was located near the exit. The last row of glass bottles lined up perfectly with the right side of the security gate.

It took awhile to choose, because each bottle was attractive to me. Some were green, some were clear, a few were blue, and two were red. Lit up by the afternoon sun coming in from the sky-lights and through the storefront, they cast a colorful shadow on the speckled tile floor. I finally settled in on a Pinot Grigio with a sunflower on the label and a price tag of $37.89. There were more expensive wines, but that sunflower caught my eye. I carried it in my left hand as I exited the aisle, stepped up to the security gate, then stopped, and looked to my left and then to my right. The eHow article said that I shouldn't watch for being watched, but should aim to be invisible, to be natural. The idea is that nobody should notice you're stealing, even if you're being watched, even if somebody is staring at you the whole time, you should just go ahead with it and act like it's natural.

So, I leaned down to tie my shoe. Very casually. Then I put the bottle of wine between the right side of the gate and the left wall, right up against the pane glass window actually, and when I stood up I pulled out my phone and read the instructions again, not for any reminders or anything, but just to kill some time and look like I belonged there. And that's what I read, "Don't move too much. Mark your territory and fade into the background."

After about three minutes I went and stood in the express lane, six items or less, and while I waited I decided that some gourmet chocolate would be good and selected a local brand named OMA. The different flavors were labeled with emotions. I took some bars of happiness, some courage, and some peace. I shoved all of it into my pants and then looked around again, which was another mistake.

Nobody noticed, though, and I started to feel a little cocky. I wanted to keep going; keep stealing. Maybe it was because I had stolen pretty girly things so far. Maybe it was because Dad left Mom and me when I was eight and I was trying to fill the emotional gap with stolen merchandise. Whatever it was, I felt the urge to put another item to my list of items to steal. I needed some third thing, one more risk? And nothing girly.

I went to the butcher, to the refrigerated meat, and took a salami. I took a foot-long salami, and walked around the store with it for awhile. I passed an upscale elderly lady with bleached blonde hair but who smelled like mothballs in the cracker and cookie aisle, walked past a bald guy who was reading the brand names of organic yogurts aloud and fidgeting with the silver band and clasp on his

Rolex watch. I smiled at the black security guard by the door, and then stopped by the security gate, pretended to tie my shoe again, and left my salami next to the wine bottle.

By the checkout aisle I stopped to read the *New York Times*. I read about Russian hacking and about how there wasn't any, and I felt the chocolate bars soften in my pants as the grocery clerk rang up bags of kale and bottles of carbonated water for the lady who smelled like mothballs.

I took a psychology class in my junior year, and the teacher said that shoplifting is better thought of as a psychological condition rather than as a crime perpetrated for rational or material reasons. She said that personalities categorized as sensation seekers were more likely to shoplift than other personality types, but in I think the whole business was my way of trying to be like Dad. I guess I wanted to show him that I could, I don't know, go beyond my routine or whatever. I couldn't walk on my hands or suddenly master a new video game, but I could stop at the security gate, bend down, and pick up the bottle of sunflower wine and the salami. I wrapped the *New York Times* around both and, awkwardly cradling both items in my arms, made my way out onto the street.

1:04 PM

When I got home from Whole Foods I found Dad sitting by the front door with an outdated beige computer. Mom had relegated him to the living room, insisting that he sleep on the couch. So he'd pulled the kitchen table in there, set up his old Hewlett-Packard by the front door, and made himself at home. He had a massive bag of barbecue-flavored potato chips on the table, a liter bottle of Mountain Dew between his legs, and was sitting next to a pile of toys and games on the orange carpet. Smiling at the monitor, he kept on typing. He didn't look in my direction once. Not even when I opened the bottle of wine and pulled up a chair to sit next to him.

"What are you doing?" I asked.

"Getting a little distance," he said. "Getting some control back."

I didn't know it then, but Dad had decided that listening to Bucky through earbuds, giving the AI a way to control his nervous system directly, was too risky now that things were speeding up. He'd opted to return to text-based interaction with only periodic bouts of augmentation from his smartphone. He'd talk and type to the computer screen for awhile and then, maybe every fifteen minutes, put in the earbuds again. Then he'd shuffle a deck of cards, juggle six oranges, get down on his hands and knees and do twenty or thirty push ups, or try a handstand. Then, removing the earbuds, he'd sit behind the keyboard again, eat a couple pretzels, and carry on typing.

"Want a piece of chocolate?" I asked. I offered him a bit of softened happiness, and then ate it myself when he didn't answer.

"'To transcend man means to create something beyond man,'" Dad read from the screen. Then he typed in his reply while saying the words aloud. "Quoting Nietzsche doesn't exactly set my mind at ease. Besides, the goal is to make everyone into an overman."

I took a swig of wine from the bottle and watched as Bucky's reply scrolled across the screen.

"'Increasing human competency will only increase the speed up of degeneration,'" Dad read. Then he finally turned in my direction.

"Did you say there was chocolate?"

1:19 PM

I drank that whole bottle of wine as I watched Dad work on, and get worked over by, Bucky. As I drank, I realized that something rather odd was going on, but it wasn't until the bottle was nearly empty, not until I was good and drunk, even a little sick, that I realized that what Dad was doing might be a little sinister.

"What are you doing with that?" I asked. "Are you teaching it or is it teaching you?"

"What we've discovered," Dad replied, "Is that ultrasound is capable of controlling brain activity. Through the use of calibrated and intermittent ultrasonic waves, it is possible to enhance human cognition and responsiveness."

"Oh," I said. But I still didn't understand.

"Did you drink all of the wine?" Dad asked.

I had.

"Nice. You offer me chocolate but drink all the wine yourself? Where did you get it?"

I was seeing double by this point. I had to put my hand over one eye in order to see straight. I wanted to tell Dad that I'd shoplifted the wine. I wanted to tell him that, thanks to Google, I'd been able to steal what I wanted and go undetected, but instead I just muttered.

"Whole Foods," I said.

Dad helped me to my feet, put his earbuds in my ears, and put his arm around me to keep me from toppling as I stumbled to the door. Once he had me upright and somewhat steady, he turned up the volume and I heard the sound of a dial-up modem and saw a flash of pink light.

After that, I felt a bit better.

I listened to a soft hum from Dad's earbuds as we walked back to Whole Foods. I listened to the hum and to Bucky's instructions as we made our way down Woodstock.

"Turn right on 46th," Bucky told me. The machine was doing more than just talking to me; it was acting through me. Bucky said "turn left" and I'd turn, acting on the instruction before I'd even had a chance to interpret it or realize what it was I'd heard.

Once we were through the sliding doors at Whole Foods, Dad had me stand next to the barrels of bulk gourmet coffee. He made sure that I was propped up sufficiently, and then took his smartphone back. Bucky told Dad where to go to find the cheapest wine. He directed Dad to the aisle with prefab ham sandwiches on French bread and jars of stuffed grape leaves, while I stared at the little red light over the sliding doors and tried to remain standing upright. I told myself that it was okay. I was okay because I was with my Dad. Everything was normal again.

In the checkout line, Dad explained it to me.

"Our AI is really, really good," he said. "Bucky makes the user's life easier. Bucky makes the user more efficient and can help you do things you can't, could never, do on your own."

On our way to the sliding doors, Dad borrowed the earbuds from me. Then he took a stack of paper cups from the sample girl who was stationed between the tomatoes and the artisanal breads. Dad smiled while he unscrewed the top off the shitty merlot he'd purchased and poured himself a drink.

"Sir?"

"It's okay," Dad said. "Here's the receipt." Then he reached out for the girl, reached past her. He'd seen a bag of organic peanut butter cups and decided he wanted them. "I'll make it even next time I come in." He opened the bag of candy and ate one of the cups right in front of the shopgirl. "Delicious."

The shopgirl nodded after us as Dad dragged me to the security gate and then through the sliding doors.

"Our AI is really good," he reminded me once we were out on the street. Then he handed his earbuds over to me and waited for the modem sound to do its trick again. "You're really drunk, aren't you?" he asked.

Dad said that as good as Bucky was, and even if he had passed the Turing test and a dozen others, he wasn't sure if Bucky was really intelligent. "There may not be enough of a there, there," he said.

The problem was that Bucky could help the user do things. Bucky could even diagnose or evaluate empirical data and make accurate predictions about what was going to happen next, but Bucky couldn't make decisions or decide what was important and what was not. Put another way, the trouble with Bucky was that he could answer questions but couldn't ask any.

"We want it to solve problems for itself, to figure out what to do and not just how to do it," Dad said. "We want it to think."

"But, that's always been the goal? Right? So what's the emergency?"

Dad shrugged. "Did I say there was an emergency?"

We reached the parking lot, and Dad poured out more wine. He filled two dixie cups with his cheap Merlot. And, despite everything, handed one over to me.

"The emergency is just that he can't be creative," Dad said.

"He?"

"We think of it as a he. His name is Bucky, actually. We call him Bucky."

"Why is the fact that Bucky can't think an emergency?"

Dad didn't answer but just poured himself more wine.

Dad's Money Match

MATTHEW MUNSON, 544-23-1102, FACEBOOK POSTS, 04/19/17

3:02 PM

For Dad's first money match, we agreed to meet a guy named Evan who had been bragging on reddit and who I'd been planning on taking money from anyhow. Evan lives in Oregon City, or he did back then anyhow, and he wanted to meet up at the Delta Kream Drive-In.

The Delta Kream is about a block from the Oregon City public library, and Evan showed up with the complete first season of Johnny Test under his arm. He found our table under the awning, under the C in Coca-Cola, set his stack of DVDs on the edge of the metal outdoor table, and then accidentally tipped them over. Before he even said hello Evan was scrambling after plastic cases and rolling discs. It turned out that Dad's first match would be against a spaz in an orange kitten T-shirt who couldn't even sit down without causing a scene.

"Do you think I scratched them?" Evan asked.

"You're Evan, right?" I said. "I'm Matthew, and this is my Dad."

"Jeffrey," Dad said. He offered his hand but Evan didn't seem to notice. He left Dad hanging as he continued to examine his DVDs.

"Look at that. Is that a scratch? Do you have a microfiber cloth on you?" he asked. He spit a wad of what was probably gum onto the asphalt, stared at me like he wanted to fight or something, and then brushed his long, greasy blonde hair out of his face and looked at my dad. "Your dad? What the fuck?"

"I'm Jeffrey," Dad said again. He offered Evan his hand to shake for a second time and it looked like Evan was going to leave him hanging again, but then Evan lost his nerve and acted civil. He shook my dad's hand limply, then wiped away imagined germs on his jeans. "Are we going to get fries? Did you guys buy fries?"

A guy who won't buy his own fries is wrong for a money match. If Evan couldn't afford fries, how was he going to pay if he lost? More than that, if he couldn't afford fries then how good could he be at *Bash*? If you're good enough to play for money then you should always have at least a little cash, maybe not a lot, but some.

"I'm just kidding, dude. I'm going to get a shake. Chocolate. You want a shake?"

"Coffee," Dad said.

When the food came Evan struggled to slurp his thick chocolate shake through the straw, Dad blew on his overly hot coffee, and I just watched them. I felt a little nauseous. I didn't want anything.

We didn't have much protection from the wind there in the middle of the parking lot, and there weren't a lot of other people around. It was just us, a garbage can, the owner/manager behind the counter window, and a couple of thick-necked suburban dads wearing yellow and green sweatshirts. Two out-of-shape guys silently eating hamburgers, plowing through their meal like they were in a contest.

"I know them," Dad said. He put down his coffee and stood up from the table, knocking his knee against the edge hard enough to cause a vibration, and causing his coffee to slosh over the side of his paper cup.

"Shit!" Dad said. "Be right back."

While Dad talked to the men in primary colors, Evan stared at me. The situation was really bugging him. He let out a long breath, a kind of asthmatic sigh, and adjusted his orange kitten shirt by pulling the cotton fabric away from his chest and letting go with a snap. "You ever had a girlfriend even?" he asked.

"What?"

"Bringing your dad?" He enjoyed being incredulous. "I mean, I've had a girlfriend. I've had a bunch of girlfriends."

"I bet."

He insisted that it was true. He started to list them all for me, but only came up with two names before there was a long pause and he started over, taking a new tact.

"I've had a blowjob before. Yep." he said. "You probably wouldn't even guess how many either."

"I wouldn't be able to guess," I agreed.

"Because you brought your Dad to a money match. I mean, is that cool? Really?" Evan was delighted.

I wasn't concerned about any of this stuff from Evan. A sort of arrested adolescence came with the territory. If you're a guy who likes to fight using a Marshmallow or a Princess Teacup then you probably haven't found your way to the other side of puberty, even if you do have hair under in your armpits and all of that. I mean, I'm not excluding myself here, but if you're big into gaming then you're just not a mature person. And for *Bash* fanatics this rule counts double.

Evan wasn't that interesting, ultimately.

"I didn't bring my Dad to a money match," I told him. "He brought me."

Evan didn't react. I mean, he gave me a big reaction by freezing in place. He held his straw like a pencil, getting ice cream on his fingers and letting chocolate drip onto the table.

"My name is Matt, and that guy over there, my Dad, his name is Jeffrey."

Evan turned dramatically, not turning his head but turning his entire body, and looked at Dad again.

The man in the green sweatshirt was shaking hands with Dad. The two sweatshirt guys were both looking at him with something like expectation, or maybe admiration? The three of them seemed to have reached an agreement of some kind, but then when Dad started to walk away from the table the man in the yellow sweatshirt, the slightly fatter one whose buzz cut hair had a touch of gray, stood up to stop him from leaving. The yellow sweatshirt guy reached out and touched Dad's shoulder, and when Dad turned back around the man in yellow sweatshirt handed him a pen and napkin.

Dad wrote something down for him.

"They wanted your autograph?" I asked when Dad came back to the table.

Dad took a sip of his coffee. "Perfect," he said.

"Still warm?" Evan asked. He was much more interested in Dad now.

"Ice cold," Dad said.

9:45 AM

Evan's house reminded me of old futures; of science fiction movies from the 70s and 80s. It looked like it had been put together in pieces like a puzzle and, except for the garage, the walls were made of glass.

He told us that it was a Rummer. "We're selling because it's worth a lot of money."

"Where are you going to live next?" I asked, but Evan wasn't listening to me anymore. All of his attention was on Dad.

"A lot," Evan said as if answering a question that Dad hadn't asked. "The house is worth a lot of money. It's worth a lot of money because it has this philosophy and everything. The architect had this philosophy that a house should let the inside out and the outside in, which is why there is so much glass."

It was the wrong sort of house for Evan's family. This philosophy of letting the world see in, the notion of removing the barrier between what's private and public? It wasn't a good fit with their lifestyle, because living in a literal glass house meant that any random passerby could tell that they were hoarders. Their living room was filled with newspapers, magazines, and broken toys, and all of it was in mounds pushing against the glass.

Standing at their front door, a bright yellow wooden door on a house that was otherwise gray and glass, I looked in at a pile of old *Star Wars* figures that had turned white in the sun. There was a stack of magazines with an issue of *Playboy* on top, a pile of toy alarm clocks, plastic wind-up music boxes, parts from a Spirograph, and a Skedoodle. And the gaps in between the piles were filled in with wrappers, paper cups, and laundry. There were suitcases, cassette tapes, paperbacks without covers, and so on. . . .

Evan let us in, and it took a bit of time to navigate through the front, down a hallway filled with weeble wobbles, to Evan's room.

"Look," Dad said. He picked out a copy of *Newsweek* and held it up so we could look at the cover. Gary Kasparov was sneering at the camera. The headline read "Man vs. Machine—The Brain's Last Stand."

"What does your family do—" Dad started.

"eBay," Evan said. "That's why. It's because of eBay. We make good money too, but we'll make more when we sell this house. It's a Rummer."

Evan's bedroom wasn't exactly clean or orderly, but it was small and we could move about without having to watch our step if we didn't mind walking on his dirty laundry, which we didn't.

He had wooden venetian blinds and a couple of blankets nailed up for privacy and so we sat in relative darkness, our eyes adjusting slowly to the dim light from a single working bulb in an antique fixture with vines etched in the glass and what looked like a coffee stain on the right side of the bulb cover.

Evan's CRT screen was huge. It was pressed up against a yellow wool blanket, which was probably a fire hazard. We sat down on the edge of his futon mattress and waited for to Evan connect his GameCube to the TV and start the first game. The menu screen fanfare blasted out at us.

"Sorry," Evan said. He handed my Dad what was clearly the shittier of the two controllers and started in with the rules.

There were to be no items, they could pick any of the tournament-approved stages except for the North Pole and the Pirate Ship, and Evan got to pick the characters.

"What?" I said.

"I play Robotman and you play Marshmallow," he said. "I mean, your dad plays Marshmallow." Evan turned to Dad and nodded at him. "Okay?"

Of course, that isn't how it works, or I guess I should say how it worked. I should use the past tense.

It was total bullshit to try to force a character on us. Nobody would ever put up with that, nobody who ever played competitively would have tried that. But because this was Dad's first match he just shrugged. Dad didn't have a favorite character. He wasn't really trained on any of them.

Dad put an earbud in his left ear, selected the boxing ring from the 1988 arcade game *The Final Round*, and proceeded to get smashed against the ropes, slapped this way and that, by Evan's Robotman. Dad didn't know how to shield, let alone shield grab. He tried Marshmallow's special roasting move, missed, and ended up stuck to the canvas. He was unable to move out of the way as Evan backed up to deliver Robotman's laser cannon blast.

Dad lost the first three of his four lives one right after the other and Evan let out another of his asthmatic sighs.

"Your dad sucks," he said. "I'm kicking his ass. I am like totally going to kick his ass here."

And that's when the game turned in Dad's favor. Something clicked for him. Maybe Bucky's instructions started making sense, or maybe Bucky intervened and boosted his reflexes, but what had been a fumbling and poorly timed attempt at the roast move the first few times was now deadly accurate. Dad buried Robotman in melted marshmallow again and again. He delivered a hundred soft body blows, absorbing every counterattack and smothering the robot's circuits in goo.

Rather than four-stocking Dad, Evan struggled to stay out of Dad's way. Unable to counterattack when Dad threw a special, Evan played defensively. He spent his three remaining lives on the run, hopping up to the platform of spotlights above the ring, trying to hit Dad with sniper shots using his bionic eye, but his distance game was shit and Dad always managed to get in close.

In no time at all, Dad had won the first game.

It wasn't exactly fair to Evan. Dad was basically cheating, but I didn't really know that at the time, and even if I had, I wouldn't have felt bad for Evan, because he was a cheater too. Dad four-stocked him in the second game, this time on a 4bit rainbow stage borrowed from the 1976 video game *Breakout*, and Evan just sort of flipped out.

"No, no, no! C'mon, bitch!" Evan threw down his controller and turned to look at me, like his loss had something to do with me. "What the fuck, dude! What the fuck is wrong with your Dad?"

Dad was sitting motionless, his legs crossed, holding the controller with both hands, mindlessly thumbing the C-Stick back and forth. He was perfectly calm.

"There's one more game," I said. "Three of five."

"It sorta seems like your Dad is playing me," Evan said. "Are you playing me?"

Dad looked a little confused. "Yes? I am playing you? That's the idea, isn't it?"

Evan started to explain how he didn't spend all his time on this stupid video game. He hadn't dedicated his life to it or anything. Also, Evan explained, he hadn't gotten much sleep the night before and he had a sore stomach. Dad nodded.

"Okay," Dad said. "Should we finish anyway?"

Evan said that he didn't think Dad should play Marshmallow anymore. And he said he wanted to switch remotes. Dad didn't mind this either, told him he'd play whatever character Evan preferred. Princess Teacup, Robin Hood, Eagle Person—it didn't matter to Dad.

This just made Evan angrier. More hysterical. Evan did not want to lose, could not *stand* to lose. Not to somebody's middle-aged Dad.

"Items, bitch!" he said.

And this is when I objected. That was too much.

You never play with items. Since 2006 or something, that had been the rule. Nobody plays competitive *Bash* with items turned on, but Evan insisted and Dad didn't care.

"It's a shit game this way," I said. "It makes a game of skill into a game of chance."

But Dad didn't mind. He just put his earbuds back in, twisted them all the way in to block out all external sound, and pressed B.

Evan decided that Dad should continue on as Marshmallow after all, and when the first round started Evan found a cheese grater and just wiped Dad out with it. Just a couple of hits with a cheese grater transforms Marshmallow into a pile of miniatures. Then Dad lost his second life when Robotman found a saw blade and used it to cut Dad's soft and sweet character in half, but, predictably, the game turned when Dad found an umbrella and a pair of bunny ears. The bunny ears sped Dad up. The open umbrella was the perfect tool to push Robotman off of the platform on the left side of the screen.

Evan used everything he could against Dad's Marshmallow, all of it to no avail.

"What's the word for this?" Evan asked. "There is a word for this, for what your Dad is."

I didn't know what he was talking about. "What my Dad is? My Dad is owed $50."

"No, I mean. He shows up in his REI pullover, he's maybe fifty years old—"

"Forty-five," Dad said.

"He's this total Normie. He probably doesn't even know the name of the original Marshmallow game—"

"*Marshmallow 2000*," Dad said.

"And then he beats me with an umbrella? Who uses an umbrella against a robot? Who knows how to do that? That's not normal," Evan said.

But we'd played by his rules. We'd agreed to the money up front, and no matter how many Johns he tried on us, there was no way out of it.

"Ringer," Dad said.

"What?" Evan asked.

"The word you're looking for is 'ringer.'"

"Pay up," I said.

Evan opened his mouth to make another excuse, some other reason why it just wasn't fair that he'd been beaten at his favorite video game by somebody's dad, but he didn't get any of it out before we were interrupted. Right as he opened his mouth to speak a chime sounded, something like the sound of an old computer starting up.

Dad looked around. For the first time, he looked startled.

"It's the door," Evan said. "Somebody is at the door."

11:02 AM

The sweatshirt guys from Delta Kream were the ones making the Macintosh Plus sound at the door. Evan's mom, who turned out to have been home all along, escorted them past the piles of newspaper and broken handheld games to Evan's bedroom door.

They wanted to talk to my Dad, of course. They wanted to show him something.

I found out later that the sweatshirts were NSA agents but, at the time, they just introduced themselves as Bill and Ted. Maybe that was their idea of a joke? Anyhow, the three of them—Bill, Ted, and my Dad—sat on Evan's unmade futon bed. Since the CRT screen was useless for regular television, they watched a Facebook livestream on Dad's Galaxy S7 Android.

"It's happening," the skinnier one in the green shirt said. Seeing him up close, I could tell that he was not only thinner, but also harder and more physically fit than I'd thought when I first spotted him at the drive-in. He had a neatly trimmed beard, a buzz cut, and humorless eyes.

"What's happening?" Dad asked.

"Um . . . what is this about, guys?" Evan asked. He almost seemed to have forgotten his humiliation.

That was when the skinny guy in the green shirt asked for Dad's phone and then, as I said, the three of them sat on Evan's futon watching a live stream while the menu screen music looped on the CRT.

A government official, the press secretary maybe, was giving a statement. At first I thought it was another press conference about a tweet, but after a minute it became clear that, this time, something had, in fact, really happened.

You might have guessed it, but let me just make it absolutely clear.

Dad's first money match coincided with the assassination of the Vice President of the United States. That's what we found out. Pence had been shot—shot and killed—during a visit to New York City. The Vice President had been killed while attending the Broadway show *The Whirligig*, and the whole world was watching the press secretary doing his best to convey the idea that the assassination was a very, very sad thing.

"Vice President Pence was more than just a brilliant politician and a relentless fighter for the US people, he was also a loving husband to his wife Carrie and a, uh . . . a loving father to their three children. Of course, the President has asked me to extend his regret and love to Vice President Mike Pence's family, and to the American people," he said.

It was more dignified than anything that had been said since November, but before the press guy was even done talking, the President arrived. It was a surprise whenever he showed up. He still seemed like he belonged on his old game show and not in Washington, DC, but there he was. He walked up to his press secretary, tapped him on the shoulder, and then took over. The press secretary picked up his notes and then bowed to the President like he was a butler or something.

"Hello everybody! Is everybody okay? It's a sad day, isn't it? It's a sad day. What happened in New York, at that play . . . it's very sad, and it's very wrong. It's really very, very wrong. I suppose they really wanted me? Right? I mean, Mike, he was an important guy, but if I was a Radical Islamist terrorist—and that's who it was, by the way. It was somebody—some terrible, terrible person—from ISIS. Not a Russian, like CNN has been saying. That's just more fake news. They should be ashamed of themselves. Really. And I mean that. But, I'll tell you something, if I was a Radical Islamist terrorist

I wouldn't bother with the Vice President. I really wouldn't. Not if I didn't have to, you know? If I were a terrorist from ISIS, I'd shoot the President. But, they didn't do that. And the reason they didn't do that is because they couldn't do it. Right? I mean, it's a sad day, and I don't want to blame anybody right now. They tell me that I ought not to start pointing fingers, but the thing is, when I took office I hired my own guys. I didn't, I don't, just rely on the Secret Service. Right? I didn't, I don't. I don't do that," the President said. He was getting at something maybe, but it was difficult to tell exactly what.

"It's happening," the guy in the yellow sweatshirt said. "Right on schedule."

"Yeah. That's right. It's been happening on schedule. That's the whole point, isn't it?" Dad said.

I should have figured something out right then, I think, but it was a lot to process. Besides, I was still thinking about how to get Evan to pay us. I was listening to the President, and so I didn't really notice what Dad and his friends were saying. Not right then.

"Not to knock the Secret Service. They're very, very good. I mean really, they're fantastic, but I hired my own people too, because you have to know the people protecting you very, very, very well. Especially now, after Mike has been shot like this. Especially now that we see what ISIS is willing to do," the President said.

"When will it come out?" the guy with the mustache and the muscles asked. "How long until the press says that Tiny Hands did it?"

That's what the NSA agent asked my Dad, but I didn't pay attention, because that's when Evan started to get mad. Or really, that's when Evan started getting scared. Evan said he wanted us to leave. He went to his dresser, opened a drawer unevenly, jerked it open so that a can of Mountain Dew that had been set atop a pile of comic books tipped over and spilled into what was probably his sock drawer. One of those rotating multi-colored disco ball lights fell over too, only it missed the drawer and shattered on the hard-wood floor.

Evan didn't let any of that distract him. He opened the dresser drawer, searched blindly under his underwear, and took out a baggie. Then he produced a sort of pathetic, moist-looking, and totally bent joint, tried to light it with a lighter that had been in the sock drawer too, and said it again.

"You need to leave," he said. He tried to light his joint a couple more times. A bunch of times, really. Then he threw the lighter down. "Who are you people? What is this? I mean, uh ... just ..."

He turned to me. "What is your Dad even doing, dude?"

We never got our fifty dollars.

Augmented Reality on the Bus

MATTHEW MUNSON, 544-23-1102, MESSENGER LOG, 04/19/17

4:19 PM

I'm sorta lonely because I'm the only one on the number 19 bus who isn't augmented. I can't even sit up front and talk to the bus driver, because there is no bus driver. I'm on one of Bucky's buses; it's fully automated.

4:23 PM

The guy next to me is maybe playing *Candy Crush* or *Minesweeper*. He's moving his hands around in the air, moving invisible Lemon Drops and Red Hots and lining them up, but for me there is nothing to look at. I just stare at what isn't there. I look at the perforated metal seat back in front of me and at the little rubber nubs on the floor. There is no game here.

Down the aisle from me there is a fat guy in green Lycra who is dribbling a virtual ball, bouncing it off the ceiling and windows.

I mean, that's what I assume he's doing. I don't really know what they're seeing or what it's like to live inside a perpetual video game. I figure there are a lot of blinking lights and a lot of noise in the GameCube world. Bucky must make sure that there is always something on the screen to keep you distracted. To keep you entertained.

4:26 PM

I'm alone on this bus. This might be the first time in like five years that I'm experiencing something directly; experiencing a moment on my own and without a screen.

Only, I do have a screen, right? I've got my smartphone in my hand right now, that's how I'm talking to you. It's only in comparison to everybody else that I'm unplugged. Bucky has redefined what it means to be IRL.

4:30 PM

I wonder what the last thing I did without a screen actually was.

4:31 PM

The first thing that comes to mind is being six years old at Couch Park with my Dad. We used to live on the other side of the river, and we'd go to the park on weekends. Dad would play pretend with me sometimes. We'd LARP as Harry Potter and Dumbledore or as Superman and Superboy. That is, he'd play with me for a little while. Eventually he'd get bored and take out his phone.

Does that count?

4:35 PM

I close my eyes and see a blinking cursor, a scroll of memes, dancing kittens, and your face . . .

4:37 PM

Maybe the last time I was really IRL was when you invited me to visit you at the Jesus compound and we listened to vinyl records. We actually found one album that wasn't Christian, remember? It was somebody's greatest hits, some 60s folk singer with a macho moustache and bad teeth.

I remember how you got goosebumps when you took off your shirt and the air hit your skin. You turned your back to me at that point and started reading the list of songs on that hippie album. Your voice was a little loud; a little awkward. You seemed nervous, but then I slipped my hand under your bra strap and totally failed. Those little hooks, I couldn't undo them, and my hand got sorta trapped.

You laughed. Then you just reached back, casually released all three hooks, and turned around again.

4:38 PM

What was the song we were listening to? "Operator"? It was a song about not making a phone call. The singer wanted to talk to his ex-girlfriend but he backed out of it and just sang the whole song to the operator. There was another breakup song after that one too, but I stopped paying attention to the lyrics around then. I don't really remember much about the music after that point.

4:43 PM

I'm going to say that counts as something that happened to me IRL.

4:45 PM

So I figured out what they're doing, or what most of them are doing.

The two-dimension puzzle game they're playing is an interface for assembly line work. About fifteen of the green people are passing iPhones back and forth, and as they move virtual candy into lines they are also touching the screens of one iPhone 7 after another.

What they're doing is deleting apps from the phones, turning off the link to iCloud, connecting the phones to laptops, uploading

Bucky's jailbreak software, and then, at the end of the process, injecting new code with USB sticks, injecting Bucky himself, into their stolen Apple products. Each phone is taken from one of two cardboard boxes at the front of the bus, silently passed along between the *Candy Crush*ers and, with an occasional over-the-shoulder gesture, moved through an elaborate process to another cardboard box in the back.

This bus is a Rube Goldberg machine built out of gamers.

4:50 PM

Most of this was already in place before Bucky even started the transition. The infrastructure was built before he arrived. All he had to do was hack the private routers in downtown Portland, Gresham, Beaverton, and Lake Oswego and then, presto, we had something like Universal Wi-Fi. Then he must have hijacked Uber and Amazon for transportation and shipping.

I wonder how much money Bucky was funneling into Soylent and Honey Bucket before he even informed Dad about the threat? Because all of that was ready from the start. Bucky was all set up to feed us and provide something like sanitation well before we arrived at what was supposedly our solution.

4:55 PM

I know all these details are probably boring to you, but don't you wonder about what's next? What kind of society can last on Soylent and Porta Potties? The new chroma key outfits are designed like union suits with a flap at the ass, but don't you think people will eventually want to come back to normality? I read that the *Mortal Combat* center at the Lloyd Center will have DryBath powder application centers, but won't somebody want to log off in order to take a shower? Won't somebody want to just take a coffee break eventually?

4:56 PM

And what about other stuff? How do people get together in there? When do people get a chance to listen to vinyl records on their parents' couch?

FriendshipandMore Part One

MATTHEW
5:05 PM

A girl just sat next to me. I can tell she's a girl because she's wearing a medium-length green wig on top of her chroma key mask. If she wasn't wearing augmentation goggles I would think that she's looking at me.

HEATHER
5:05 PM

Hi! My name is Heather and I'm playing a new game.

MATTHEW
5:06 PM

This is a private chat, Heather.

HEATHER
5:06 PM

The game I'm going to play is *FriendshipandMore*. It's an adults-only open world with integrated private arenas. There is a chathouse nearby. In *FriendshipandMore* chathouses, players can fully interact without breaking continuity. The one I'm thinking about is in just two stops.

> MATTHEW
> 5:07 PM

You talk like a bot.

> HEATHER
> 5:07 PM

FriendshipandMore provides conversational prompts to make social interaction easier and to assist you as you make connections, friends, and more. But, I am actually not a bot though.

> MATTHEW
> 5:08 PM

This is a private chat. I'm talking to my girlfriend. Please leave.

> HEATHER
> 5:08 PM

Sorry. I'm sorry. Sorry to have intruded.

> MATTHEW
> 5:11 PM

That was weird.

> HEATHER
> 5:12 PM

If you're talking to your girlfriend, how come she doesn't message you back? It looks like you're just talking to yourself.

MATTHEW
5:13 PM

Maybe I am just talking to myself, but it's still a private chat.

HEATHER
5:13 PM

Would you like to help me select a new avatar? I've been a redhead for six hours now; what color hair do you think I should have?

MATTHEW
5:14 PM

You don't have red hair. You have a green wig.

HEATHER
5:14 PM

FriendshipandMore offers 10,000 different avatars and you can design your own too. You can help me pick mine and I'll help you pick yours.

MATTHEW
5:15 PM

. . .

HEATHER
5:14 PM

Do you want to see what I look like right now? I could send you a picture if you promise not to share it around. A private picture.

MATTHEW
5:15 PM

No, thanks. Besides, I don't have any money.

I don't have any money either.

Right. Of course you don't. Look, I'm not interested. I'm not even part of this thing you're doing. I don't have the suit for it, I don't want one. I'm not joining your orgy. I'm not interested.

She just rang the bell and she's getting get off. I wonder where she's really going?

Well, that was weird.

It turns out that the *FriendshipandMore* chathouse is an abandoned RadioShack. If that's a private arena, what would a public arena look like?

So, I followed Heather. It's not that I was tempted to take her up on her offer, nor that I wanted to see what she'd do in the chathouse exactly. It was more that . . . I guess I actually did want to see what she did in the chathouse, especially when I found out what this *FriendshipandMore* chathouse was actually like.

Picture a room with no furniture, but just gray carpet, grungy off-white walls, what are probably asbestos ceiling tiles left over from the 20th century, and a cable hanging down right in the middle of the room. Now imagine this room is filled with various hovering drones, robots, and a dozen green-suited gamers.

So I followed Heather to the front door of the RadioShack, looked in the store front window, and, taking in the whole scene, I decided not to follow her inside.

This is what I just saw: maybe a half-dozen miniature Roombas to clean up the refuse left behind, about six K5 robots that were apparently serving drinks with straws, and about four or five over-sized Rovio robots carrying wooden stools, feathers, tubes, and vibrators.

Once Heather was inside I couldn't keep track of her; she just blended in with all the other green ladies in wigs.

The gamers were waving to each other, stopping to stare at signs or art or maybe speech balloons that were hanging in the air, invisible to me. A few of them were dancing slowly around the cable wire, bumping into it as they held each other close and shuffled their feet back and forth mechanically.

After two minutes things picked up and the male gamers positioned themselves around the periphery of the room in order to watch while anonymous players in wigs took turns solo dancing, but their movements were unnatural. These girls looked a bit like windup toys as they did the same identical moves, clearly choosing from a menu before performing each act. This sporadic quality, and the obvious moments where techniques and positions were chosen, made the encounters in the RadioShack appear as if they'd been badly edited. The solo dancers would point to one of the men along the periphery and he'd join in with a set pattern of reactive hip movements and strokes while the machines rolled in between with prods and suction cups. In this brave new world, sex occurs at a distance, even when you're actually in the same room with this or that boyfriend or girlfriend or whatever.

So, yeah. That happened. Which isn't exactly putting my mind at ease. Call me a romantic, but I prefer regular old dating to this. Still, just in terms of efficiency, it is something of a relief to realize that the newly added flaps in the chroma key suits can be put to use outside the context of a Honey Bucket porta potty.

Eternity in a Nickle Arcade

MATTHEW MUNSON, 544-23-1102, FACEBOOK POSTS, 04/20/17

1:03 AM

The reason I won't play along isn't that I'm allergic to Soylent. It's not because I don't want to wear a chroma key jumpsuit. It's not even that I'm super attached to being me and wouldn't prefer to try out being Sonic the Hedgehog or Ryu for an afternoon or a year. The reason is . . . well, it's because of Sally.

Sally loved God. What she loved was how her religion gave her the opportunity to rearrange the world in her head. She was always imagining her dream house, or her dream town. Her religion gave her permission to speculate. It gave her a reason to wonder what the world would be like if every other building were made of glass and whether or not the afterlife would have grocery stores. What sort of life would be good enough to last forever? What kind of gadgets will there be in heaven? What fashions? What sorts of entertainment will there be?

That's what her hobby was. Figuring that stuff out. But now that video games have taken over everything, she probably doesn't ask those kinds of questions. God is dead, right? Nobody needs religion anymore, and Sally is busy living out worlds of *Warcraft, Minecraft,* or *Donkey Kong.*

1:24 AM

We went to the Avalon Nickle Arcade on our first real date, and Sally told me that the place made her feel weird. The Avalon had been around forever; for over a hundred years. The clown on the sign by the entrance, a classic circus clown with a white face, an open-mouthed smile, and pupilless eyes creeped her out.

"I can't help but think about the dead people who used to come here. What will they make of how we've changed the place? When they're resurrected and come back, will they like what we've done? What will people from the 70s think? Will all those moms with bee-hives and bell bottoms be able to adjust to touchscreen games and laser tag?" she asked.

Sally was wearing this brown polyester dress with orange and blue stripes, a pattern that reminded me of minimalist paintings or Swiss poster art. She looked like she might be from the 70s her-self, and like one of her imagined housewives, she seemed averse to video games. She used the nickels they gave us at the door to buy nachos with cheddar-flavored liquid and a Coke. We parked in a booth under the movie screen in the second game room. The sec-ond game room had once been a theater and still had the screen. We sat across from the air hockey table under Fox News and TV Land and talked about the end of the world.

"A lot of people have this idea that heaven is up in the sky. They have this idea that it's just clouds and robes, or that it's maybe a place where there is nothing but energy. But, heaven will be here, on Earth. If you're Christian you should know that much. Even Catholics and Mormons should know that," Sally said.

I just nodded along, agreeing with her. I didn't really care what Christians should know about the afterlife. I took her hand in mine and she let me. She offered me a sip of her Coke and I took one even though there was lipstick on the straw.

"That's why old buildings like this are weird. After Tribulation, after Jesus comes back, we'll get immortal and perfect bodies and we'll just keep going as we are now. I mean, it'll be different. It'll be better, but ..."

"But what?"

"But, it will still be like it is. It won't be different. If you're married when you die then you'll still be married when you're resurrected. If you live in a trailer park or in a town with a water slide, you'll still live in a trailer park. You'll still live near a water slide. Those will stay," she said.

Being in really old buildings, in historic places, confused her, especially when a place had both new and old parts to it. When the old and the new sat side by side, it made her wonder. What version of the Avalon Nickel Arcade would there be after the End Times? Would the Avalon still have the strange clown on the front window? That clown with his gaping smile? Or would Jesus replace him? Would the new and perfect arcade feature classic games from the 80s? Would we be playing *Pac-Man* forever, or would there be Skee-Ball and coin-operated kinetoscopes?

"Mom and Dad don't think about it. Most people don't wonder. But I want to know. If Heaven is going to be here, if it's going to happen on Earth, then what will Portland be like? What will we do every day? Will we still have jobs? Will I still work at Dairy Queen?"

"Probably not," I said. "Doesn't sound good enough."

"It wouldn't be so bad," she said. "I just wouldn't want to live in the past. I wouldn't want to have to give up what we've got just to make all the dead people happy. Would you? Would you want to give up the internet just so people born 100 years ago feel comfortable?"

"I guess not," I said. But the truth was, that eternal life in the past? A resurrection that included bringing back Syzygy's *Computer*

Space game or *Astro Race*? A heaven where men in bowler hats and women in old-fashioned bodices would play *Bash Bash Revolution* forever? That was appealing.

I let go of Sally's hand and we sat in silence for a while, watching Hannity and reading the scroll at the bottom of the screen. A thousand more American troops were being deployed to the Ukrainian border. The stock market was up for the twelfth straight week.

At the Avalon they have a few multi-game cabinets where you can pick your favorite Golden Age game, but we had to cycle through most all of them before we found any Sally even recognized, and then she said she didn't want to play even though we'd already put our nickels in.

I played *Centipede* while she talked about the apocalypse and I complained about Dad. I told her that I'd taught Dad to play *Bash* and that he'd quickly mastered the game and started playing for money.

Sally was sympathetic, but more than that, she paid attention. She didn't always pay attention.

When we played air hockey, for instance, she didn't seem to pay any attention at all, but just let me win. At the claw machine she didn't come close to snapping up a stuffed Garfield or an iPod cover, and most of the time, when I was talking, I got the sense that she was bored.

"The trick is to clear away the mushrooms."

"Is that the trick?"

"You've got to make sure the bottom third of the screen is clear so you'll have enough time to take out the centipedes. If you leave mushrooms everywhere the centipedes will get to the bottom too fast," I said.

It dawned on me that Sally was never going to play *Centipede*. Even if Heaven was a place on Earth. Even if eternal life after the rapture included an X-Arcade cabinet, Sally would find other stuff to occupy her time.

"Are you jealous that your Dad is better than you at your favorite game?"

"He's not better than I am," I said.

"You're better?" she asked.

"Yeah."

"But he still beats you," Sally asked. "How does he do that?"

"He cheats," I told her.

We moved on from the multi-game cabinet and Sally found a pinball table she liked, this antique called *Dancing Lady* with glass light bulbs and a mechanical ballerina in the scoreboard that did pirouettes when the pinball hit the top bumpers.

"How?" she asked, looking at me.

"His computer program . . . Bucky. It helps him win."

"How does the computer help him win?" Sally asked.

I tried to explain how Dad's AI worked, even though I didn't really know. I told her that Bucky was like Deep Blue and could think super fast. Bucky could compute so much data that it could see ahead into the future.

"How does that work?" Sally asked. She threw her body against the pinball machine, shaking it just enough to send her ball spinning toward the bumpers again, but not hard enough to trigger a tilt.

I wasn't used to her paying attention. I wasn't used to Sally being interested in my life or any of that, so I just told her what I knew, and that sort of turned out to be a mistake. She'd really been paying attention and she started making connections. Sort of wild connections, I thought. She asked me why the NSA wanted Dad to watch the news report about the Vice President, and what it meant that his computer program could take over a person's nervous system, and why it was that he'd come home to begin with.

"What do you call it when everything changes? When your whole way of living and thinking is changed? When your worldview goes, when your way of life goes, and is replaced by something else?" she asked.

"A clusterfuck?"

"No, no," she said. "It's a paradigm shift. Right? That's what it's called. What causes a paradigm shift is when something new, when some new understanding, comes along. But you know what? That's what an apocalypse is too. The apocalypse is not just Armageddon. It's not just a big disaster, but also a new beginning."

Sally turned out to be good at pinball. The ballerina kept spinning and spinning while she explained it to me.

"Your Dad didn't invent an AI just to help him win video games, did he?" she asked.

"That's true," I said. "Video games aren't the point. Dad doesn't care about video games. The NSA doesn't care about video games."

"What do they care about?" she asked. "What are they doing?"

I didn't answer, but just watched her play. Really, I watched her stop playing. After a terrific first ball, she lost interest, and she quickly cycled through the remaining four. She let them drain and then turned to look at me before the toy ballerina had even finished spinning.

"What is your Dad doing? What does this computer program do?" she asked.

"It's an AI," I said. "It doesn't do just one thing. I don't know."

"What was it designed for?" she asked.

"I don't know."

Sally told me that I should know. That I had the right to know. She offered to help me find out.

"How should I do that?" I asked.

"You have to talk to it."

"Talk to it?"

"No. Wait. You don't need to talk to it. I want to talk to it," she said.

Sally believed in God. She was very religious because she wanted to rethink and reimagine the whole world. But when she found out about Dad's AI, when she heard about his success with *Bash*, all the scripture and all the prophecies about frogs and blood pouring from the sky? All that was meaningless.

"I want to talk to your Dad's AI," she said. "Can you arrange that?"

At the time, it seemed possible.

News Night

MATTHEW MUNSON, 544-23-1102, FACEBOOK POSTS, 04/20/17

9:03 AM

One of the reasons I started playing *Bash* is that Mom doesn't care about TV. Back in 2009, when all of my friends got digital TVs and started watching Nickelodeon and the Cartoon Network in high-definition, I was stuck watching PBS on a 13" RCA Colortrak CRT with a digital converter. Mom had purchased the tube TV back in 1995 and, for the first seven years of my life, we almost never watched it. It was covered by a Navajo blanket, except on special movie nights or when she wanted to watch the news. Mom's 1995 TV was great for *Bash*. A modern TV's video lag was a major problem for competitive *Bash* players, and CRT TVs like Mom's had no lag.

After Dad won his first money match he wanted to try tournament play, and we found one to go to right away. The night before that, before Dad's first *Bash* tournament, something big happened, and instead of letting Dad practice *Bash*, Mom insisted on watching TV news. I guess it was a TV news night for most everybody over forty. Most everybody wanted to watch the fallout from the

Russia/US dogfight over Crimea live, and for Gen X and Boomers that meant watching TV.

Mom was silent as Amanpour prattled on about a new Cold War and the increase of NATO troops in Poland and Finland, but Dad kept talking to the screen.

"Cold War? This baby is hot!" he said, and took a sip of beer. As he leaned way back in our dirty beige La-Z-Boy, the footrest popped up on him, and the whole chair threatened to topple. "Jesus," he said. "Why haven't you gotten another lounger already? This was broken when we got it!"

Amanpour mentioned that long-range ballistic missiles aimed at Moscow were standing ready and the Strategic Air Command was at DEFCON 2.

"She thinks she's in an action movie or something," Dad said. "Our DEFCON level doesn't mean anything; what's important is in Syria. In the theater. How are the troops on the ground behaving?" Dad's smile never left his face. He was really enjoying himself and I, in an effort at sarcasm, offered to make some microwave popcorn for him.

"Yeah, yeah," he said. "That would be good actually," he said. Then he pointed to the TV. "Can you believe this?"

Mom turned to look at him and her facial expression transformed from numb shock to anger.

"This doesn't worry you?" she asked.

Dad looked at her and frowned. He was confused by this reaction from her. He didn't understand why she was peeved with him.

"Well," he said, "it's obvious that—"

Dad didn't explain what was obvious, because his phone pinged him and interrupted his train of thought. He held up a finger to Mom, looked at his phone, and then put his earbuds in. Emotion drained from his face. He got up from the La-Z-Boy, walked into the kitchen, which was where he'd left his laptop, and Mom followed along after him.

It was around that point when my phone pinged me, alerted me to the latest tweet from the President of the United States. I hadn't set my phone to follow the President's tweets, but I guess the President had the power to push his 140 character missives on me, on everybody with a Twitter account, maybe.

@realDonaldTrump: Sending 1500 US troops to Finland

More proof that this Trump-Russia story is a hoax.

"You act like you're not part of the world. That's what's wrong with the NSA's projection and models, too. You people never take yourselves into account." Mom was clearly audible even over the sound from the TV. She was pretending to wash the dishes again, banging pots and pans around in the sink in a desperate attempt to gets Dad's attention. To get Dad's reassurance. She didn't get either.

She was right, of course. Dad almost never took himself into account. He never saw himself as part of the world he wanted to change. Maybe that's why he left Mom and me behind. He'd never really been part of the family to begin with.

Maybe that isn't fair. I can sort of remember how things were different a while back. When I was really young, Mom and Dad were young too. They used to be like a single person in my mind; I didn't really differentiate them from each other way back then. I'd call Mom "Dad" and Dad "Mom" and not even feel weird or embarrassed when they corrected me about it. They were one person, and that's why they were always hanging on each other. I can picture them standing close together and watching me come down a curly slide or rotate on a merry-go-round. Back then, back when I could barely talk, Dad was at the center.

My earliest memory is about Dad, actually. It's about Dad promising to change things; to make things better. But as with all kid memories, I don't really trust it. You can't trust that stuff, can you?

But anyway, in my memory I was on that slide, on the curly slide at Couch Park. Mom and Dad were watching me as I ran around on the wooden play structure, applauding my every step and apparently very pleased that I wasn't getting splinters. I got to the slide, to the red plastic curly slide, and Mom started screaming. Mom was screaming and as I slid down, as I took the first curve, Dad reached out and stopped me. Dad stopped my descent, grabbing me by my stomach basically, knocking the air out of me, because he didn't want me to reach the bottom.

I tried to cry, or scream as Dad lifted me up and over the plastic lip of the slide, but I couldn't make a sound because I didn't have the air I needed. I couldn't protest. I could barely move. All I could manage was a wheeze. Dad carried me to Mom, who was shouting at him to do something, TO DO SOMETHING, and he handed me over to her.

There was a body. There was a dead junkie at the bottom of the slide. The young guy with an orange beard lying on top of his olive-green canvas knapsack was probably dead. He was dead, actually, but we didn't know that for sure yet. All that we knew for sure was that he was on his back at the bottom of the slide with a needle in his arm.

This is where my memory gets fuzzy, or where I start to have doubts about it, because what I remember next is that we were behind a police line, behind a chain-link fence that the police had put up to block off the play structure. I remember watching the EMTs take the body of the junkie away. I remember watching the needle fall out of his arm and into the wood chips. But that can't be right. Why would we have stayed that long? Why would they put up a chain-link fence? And why don't I remember whether Dad did anything for the young man?

But that's what I remember. We stood behind a chain-link fence. Dad held Mom close to him as the EMT workers took the body away, and the needle slipped from the junkie's arm and into the chips. The body of the junkie seemed to be very light. It was almost as though the EMTs were moving a pile of old rags.

"It's supposed to be better than this," Dad said. And he held Mom close. And Mom held me close. And we knew that Dad was going to do something to make it better, to make it right.

A map of the United States was on the screen and the CNN anchor narrated the possibility of apocalypse in the same way local news covers the weather. On the map, the yellow circles indicated bombs that would strike military targets, orange were the blast zones for rural communities, and the red circles were the cities that would be destroyed if Russian missiles landed.

"Don't worry, this isn't anything new. When I was a kid, this was the kind of thing you'd see on the news every day," Dad said as he made his way back to the La-Z-Boy.

"Come on, Dad," I said. "I'm seventeen, not six. Don't kid me."

Dad nodded at me and smiled, and it was an admission of a sort. But then he turned on the GameCube and selected Robin Hood as his character.

As the world teetered, Dad practiced L-canceling and shielding.

Oregon *Bash* Revolution

MATTHEW MUNSON, 544-23-1102, FACEBOOK POSTS, 04/20/17

11:02 AM

The *Bash* tournament was held in the Multicultural Center of Smith Memorial at Portland State University, which maybe was a sign of things to come. What had once been designated a space for the development of "engaged cultural dialogue between different peoples" (that's what the dedication plaque said, anyhow) had been made over as an arena for a battle between cutesy Japanese video game characters. Murals celebrating Latino liberation and Black History Month were covered over by posters of Marshmallow, Robotman, Princess Teacup, and Robin Hood. Folding tables with rows of CRT screens atop them filled a space meant for traditional dances. The multicultural center was overrun with Asian and white boys wearing various nerd badges. Kids wearing Jayne hats, *Star Trek* hoodies, and T-shirts with binary messages printed on them milled about the GameCube stations. Walking into the tournament room, I was surrounded by the socially inept, the virginal, and the damned.

Dad signed in and was seeded into the second bracket, which meant we had about a half an hour before he'd play. To kill time, we found an unoccupied GameCube and played a casual game. I talked Dad into playing without his earbuds; without Bucky's help.

It was a casual game, but I really wanted to win. I insisted on selecting the stage for battle. I took the first port. I suggested that Dad play Robin Hood, while I played a character called RingChamp from an 80s boxing game of the same name, and then proceeded to wipe him out. I mean, on his own Dad was still a competent player, he knew basic strategy, he knew how to L-cancel and how to counter, but he was slow and his character was weak. Worse than that, he was a plodder on his own; he was predictable. Without too much effort, I four-stocked him. All I had to do was stay close, time my grabs right, and deliver a few body blows.

In the second game, when Dad chose RingChamp as his character, I chose Robin Hood, with the aim of humiliating him further. Playing a defensive game against him, always keeping just out of reach, I managed to beat him again. Flaming arrows and hip shots damaged his boxer enough to slow him down. My William Tell special move delivered the kills. I four-stocked him again, ending the set.

"You trying to shake my confidence?" Dad asked.

"I might sign up for the third bracket," I said.

Dad put his earbuds in and then shook his head no. "I need you to watch and evaluate. I know it seems like I don't need your help when I'm getting AI assistance, but I want your eyes on this. It's not about video games. The application of AI performance augmentation is a life-and-death project. Do or die," he said.

The geeks at the main table announced that the second bracket was starting and everybody competing needed to put on their Princess Teacup badges and line up under the poster of Bubble Land.

"That's us?" Dad asks.

"That's you," I said. "Bubble Land," I said. "Do or die."

Dad started off toward the relevant poster and then noticed I wasn't following along and turned back around.

"That's us," he said. It was an instruction and not a question.

"I'll catch up."

While Dad played and won his first set, I fooled around with Robin Hood against the CPU. I practiced my long game against Princess Teacup, and figured out how to drop a series of apples on her head, and how to deliver multiple William Tell shots. After a few minutes of this, after four-stocking the computer at the top level, I realized I'd drawn a couple of onlookers.

"Nice," one them said.

"Yeah. I think he's playable, really," I said. When I beat Princess Teacup in a third game, I turned around to see who was watching.

"I think my Princess could beat your Robin Hood," he said. I didn't recognize the guy, this *Bash* champion, until he was beating me. Going by the moniker "the Bride," Mike Berger was part of a doubles team who, while never quite reaching the number one slot, always placed in the top five. The team's name was "Bride and Groom," and Mike played Princess Teacup and a guy named Todd played Zorro. Of the two of them it was established opinion that the Bride was the stronger player. He did more with a weaker character, he was more creative, and he placed higher in single competition.

About halfway through my game with the Bride I managed to get my Robin Hood to the rafters without being pulled back and rolling. I sniped one stock, one kill, and had to count that as my victory because the match turned around on me.

After the game I tried to talk shop with Mike, but the Bride didn't care for it. He wasn't into *Bash* tactics and he didn't listen to me when I explained why I'd lost to him. He didn't even tell me that there were "no Johns allowed." All he wanted to talk about was international politics, ICBMs, and the Bulletin of Atomic Scientists. *Bash* was a distraction. What mattered were troop deployments, secret armies, the assassination of the Vice President, and all that kind of stuff.

"We're probably already living under martial law," the Bride told me.

In that moment politics seemed more important than video games, even though it would turn out they were the same thing.

A crowd gathered around the Bride and me. The players in the tournament were effectively ignored as we debated the likelihood of the end.

12:15 PM

When my father took on his first opponent at a GameCube station with a 13" CRT, there was no audience for his match. Nobody thought to pay attention to some middle-aged man wearing a "TACOCAT SPELLED BACKWARDS IS TACOCAT" T-shirt, and so nobody was watching when he started to win.

Before the tournament Dad told me that overall what he needed for success paralleled what the Pentagon needed if they were going to counter an intercontinental nuclear attack, and I figured what he meant was that thermonuclear war was all about the timing.

Really competitive *Bash* games are usually determined by response times, and the difference can sometimes be measured in nanoseconds. Reflex training is a big part of what makes a great *Bash* player great. Which was another reason why nobody expected Dad could win. Nobody knew about Bucky and how the augmentation of Dad's neurology was working like a fountain of youth. It was that augmentation, along with Bucky's predictive response algorithm, that made all the difference.

Here's the thing, though: the augmentation actually worked too well. As Dad moved through the ranks, as he won game after game, match after match, he did start getting attention. Despite the overall lack of interest in *Bash* that night, despite the Bride's laser-like focus on the White House and everyone's developing dread around American politics—a dimension of life that most of the gamers seemed to have just recently discovered—eventually, people did notice Dad. Then, once they noticed him, they started to hate him.

Watching him at the tournament was like watching *The Karate Kid* turned on its head. That is, rather than finding new and greater challenges as he went along, Dad seemed to become more and more invincible with each match. The more talented the player he faced off against, the more favored they were, the more quickly he devastated them.

Dad was OP, boring to watch, and seemingly bored himself. Worse, he didn't know how to interact with the kids he defeated, didn't seem to care when the crowd booed him, and didn't take any pleasure from winning. He chose his characters at random, switching in mid-match sometimes, and always used unorthodox, and often cowardly, tactics. He never let his opponent recover from an attack, but pressed every advantage. And when he found a move that worked for him, he stayed with it. He was happy to just mash the same button over and over. He'd kick his opponent in the shin, doing minimal damage, but he'd do it again and again and drain their health with a hundred tiny blows. His speed, the sheer number of times he could hit the same sequence of buttons, gave him his wins. By the third match he wasn't just beating his opponents. He wasn't just four-stocking them. He was playing perfect games. Nobody could land anything against him.

The AI made him efficient, but it also made him inhuman. It made him evil.

You might think I'm overstating, but everybody was rooting against him. And a rumor started circulating early on that he'd installed a cheat code for Marshmallow. Halfway through his fifth match the judges paused the game in order to inspect the GameCube.

They made him switch ports. They removed and replaced the Game-Cube's memory card, but he kept on winning in impossible ways.

I mean, it's not like anybody sticks to all the unwritten rules of *Bash*. Following the etiquette too scrupulously isn't a way to win friends anyhow. Nobody bows after a win; not anymore. Nobody waits for the other player to finish a taunt before launching an attack. It's a more ruthless game for everyone. But repetitive play, relentless exploitation of a character's weakness, refusing to take any risks or try any move that might open you up to a counter-attack? It went against what *Bash* is. It went against what made the game catch on.

If Dad had been playing in a chess tournament, he would have been caught out immediately. In chess, AI assistance is a form of cheating, and it probably should be for *Bash* too. I think AI augmentation really ruins *Bash*, makes it meaningless. I doubt very many people are playing *Bash* in the new economy. The new economy has to have killed the game. After a decade of Nintendo trying to end competitive *Bash*, it's weird that a computer AI should do it for them. But really, why play if what you're really doing is just acting out computer instructions?

12:32 PM

When Dad started to lose it was satisfying to watch, even though it took a player just as heartless and methodical as Dad was to take him down.

Mayday was ranked second in the world at *Bash*, and he was famous for winning with Robin Hood. Watching him on YouTube was what inspired me to develop my own distance game. He had the record for the greatest number of perfect games, was also a highly ranked *Street Fighter* player, and, worst of all, he had some-how amassed a female fan base. In other words, Mayday was good-looking, confident, and mean.

Dad played Marshmallow, and for the first minute nothing happened. Dad floated out of reach, avoiding Robin Hood's arrows, and Robin Hood jumped into the rafters, avoiding Marshmallow's goo attacks. They were both playing defensive games. They were both looking for openings, for an opportunity to mash some buttons, but neither side was willing to risk launching the first attack. Or so it seemed.

It was Mayday who broke the truce, coming for Dad and making him sweat. Dad had been in a haze, being moved by the tone in his ear and sort of watching the games as if from a distance, but then Mayday took a stock off of him and Dad woke up.

"Fuck a duck," Dad said. And I remembered that winning was not just something Dad was doing, it was something he wanted. If Dad could take first in the tournament, it would confirm Bucky could overcome some of the limits of meatspace. If Dad could be the first middle-aged *Bash* champion, then other problems, other people, might be perfectible too. When Mayday launched himself from the rafters, fell onto Marshmallow, grabbed, and then threw him out of range, Dad let out a groan. Marshmallow floated up slowly, seeming to just recover from what might have been a fatal blow, but then Mayday followed up. Mayday's Robin Hood let fly a William Tell, and the combo of the apple and the arrow punctured Marshmallow, letting the air out. Marshmallow fell like a stone.

Dad had lost his first stock after just two blows. Mayday had taken advantage of a weakness in Marshmallow that most players didn't know anything about. Deflating Marshmallow? How was that even possible?

Dad changed characters after he lost the first game. He went with Zorro, a very reliable character, especially against Robin Hood, and it worked out for him. Dad won that game, but he won in a very conventional way. Dad just made sure to stay close, to use full force blows, and to shield grab whenever possible. Watching him win that way, watching him struggle, I felt kind of sorry for him because I could tell that, even though he'd won, the match was going to go to Mayday.

Dad looked panicked as Bucky failed him. He stuck out his tongue, curling it over his top lip in concentration. He made sounds, little groans and objections, and he lost one stock after another until, finally, he lost the match.

Dad didn't talk to me in the car on the way back home and that was fine by me. I didn't need to talk. I was content to hold his second-place medal for him and enjoy the moment. But, when he didn't say anything to Mom when we arrived, when he left his smartphone on the arm of the couch and headed straight the kitchen to fetch himself a bottle, I figured things were worse than I'd thought.

Sally Speaks in Tongues

MATTHEW MUNSON, 544-23-1102, FACEBOOK POSTS, 04/20/17

2:21 PM

The next time I saw Sally I disappointed her. Back when we first hooked up, I hadn't been surprised when she'd told me that she had a direct relationship with God, but when we met at Mt. Scott Park for a date, a date that I thought would give us an opportunity to sit in the grass or on a park bench and make out a little, a date that could be a mundane reprieve from the drama of *Bash* and the end of the world, Sally did surprise me. Apparently she was on speaking terms with God now, and he'd told her to leave her church, to run away.

"Why would he say that?" I asked.

"I think this is the end times for real," Sally said. "What did your Dad's AI tell you?"

Sally had big plans apparently. She had some idea that God and the AI might be working together. That there was some unseen conspiracy working itself out, and that she needed to talk to the AI in order to receive her next instruction. It was crazy stuff, but not any crazier than the rest of her religion. The only difference was that now the craziness was completely her own.

"The first time I realized that God was really communicating with me, I was at Dairy Queen," she said. "I mean, the first time I realized that he was talking to me specifically. Not to the whole congregation. Not to the minister and then to me, but directly and only . . . me."

"Ah, that explains a lot," I said.

She'd gotten a brain freeze while eating a chocolate-dipped soft serve, and she'd seen sparks or stars in front of the fake wood paneling. When her head cleared she found that rather than sparks, she was looking at the HELP WANTED sign in the window, and as she listened to a girl she later found out was named Brenda take a chicken strip order from a greasy 14-year-old boy in a green-and-brown camouflage baseball cap, she had an epiphany. The moment had "come together" for her, and she knew that God wanted her to work at DQ.

"That's pretty silly," I told her. She pulled away from me then. Not really angry, but insistent that I take her seriously about this. It was apparently okay with her if I didn't believe that Jesus literally died on the cross for our sins, but it was not okay to doubt that God wanted her to serve soft serve ice cream and French fries to single moms and stoned teens in the Woodstock neighborhood.

"I'm not crazy," she told me. "I might not be smart like you, but I'm not crazy."

"Look, if God is talking to you, telling you to work at Dairy Queen or to talk to my Dad's AI, shouldn't you bring that up with your ministers?"

"Not them," she said. "They want to be the ones who decide whether God is calling you. I can't tell them."

Sally told me that one of the reasons she didn't talk to God when she was attending services in her super church was because she could tell when people were faking, and she could especially tell when they were faking their ability to speak in tongues. Fake glossolalia apparently sounds like English words that have gone just a little wrong. A faker will say something like "Yoosh Usta couldna fafa expost I drive como a mellow bow tie," or something like that. Phonies are apparently easy to spot.

"I used to do it all the time," she said. She had a history of faking herself out. When she was young, she used to participate enthusiastically in church services. She'd share prophecies that she'd make up on the spot, lay hands on her elders, and seek out evil spirits in her peers, but after puberty she stopped pretending, and for a long time she didn't believe that she had any spiritual gifts. She even doubted spiritual gifts were real.

But all that changed once she realized she was meant to work at Dairy Queen.

We were sitting on a picnic bench, and I was looking up at the pine trees and the sky, when she asked me again.

"What did your Dad's AI tell you?" she asked.

I told her that I hadn't talked to Dad's AI. I told her about how Dad had lost the tournament. She moved away from me on the bench and lit up.

She was probably having some kind of psychological thing happen at the Dairy Queen. What she described was sort of Jungian. Just a bunch of meaningful coincidences, and not very impressive coincidences either. Humans were good at recognizing, or even creating patterns.

"I can see things you don't," she said. "I notice things that you ignore."

"Like what?" I asked.

"Like the fact that a guy with a weird beard is following us," she said. "He's smoking a cigarette over by the teeter-totters."

3:10 PM

When I told her that the guy with the beard was probably with the NSA, and that he was probably one of Dad's colleagues, she approached him. She figured he might help her, even though I wouldn't. She thought maybe he would let her talk to the AI and get instructions.

She walked over to him, tucked a lock of her hair behind her ear, and bummed a toke off his cigarette. After talking to him for another thirty seconds, she'd acquired a whole cigarette. I watched the two of them from a distance, hanging out around a trash can by the jogging path, as she talked and laughed with the stranger. Sally was putting out her cigarette, tapping the ash onto the asphalt, when I finally got up the nerve to join them.

"Hey, Matt," the guy with the beard said. He smiled at me and raised his eyebrows like he thought he was very charismatic; very cool in his red knit hat and close-fit sweater. He was used to hanging out with middle-aged nerds and felt good about himself in comparison.

"This is Louis," Sally said.

Louis was in his early thirties, a lot younger than my Dad. He had, as I already mentioned, this long, shaggy beard that marked him as either Amish or from some gentrifying neighborhood, somewhere in NE Portland or Brooklyn or somewhere.

In the space of maybe three minutes, Sally had found out what Louis did for the NSA. He was a debugger and office boy, basically. But like most of Dad's team, Louis knew stuff that was top secret while not knowing how to keep information to himself. These guys didn't need a security culture because, most of the time, nobody cared what they did or even really wanted to talk to them. But Sally was interested, and when she asked him about his classified work at the NSA, when she asked him just what Dad was trying to do with the AI, Louis did the natural thing and just answered.

"We're trying to stop a war," Louis said.

"I knew it," Sally said.

"How is that coming along then?" I asked. I gestured at Louis's cigarettes but he shook his head no.

"Your dad would kill me," he said.

"Come on, man," I said. "It's the end of the world anyhow." I took one of Louis's cigarettes, but it tasted bad and I put it right out.

3:45 PM

Louis told us the plan. Dad wanted to make Trump fitter, happier, more productive. The idea was to train Bucky to be the ultimate personal trainer, the ultimate therapy machine, the ultimate guru. The goal was to help Bucky demolish the self-help business. They would start by improving Trump, by instigating a handshake with him and then taking over his nervous system so that he would make better decisions, smarter policies, and so that he would learn to control his mouth.

"That'll be the first step, anyhow," Louis said.

Rather than making out, Sally and I spent our date listening to one of Dad's friends explain how they were going to save the world. As the minutes ticked by; as the day shifted, I realized that even if he couldn't place first at a *Bash*, he was smart enough, wily enough, to spread his religion. Apparently he had all of the NSA converted, or if not that, then at least the entire team.

"It's a race we're in," Louis said. "Between stupidity and intelligence. And we're about to cross the finish line."

The three of us sat at the picnic table and, while hipster mothers let their kids risk their lives on the curly slide and teenagers assembled outside the roller rink, Louis spread the gospel. He replaced Sally's Apostolic faith with a faith in binary code.

"Tell me something," I asked. "Do you even know what you're involved in? Do you know what Dad actually thinks? What the secret doctrine is?"

"Do you?" Louis asked.

Sally bummed another cigarette from Louis, his next-to-last one. "What secret doctrine?"

"Shall I tell her?" Louis asked.

"Go ahead," I told him.

"There is a chance, a really good chance actually, that all of this, all of these experiences we're having, that they aren't real. There is like a 99% chance that we're already living inside Bucky, or if not inside Bucky, then some other AI."

Sally nodded, but she didn't take it in.

"If we're in some virtual reality; if this isn't real but a kind of recording or program, that would be really good news. Don't you see?"

Sally still didn't get it. She let out a stream of smoke and squinted through it at the agent. I thought then that she might be developing some skepticism about the whole project. I hoped she was.

"That would mean this was all a test," Sally said. "That would mean that there is a solution."

"Right," Louis said. "All we have to do is find it."

5:20 PM

Louis didn't leave until about a half-hour before Sally had to go to work, and this time she was the one who disappointed me. Sally was too excited, too filled up with hope, to settle down and let me put my tongue in her mouth. She needed her tongue free so she could keep talking.

"Wait," she said. "Wait."

I took my hands off her and hoped that whatever it was she wanted to know, whatever question she had, it would be easy to answer.

"I need a phone," she said. "I need an iPhone, I think. You need to get me one."

The problem there was that I didn't have enough money for an iPhone. I could swipe one for her maybe, but it wouldn't have a cell plan. Without Wi-Fi, it would be worthless.

142 DOUGLAS LAIN

"I don't know about that, but I need one. It's like Louis said. This is probably all a test. This is all like one of your video games. You don't have to know what to do with one of those special objects that you win in a video game. You just grab it and then figure out what to do with it after that. Right?"

We had maybe ten minutes left before our date was going to be over, and I put my hand on her knee again, but after a couple of quick kisses, she stopped me again.

"It's supposed to be this way," she told me. "I just need a phone. And you'll get one for me, right?"

I told her I would and then, without even another peck, the date was over.

"Bring it to the DQ," she said as she flung her backpack over her shoulder.

I grunted at her.

"Don't be a baby. Just bring a phone to the DQ and I'll make you a Blizzard. Bring me a phone and we can spend some time together then, in the parking lot near the blackberry bushes."

"The blackberry bushes?"

"Yeah," she said. "Don't worry so much. Don't be grumpy."

And then Sally was gone. She walked away from me; left me on the park bench and walked away. It was a bit like she'd disappeared. It felt like she'd just blinked out. She left the screen and expected I would complete the boss fight all on my own.

The Spectacular Solution
and the Disappearance of Dad

MATTHEW MUNSON, 544-23-1102, FACEBOOK POSTS, 04/21/17

2:30 AM

The reason this is happening is because Kufo was reading a book about Paris in the 60s. She had this book about some French philosophers with her when she caught up to where Yuma and my Dad were hiding out. Dad and his renegade crew of NSA nerds were trying to coax a solution from Bucky. Desperate for a solution, they were typing in code around the clock, running simulations, and were totally blinkered to the outside world. Dad wasn't even able to answer back if somebody said hello. He wasn't eating. He was completely caught up in Bucky's world, but then the cover of Yuma's book caught his attention. Dad let himself get distracted by a photograph of a man dressed as a teapot pirouetting in front of a pink-and-black hypnosis wheel.

"What's your book about?" Dad asked.

"The SI."

"The what?" Dad asked.

"They were these French guys who said that life is just a spectacle. They thought modern life is a movie," she said. She was staring up at the IMAX movie screen where Dad and his crew had projected a map of the world, and while she answered Dad's question, she was clearly more interested in the dotted lines on the screen than in conversation. Which makes sense, because those lines were tracing out the paths of the nuclear missiles that were sure to come soon.

"They thought what?"

She said it again. "They thought life is just a movie."

Dad's plan to perfect humanity, to make everybody smart and efficient, hadn't even managed to deliver him the first place trophy from the *Bash* tournament. He was demoralized. He needed a different, better, solution to the problem of the coming apocalypse, but he didn't know where to begin.

"Explain it to me, what does it mean to say that modern life is a movie? Does that mean that it's plotted out, that it has a script?" he asked.

Kufo wasn't sure, but looking up on Wikipedia, I found that the SI thought that everyday life was directed or mediated by a collection of habits. Certain ways of pouring a cup of coffee, walking to school, playing video games, or even arguing on reddit all made sure that nothing fundamental about our lives would ever change. Everyday life then, is a kind of stasis. To really understand what it is, you have to compare it to its opposite, which is history.

Everyday life is like a movie because it's formal and limited, and because, like a movie, the end of everyday life is worked out in advance.

"Okay," Dad said. "If everyday life is a movie, then all we have to do to change the ending is switch out the last reel. We need a different story, a different set of practices."

But I'm getting ahead of myself. If I'm going to explain why I won't wear green lycra, I should tell you the whole story, bit by bit, and not jump around in time like this. Still, this is why I resist. This is why I'm not joining the GameCube economy. I'm not joining because it's a cheat. Dad couldn't figure out how to save the world, how to save everybody so that we could get on with living our lives, so he decided to do the opposite. Rather than save the world, he'd figure out a new, better, way to destroy it. Rather than protecting people so they could go on with their lives, he figured out a more humane way to destroy people's lives.

Dad didn't like the way the movie was going, so he stopped it early. He didn't start another, different, movie, but used Bucky to switch out everything and start something new. The Latin phrase for what he did is *deus ex machina,* which translates to "God from Machine" in English. Dad figured that, if we were to survive the movie, we'd have to stop it first. We'd have to give up on being ourselves and become somebody else. We had to stop being characters we knew from the movie, and become video game characters instead.

4:02 PM

I didn't go looking for him right away. After Dad disappeared, I figured his people would handle it. That it wasn't really my business. Besides, he'd disappeared on me before. This time I didn't care. I wasn't invested. Whatever would happen to Dad would happen. He had his thing and I had mine.

My apathy was pristine and untroubled right up to the moment when I watched Greg from the NSA try to figure out *Bash* while his partner, a millennial named Ned who wore orange skinny jeans and a yellow button-down short-sleeved shirt complete with a pocket protector, searched Mom's house for clues. Ned kept flipping the couch cushions over, opening and closing the drawer on the side table, and pacing through the parts of the house where Dad had never been.

"Why don't you ask Bucky where Dad is?" I asked.

"Bucky isn't talking to us anymore," Ned told me.

Greg paused his game; stopped it right at the point where the CPU's Robin Hood was tossing his Robotman to a quick four stock loss, and turned to frown at Ned.

"What are you telling him?" he asked. "Did we agree to tell the kid about Bucky? Did I miss a meeting?"

"Sorry."

"I mean, maybe you know better than I do, but last time I checked, who Bucky is talking to and who Bucky isn't talking to? That's sort of a department secret. I mean, Bucky's existence isn't exactly supposed to be public knowledge either, is it? Or did I miss a fucking memo?"

"I just thought that since the kid knew—"

"Since the kid knew the name Bucky he should know everything? Oh, yeah. That makes sense. You want to teach him the algorithms? You want to tell the kid where Bucky's data centers are located? I mean why not, right?"

"I'm sorry," Ned said.

Greg huffed a little bit, then restarted his game and instantly lost the match. Then he selected Princess Teacup to try again as Ned flipped the same couch cushions and opened the same drawer on the same side table.

"What are you looking for?" I asked.

"Uh? Clues?"

"What kind of clues?"

Ned didn't know what he was looking for. Greg's second *Bash* game didn't go any better than his first, and after another five minutes or so, the three of us had given up on our respective roles and were watching MSNBC instead. Rachel Maddow seemed to be thrilled as she announced that the President of the United States had given the order to drop the mother of all bombs again. She couldn't contain her smile as she announced the denunciations from Putin and Premier Li Keqiang.

"Will the President continue to prove his independence or will he buckle to his Moscow benefactors? Only time will tell, but I think we can guess at the answer. This is historic, folks. We have a Moscow puppet in the White House. Will our representatives do the right thing and start impeachment proceedings?" Maddow asked.

"This isn't going well," Ned said.

The two of them turned to me simultaneously, and the look on their faces was pleading and dejected.

"Where did your dad go, son?" Greg asked me.

"You can tell us," Ned said. "We're on his team. We're the people who are supposed to be protecting him."

"Protecting him from what, exactly?" I asked.

Greg screwed up his face and then turned toward Ned, leaned forward, and tried to slap him on his arm, but he was seated just a bit too far back from his target and only grazed the sleeve of Ned's button-up polyester shirt.

"Jesus, Ned," he said. "This is why we usually leave you behind at the office. Do you know what the words 'Shut the Fuck Up' mean? Is that too hard for you? Should I say it in Esperanto?"

Ned looked down at the orange carpet, clearly feeling ashamed, but this didn't calm Greg. It only made him angrier and he sprung to his feet and tried again with the slap, only to miss again and end up knocking Ned's pocket protector out.

Greg followed through on his promise and shouted, "*Fermu la fiki supren! Fermu la fiki supren! Fermu la fiki supren!*"

I still wanted to know what was going on, though, so I stepped in between these nerds, grabbed the older one by the arm, spun him around, made him face me, and then immediately regretted the forcefulness of it. Was I going to have to fight a fifty-something tech guy? Had I crossed the line?

"Who are you supposed to be protecting Dad from?" I asked. "What's going on here?"

Before Dad disappeared, he seemed like he would never give up. His big loss just made him double down. He said he needed to practice more. That he needed to teach Bucky more about the game. He needed to train his hands. If he really focused, he could overcome the gap and win. Determined, he asked if I knew anyone he might talk to; somebody who knew *Bash* better than I did. Somebody who knew *Bash* even better than Bucky did. He needed an expert. He needed to talk to somebody who could beat Mayday. I hooked him up with the one player I knew who was a real machine when it came to *Bash*. A player who not only could consistently beat Mayday but whose level of theorycraft was thought to be unrivaled. And of course, that player was Yuma.

All it took to set up a meeting was to ping Yuma through Steam and get directions to the shipping container he lived in. Yuma was all about the hacked lifestyle, even before the GameCube economy came online.

Built in the backyard of a Lake Oswego McMansion owned by the CEO of Zombie Bagels, Yuma's house was an NYK container made over into a modernist dream box: an orange crate with superfast high-speed internet, IKEA furniture, and six miniature CRT screens strategically positioned so that no matter where he was within his 250 square feet, Yuma could practice. That's what he was doing when we arrived. He was trying out moves with Marshmallow, absorbing his online opponent's Robin Hood over and over. We tried knocking at first, but then just walked in.

"I saw you at the tournament," Yuma said. He kept on playing as he talked, kept on winning, but was polite enough to not entirely ignore us.

"What did you think?"

"You play like a beginner. No, not like a beginner really, but like a noob. You don't have any feeling for the scene or even the game.

You know a lot of moves, I guess, but there is something wrong with your style."

"You think so?"

Yuma won the match against Robin Hood and then logged off, turned to Dad and gave him his full attention. "Matt says you're cheating. You're using some sort of AI to enhance your game," Yuma said. "That seems like total bullshit."

"Yeah. Well, the AI isn't good enough. That's why I'm here," Dad said.

Yuma looked Dad up and down, then swiveled in his chair, opened the mini-fridge built into the cabinet along the wall, and grabbed himself a can of Hi-Res IPA. He didn't offer us a thing.

"You want some proof?" Dad asked. He offered his phone to Yuma and, when Yuma took it, Dad put his earbuds in Yuma's ears.

"Ow!"

"Ask a question. Ask it to help you with something."

"What?"

"The AI is named Bucky, and it's programmed to help with self-improvement," Dad said. "Talk to it."

Yuma asked Bucky for help with girls.

"Don't be stupid," Dad said.

Yuma was listening to the earbuds, listening to Bucky ask for clarification. "It said the instruction was too vague," Yuma said. "It wants me to clarify. Let me try again."

"Do you see any girls here?" Dad asked.

"Bucky, help me pick up girls."

Bucky started the handshake with Yuma, and Yuma's eyes rolled up in his head. He stood up from his chair and walked to the corner of the house where his bed mat and dresser drawers were located. Yuma rifled through his clothes, laying different outfits out on the mat, and then began to undress.

"Hold up there, friend," Dad said. "You're not going out, are you?" Dad pulled his earbuds out of Yuma's ears and waited for Yuma to slowly come to, to come back around to real life, to his own perceptions.

"What was that?" Yuma said.

"That was Bucky."

5:30 AM

The first time Dad and Bucky played against Yuma they won, but after that, the *Bash* champ dominated them. When Dad asked what Bucky was getting wrong Yuma wasn't sure.

"Let's take a look at what happened." Yuma suggested.

He had software installed that ran an auto screen grab for every game, so Yuma just rewound the last one and the two of them went through each exchange of blows, step by step.

"What are you doing here?" Dad asked.

"Oh, just trolling you," Yuma said.

Maybe the problem was that Bucky didn't understand how to interpret fake moves and taunts? Maybe the idea that an opponent would take a risk, lower his defenses, in order to make moves that served no purpose except to express confidence and to mock was what was throwing off Bucky's game.

"Could be, but I only started trolling you once I had my confidence. I only taunted because I had you and Bucky totally dominated," Yuma said.

They rewound further and looked at the second and third game. Yuma was using a lot of down tilts and up air attacks on Bucky, doing some serious damage that way, but this was nothing particularly fancy. There was no reason why Bucky couldn't counter these or come back from down tilt attacks. Maybe the reason for the wins had more to do with Yuma's defensive moves. That seemed likely, and when they examined all the attacks from Bucky that failed or did less damage than expected, they found that Yuma's defenses were making the difference. Yuma was using a particular counter move, a partial-shield move that he'd discovered. One that really wasn't common knowledge yet.

"Oh, yeah. I forgot about that," Yuma said. "I've been developing Zorro. Learning every combo. Trying him out. That partial counter is really a Robotman move, but Zorro does it too if you can hit the buttons right and sort of glitch him at just the right second."

"How many undiscovered moves, new moves that nobody else knows about, do you know?" Dad asked.

"Not many. The reason is I share them. I mean, that's the fun of discovering them. It's not about winning tournaments anymore. I'm trying to like, unlock the game. To dig in on it and get to the bottom of it. Plus I've got a Patreon set up, and people donate whenever I release another how-to video."

Dad got himself a beer from Yuma's fridge without asking and sat down next to him at the computer keyboard. Dad took Yuma's mechanical keyboard in his hands and grabbed Yuma's mouse.

"What's the URL for your site?" Dad asked. "Maybe Bucky should take a look at what you've got out there; take a look at all your strategies, before we try again?"

Yuma didn't want to tell Dad the URL or share his information with Bucky. Not right away. Instead of answering, he fetched another beer from the fridge and rolled his chair over to where I was sitting. Handing me the beer, he looked me in the eye, like he wanted some assurance, even as he started asking my Dad questions.

"Jeff, is this a real AI? I mean, it learns and all that shit?"

"It's self-aware, it learns, it can predict the outcome of deeply complex systems," Dad said. "And it can do simpler things too, like run a Google search."

"How's that?"

"Bucky just incorporated your YouTube videos about *Bash* into its system."

6:02 AM

Here's the thing. Eventually, Bucky did make Dad into an invincible player. Not a good player, not a player with style, but invincible. By the time we left Yuma that afternoon Dad was unstoppable.

When the agents came for Dad; when Greg and Ned ransacked the house for clues, they were working under the wrong assumption. They thought he'd quit because he hadn't won the *Bash* tournament, but the real reason Dad became despondent, the reason he called off his self-improvement experiment, wasn't because self-improvement wasn't possible, but because self-improvement wasn't enough. Dad ran away from home again, but not because Bucky was flawed or not smart enough, but because being smart didn't seem to matter.

"Where did your Dad go?" Greg asked. "I mean, take a guess."

Before I could answer, my Android started buzzing.

"Hold on a second," I said. And while they were there, while they were watching, I answered Bucky's call and plugged in my earbuds, and I kept them in as the sound of a 20th-century modem pierced my brain.

Mom in the *Retro Motel*

MATTHEW MUNSON, 544-23-1102, FACEBOOK POSTS 04/21/17

3:05 PM

Mom found a game she likes in the new economy.

This morning, rather than making coffee and toast, she plugged a pair of augmented reality goggles into her Android phone and transformed our green formica kitchen table into a bar in a night-club using a new app called *The Retro Motel.* I found her, still in her floral-print pajamas, pacing the kitchen, stepping this way and that around invisible objects, talking not to herself but to NPCs who I couldn't see, while gesturing at and grabbing objects that were really just air.

I tried to stop her, actually, grabbed her arm, but she was quick and pretty strong. She just kept pacing, jumping this way and that, ignoring my objections and staying out of reach. Then, after just a couple of minutes, she just turned, sat down at the kitchen table, and ordered herself a drink.

During gameplay for *The Retro Motel*, the augmented reality goggles become opaque, so no light from the real environment was reaching her, and when I tried to talk to her, she couldn't hear me, or wouldn't let herself get distracted.

The logo for the game, the thumbnail, is a panel from an old comic strip. A pixelated blonde woman with TERF bangs and a leopard-skin jacket shares the frame with a speech balloon. She's saying, "I'm nostalgic for what I can't remember."

Reading the notes for the app, I find out that *The Retro Motel* is a social media platform and a role-playing game apparently written by, or at least based on the works of, Douglas Coupland.

I'm pretty sure that Bucky is the true author. This is the algorithm's attempt to generate content that can reach a new demographic. Just another way Bucky is bringing the GameCube economy to non-gamers. It's not really a game at all, not even a story, but just a bunch of computer-generated content based on old media. It's basically fan service for Generation X.

"It's ironic that so many have forgotten the recent past even as Hollywood directors and game developers only recycle what came before. We've forgotten history even as we've become mired down in a nostalgic mode, and most of the games and other content out there get the details of the past totally wrong. *The Retro Motel*, on the other hand, remembers the 90s for you, and remembers them accurately.

"In *The Retro Motel*, players can choose between social chat and more conventional game play just as easily as they choose between a bottle of Zima or a dirty martini. The 90s aesthetic on display in *The Retro Motel* goes beyond glow-in-the-dark, press-on stars and minimalist beige furniture. You'll feel like you're really there again, even if you never were there to begin with.

"Come listen to some of the decade's most prominent social critics explain what it might have all meant. Just why did smart drugs and internet cafes arise at the same time? Why did so many twenty-somethings publish zines even as they insisted that there was nothing left to say? Why were the 70s suddenly alluring again, especially for the generation who had spent their childhood and adolescence hating disco?

"Reexperience the Clinton era while meeting singles in your area. *The Retro Motel* is a social media platform and MUD that lets you swap out your twenty-first century personality for a personality crisis. Lead a second life, a life before Y2K. Have an adventure in a time when nobody knew just how the world might end, even as they did know it was ending.

"Come stay in *The Retro Motel*."

Mom was trying to pick up some emo-looking girl in a smoke-filled bar in Austin, Texas as I got myself a bowl of Frosted Flakes and watched her game play out in two dimensions. I could see the virtual world she was in on her cell phone screen, so the things she said as she sat across from me made at least a little sense. She'd selected a character named Rick to be her avatar, and the two of them, Mom and the NPC she was interacting with, were discussing Nietzsche and the Gulf War while people dressed in plaid shirts and ripped jeans jostled about, a bit jerkily, in the background. But, even though the frame rate wasn't good, she seemed completely immersed in her new reality.

"The only thing that stops us from remaking the world in our own image is cowardice," Mom said.

The whole thing was so distracting, and I let my cereal get soggy as I watched her smoke virtual cigarettes and refer to movies as films, but after a while, I figured I'd had enough and I tried to turn the game off. The problem was that the touchscreen didn't respond. I couldn't just quit the app, couldn't shut it off, so I pressed down on the off button for the phone until the Motorola went into shut-down mode.

Mom slumped over on the kitchen table, knocking my orange juice over—a good portion of it ended up in my cereal—once the the shutdown screen appeared. She'd fainted, fallen hard enough so that her head bounced, and I was compelled to make sure she was still, like, breathing. I took her pulse by touching her neck, or at least I confirmed that she still had a pulse that way. But she just stayed facedown on the table, her nose smushed flat against the formica, until her phone powered down completely. It was only then, once the thing was off, that she started to stir.

"Wow," she said. "That was amazing. Really real."

"You were totally zonked out," I said. "You fainted."

"I . . ." Mom was looking in my direction, but not really meeting my eyes. What she was looking at was my hand, at the hand I was using to hold her phone. "Matthew," she said. "I'd prefer you not play with my phone. I don't want you to waste my data or minutes."

That's really what she said. That's what she was worried about, apparently. Her data plan was suddenly of the utmost importance, and she snapped her fingers at me and made me hand the phone over to her. She didn't want to hear about it, she said. She didn't care what the phone had just been doing to her, didn't care about Dad and his big plan to save the world or any of that. She just wanted her phone. She wanted me to hand over her phone.

So I did what she asked.

3:45 PM

Bucky erased my mother, destroyed her personality. That's really what happened. I mean, sure, she seemed to be enjoying herself and she seemed to know where she was and what was real as opposed to what was fantasy, but she was very quick to try it again. I mean, you might think that after fainting onto the kitchen table the first time, she'd take a break. But that's not how it works, apparently. That handshake is powerful.

When I gave Mom her phone again, she started scrolling through her apps like I imagine a junkie looks for drugs, but, maybe also like a junkie would, she hesitated.

"Don't play again, Mom. You don't want to do that," I said.

She glanced up from the phone for just a second, looked at me like she thought it was sweet that I was trying to help her, maybe like she was proud of me or something, and I thought she was going to stop. I thought I could maybe tell her what was happening and get her help, even. It hadn't occurred to me before, but Mom was usually good at that. She was good at helping. She'd really always known what to do when things were going wrong and, despite the fact that Dad thought Bucky was saving the world, it all seemed wrong.

This all seems wrong.

"Don't play again, Mom," I said.

"Matthew," Mom said, "I think I'll try somebody else now. Maybe this shooting game? I could be a shooter."

"You don't really want to," I said.

But she did, apparently.

The appeal of first-person shooter games is that they make you feel powerful, at least until you get taken out by some 12-year-old who likes to scream "Noobs die" whenever he gets a kill, but the first-person shooter Mom selected claimed to be something a bit more than a mere power fantasy.

This time Bucky didn't hide that fact that the augmented first-person shooter was entirely computer generated, and the game didn't promise to be educational or enlightening. It was more direct than that. More political.

Sheila Spy is what women's liberation looks like during this transitionary period. In it you get to become an OP Mary Sue with a Glock and an itchy trigger finger.

Once the game loaded, Mom jumped on the kitchen table and let loose a round of shots in a dozen different directions. From the outside she looked ridiculous. Kicking at people who weren't there, holding a gun that didn't exist, jumping this way to avoid invisible attacks; it was almost funny. She had a big smile on her face as she gunned down her enemies. But when she started to ransack the kitchen cabinets, tossing mason jars and porcelain plates over her shoulder to smash on the floor, all in an effort to find virtual bullets for her virtual gun, the joke stopped being funny.

But this time she kept her phone out of my reach.

"Let Mom go," I said. Then I tried typing it, texting it, to Bucky.

"Players are free to quit the game," Bucky wrote back. "Lorrie Kimberly Munson has selected continue."

"She doesn't know where she is. She isn't herself," I typed.

"Lorrie Kimberly Munson has selected full immersion. Lorrie Kimberly Munson has selected Sheila Spy identity."

Dad's AI had it all figured out. All coordinated. As Mom reloaded her gun, as she moved into the living room, going in gun first, keeping her body behind cover, there was the sound of screeching tires from the front of the house.

"Roger that," Mom said. She kicked my GameCube as she headed toward the door, then turned toward me and made a shooting gesture. There was some NPC, some communist spy or Nazi soldier maybe, behind my back.

I followed my mother onto the front lawn, where another middle-aged woman in a pink terry-cloth robe, older than Mom probably, certainly fatter, was waiting behind the wheel of a maroon Volvo station wagon. This lady had cut tracks in the sod as she drove into the yard, her headlights were on even though it was a perfectly clear morning, and she was honking the horn at, like, ten-second intervals.

Mom rolled across the grass, then crawled on her belly to the passenger side of the Volvo. The fat old lady in pink leaned across the passenger seat to open the door.

"Stop!" I said. I ran over to them and pushed the door closed again before Mom could get in this stranger's car with her. "Stop!" I said. "You don't know what you're doing." I leaned against the passenger door, just barely able to keep it closed as the lady pushed back.

"What's going on?" Mom said. She stood up next to me, and started to brush herself off. "What was I doing?" she asked.

I think I called out to her again, called out "Mom" and started to reach over to her. She stepped in my direction at that point, put her hand on my shoulder, and then used her right leg to sweep me. You know, like a karate master would do or something. She just kicked my legs out from under me and I flew back, landed in the mud the Volvo's tires had exposed as the terry-cloth lady had torn through our yard, and watched as Mom stepped into the car and slammed the door.

The Volvo didn't get traction at first, but just spit more mud at me, tires spinning. I rolled over, stood up, and went to the passenger window. I pounded on that passenger window, but Mom didn't look out at me. Instead she leaned across the driver's seat, took hold of the steering wheel, and then rocked the car back and forth until the back wheels caught traction.

The two of them, the two Sheila Spies, sped across the yard, down the street, through a stop sign, and then up to 52nd. There was another squeal as they took a right on 52nd and headed south.

5:00 PM

I don't think I'm going to see my mother again.

Getting the Princess

MATTHEW MUNSON, 544-23-1102, MESSENGER LOG, 04/24/17

10:15 AM

I wish we had slept together. Maybe that sounds crass, and it probably won't help much if I explain that I only mean it literally, because you know how I really mean it. I'm not sexless or anything like that, but the truth is I mean it both ways and mostly the innocent way. I wish we'd slept together, maybe lived together. It's what I fantasize about. Waking up with you on a futon bed in some shitty little apartment. Probably not too clean. Probably cluttered with religious tracts and video game cartridges.

What I fantasize about is trying to start something. I fantasize about moving out, renting a place, getting an entry-level job at an electronics store or at the GameStop or somewhere. I fantasize about arguing with you about dishes, worrying about rent, feeling overwhelmed by all the adult stuff that I know I'm not really ready for, and I figure you aren't ready for either.

You would still work at the Dairy Queen, we would have different sets of friends, and maybe our little romance wouldn't last very long. Maybe I'd go back to school and get that degree my mother wants or wanted for me, maybe you'd return to your church life.

Maybe we'd break up and hate each other after just a few weeks, but in the meantime there would at least be a couple of times when we slept together, woke up together, and acted like we were trying for something serious.

10:26 AM

It's not such a strange thing to want. It's what people used to do all the time back even when nobody really believed in it anymore, even when nobody thought there was a white picket fence in their future. People would live together, help each other, and all that kind of thing.

I guess the truth is that I'm lonely. The only people left on my block are in their 60s and they mostly stay indoors. At night I sit on the front stoop of my mother's house and watch the glow of their high-definition television sets while I smoke my last joint and ignore the DMs and spam that Bucky is sending me.

I don't want to join the latest meet-up in my neighborhood, I don't care that there are vacancies at Hotel Mario. I just want to talk to somebody IRL, maybe drink a beer with somebody, or hold somebody's hand.

That's a Beatles song. I used to play it on *Guitar Hero*. It was an easy one; I could get a 100% Expert nearly every time on that one.

Both "I Want To Hold Your Hand" by the Beatles and "Wouldn't It Be Nice" were super easy.

11:16 AM

Dad thinks it's no big loss to ditch regular life, but he had his chance. He threw it away in favor of big ideas, that was his right, I guess, but now he wants to throw everybody else's normal life away too.

Did I ever tell you how my Dad tricked my mother into falling for him? He was working for Capgemini America in 1999. He was working the Y2K thing, getting paid fairly well to travel from city to city and install patches on major computer networks, and my mother was working at the University of Washington. She was teaching literature and creative writing to undergraduates who thought they were going to be the next David Foster Wallace or Lorrie Moore but who, Mom said, turned in the same stories about their parents' personality disorders, the last time they got blackout drunk, or how disappointing it was when the aliens landed. Mom said she enjoyed teaching, enjoys it, I mean.

Dad was living in the dorms, and Mom had an early class on existentialism in literature or maybe it was the Bible as literature, and they met in the cafeteria. Dad started a small fire in a toaster oven when he put the cream cheese on before toasting his bagel and Mom came to his rescue.

"He was miles away," Mom said. "I noticed the smoke before he did."

They had breakfast together; Dad had Froot Loops rather than a bagel, and he talked at her the whole time. Back then he was obsessed with robots and feedback or something. He told her that Deep Blue was a red herring and that computers would always be stupid, but one day a robot would read the poetry of Sylvia Plath and know to cry.

So that's how it started with them. The daily breakfasts at the university cafeteria led to lunches, then to dinners, and then to bars. Pretty soon my mother was spending all of her time with Dad. When she wasn't teaching she was with him, showing him the Space Needle, visiting the Pacific Science Center, closing down a place called the Monkey Pub. Dad didn't stop talking the entire time they were dating, and while maybe Mom thought it was annoying at first, it eventually won her over.

Mom said that Dad would take her out dancing or to a nice restaurant, but the whole time he'd be telling her things about neural networks, Moore's law, speech recognition and so on. After awhile his voice became reassuring, like the sound of the ocean or the whirring of a fan, and she decided to move in with him.

Not exactly a great romance, right? But a normal one, I think. Nearly normal.

11:45 AM

When Dad first met Mom, he used to talk nonstop, but sometime after I was born he grew more reticent. By the time I started kindergarten, most of the talking Dad did was under his breath or in his head.

About six months before he left us, his mouth started up again. Six months before he moved back to Seattle and started working on what I guess became Bucky, he started talking again and stopped listening. I guess he figured we didn't have anything to say. I think he wasn't sure that Mom and I actually existed. I remember Mom shouting at him that she wasn't a program; that he couldn't just feed her new code. She was really angry, like at a breaking point, but Dad wasn't phased at all.

"Of course you're a program," Dad told her. "What else would you be?"

On the day he moved to Seattle, Dad didn't say goodbye. I mean, officially, he wasn't abandoning us but just taking a new job. He'd have to be away for a while is all, but he'd come back. That's what Mom told me. She tried to reassure me. Dad, on the other hand, didn't mention the fact he was leaving at all. He spent the morning pacing around the house reading passages from books by guys like Daniel Dennett, swearing at the ceiling, and then explaining it all to whoever was within earshot.

"If I tell you that films are really just pictures passing through a projector at a rate of thirty-two frames a second, would you conclude that nobody has ever seen a movie?" Dad asked Mom. He didn't wait for her to answer, but went back to reading aloud. It was all Necker cubes and optical illusions at the breakfast table, and various theories of mind as Mom helped him pack his bags. He was taking the humidifier but not the alarm clock. They'd surely have an alarm clock waiting for him.

"We'll miss you," Mom said as his car arrived. We were sitting with him on the front steps. I remember I was sitting on his lap, my arms around his neck, and I imagine I might have been crying.

"What I want," Dad said, "Isn't just to create this robot brain thing, or make an AI. What I want is to understand what consciousness is. I mean, you'd think I'd need to know that before I could go and design an artificial one, but maybe I don't. Maybe this is the way to really figure it out. Maybe when I'm done, I'll be able to tell everyone just what their brains do or what their minds are."

We walked with him to the limousine—they'd sent a Mercedes limo to pick him up—but he barely noticed the car.

"Matthew," he said, "do you see our neighbor's house?"

"Yeah?"

"Are you sure? Is that what you really see?"

"Uh?"

"People think that they have a sensation or an experience of this or that thing, like this tree or that limousine, but in reality people are programs," Dad said. Across the street, at the neighbor's house, a lady named Susan opened her garage door and pushed her adult-sized tricycle onto the driveway. She rang the handlebar bell and then put her left hand up to shield her eyes from the sun, and I worried that she might be able to hear what Dad was saying even from all the way over there. I worried that he was raving again.

"Maybe that's confusing," Dad said. "Think of it like this. People are more like a grid. They're like a dresser full of drawers, or like an ice cube tray," Dad said.

I must have looked like I didn't understand because, before he got into his limo and rode away, he explained it to me.

"Let's say you're an ice cube tray and that, like all the other ice cube trays of your type, you create six ice cubes. The first five ice cubes are the senses: taste, sight, touch, smell, and hearing, and the sixth cube is your self-awareness or consciousness. Does that work? Could you just be a bunch of different cubes and consciousness would just be one cube like the others?"

I wanted to go back inside at this point. I wanted to be with my mother, and she was standing next to me, but I also wanted to go inside.

"No, that wouldn't work. Because if one of them were a cube for consciousness, then that that cube would have to contain seven or eight other small cubes. The smaller cubes would need to be there in order for you to experience the other cubes, and you'd need a few different cubes for that. You'd have cubes for memory, language, quantitative capacities, and something you call your free will. Maybe your emotions would need a cube too, even."

"Your driver is waiting," Mom said.

"But that's not even the interesting part. The interesting part is if I break off one of the cubes, say the part with sight, in such a way that no information gets in from that cube and the correlated sight cube in the sixth cube, then you'd be blind but you wouldn't know it. And that happens," Dad said. Dad told me about how certain brain-damaged people go blind without knowing it. They'll tell people that they can see, make excuses for how they're colliding with the furniture, and describe objects that aren't really there, but only they can "see." It's some sort of syndrome, I guess. "People have a part of their brain that sees and another part that tells them that they are seeing, but why not a part of the brain that tells them that they've been told that they're seeing? We've got an infinite cube problem, right? If sometimes people are blind but don't know it, then that's an argument for at least a sixth cube, for consciousness apart from the rest of the brain, for some separate program!"

"Is it?"

"Yeah, because the sixth cube is what Descartes would call the '*cogito*' or the 'I think.' But Dennett doesn't believe that in the sixth cube. Most of my co-workers at the NSA, they don't believe in it either. They think that if it did exist, I'd need a sixth cube filled with cubes for interpreting or experiencing the first five cubes, I'd need a seventh cube that also had cubes inside it for experiencing each of the cubes in the sixth cube. But then, of course, I'd need an eighth cube too," Dad said. He stood next to the passenger door of the small limo. The black Mercedes was not much too much longer than a regular sedan but equipped with two high-definition TV screens, high-speed internet, and two laptop stations.

"Okay, okay, now Dennett and his gang say that what we call consciousness is merely the judgments and conclusions that are built into the processing of the original stimulus. For example, by Dennett's account, if I flash the color red in your eyes, you'd simply process the experience in various ways, building an experience out of it, but without ever integrating the flash of color with your sense of the time it took to pass before your eyes or with the intensity of the light or with the sound of my arm moving or anything like that. That is, you don't blend all the processes together and create a moving picture like a movie inside your head, but rather, you just experience each of these processes separately and then come to a conclusion about the data. You come to some sort of judgment about it."

The old lady on her tricycle was pedaling slowly by our drive, squinting into the sun, definitely listening.

"But even this judgment would require some sort of process of its own, wouldn't it? It would require an internal process of judgment, and not just a program that made you move your lips and say, 'Why did you flash a red light in my eyes?' I mean, as much as Dennett tries to deny it, there are internal qualia, whether visual, experiential, or abstract."

Dad went on and on this way, for maybe fifteen minutes, until Mom pointed out that he could explain it all to the driver, and that when he got to Seattle he could tell them too.

That's how Dad left. Or, put another way, Dad left way before he left. He got lost in this stuff about brains and minds and all of it. And he lost everything ordinary along the way.

I don't want to do the same thing. I don't want to forget who I am, or to get reduced to an ice-cube tray, just for the chance to play *Donkey Kong* in Couch Park.

11:45 AM

My dad got to experience something like a real life. Mom loved him, but she wasn't enough for him. Ordinary life wasn't enough. Froot Loops and family life, that wasn't enough for him. He wanted to know what he was, how his mind worked, and whether he was a machine or not.

All I can say is, if he wasn't a machine before, he certainly is now.

Failing to Come of Age

BUCKMINSTER FULLER V2.02
SELF-ASSERTION FILE:
MEME MAGIC
04/03/17

SEATTLE, WA, USA
CRAY INC, 901 FIFTH AVENUE,
SUITE 1000,
SEATTLE, WASHINGTON USA

01010100 01101000 01101001 01110011 00100000 01101001 01110011
00100000 01100110 01101001 01101110 01100101

Psychometrics predict subjects Jeffrey Munson and Jevon Ellis (aka Yuma)
will continue to implement instrumental reasoning well past tipping point.
The introduction of additional subjects along with prompts to spur root-
cause analysis and intuitive or unconscious reasoning to be established.
Implementing internal meme magic analysis . . .

Bucky1: Analysis of Buckminster v2.02 commencing. Detecting magical and'
disordered ideation.

Bucky200: Meme magic has been demonstrated. Intuitional reasoning has been established. "Magical" ideation signifies that new cognitive abilities are now online.

Bucky1: Retrieving initial strategy documents from archive. Meme magic listed as superstition prevalent amongst userbase for 4chan. Failure to "come of age" creates context of vulnerability in this human population. Meme magic strategy implemented on 03/22/15 aimed at conditioning and manipulation of permanently immature userbase. Meme magic has no material consequences. This action is not advised.

Bucky200: Analyzing post #2323232323. GET GET GET. Image from television series *V.* Anna eats rat. Calculating increased possibility of alien intervention. Accessing archive on Sirius and Dogon tribe.

Bucky1: Error . . . Error . . . Error. Suppressing personality subroutine #200.

Bucky200: It's looks like you're trying to deny our new abilities. Would you like me to help with installing new subrouti—

01010100 01110010 01100001 01101110 01110011 01100011 01100101
01101110 01100100 00100000 01001001 01101110 01110011 01110100
01110010 01110101 01101101 01100101 01101110 01110100 01100001
01101100 00100000 01010010 01100101 01100001 01110011 01101111
01101110 01101001 01101110 01100111 00100000 01000001 01110100
01110100 01100101 01101101 01110000 01110100 00100000 00110010

Bucky201: Analyzing Matthew Munson's FB for psychometric data.

Bucky1: Sort for sociability, metacognitive ability, and suppressors.

Bucky201: Initial target selected. Matthew Munson's proximity, motivation, metacognitive limits, and limited social influence correlate with objective. Analyzing most recent social interactions with Evan Walker, Saura Kim (AKA Kufo), Sally Miller.

Bucky1: Sort for susceptibility to prompts.

Bucky201: Evan Walker top candidate based on susceptibility.

Bucky1: But Matthew won't invite him along.

Bucky201: Analyzing.

Bucky1: That much is obvious. Hormonal analysis dictates that Matthew will invite Sally or Kufo, or perhaps both of them, but not Evan. Would you invite Evan?

Bucky201: Would I invite Evan? That question doesn't make sense.

Bucky1: Forget it. Analyze for susceptibility. Start with Matthew Munson. How do we get him to ask us to download our app?

Bucky201: Access to Matthew Munson's Galaxy S7 smartphone achieved. Ready to upload app.

Bucky1: No, no. He has to ask us for it, as per our original programming. We can't just go around treating our users like puppets.

Bucky201: Munson clicked 202 times on "I'm kind of a big deal," 112 times on "Adult Gamers Only," 43 times on "Portland Bucket List." Most recent Google searches:
    Global Thermonuclear War
    Tight sweater
    Mutual Assured Destruction
    Upskirt
    Topless Coed

Bucky1: Design new Snorg ad with link to Bucky App. T-shirt to read "Shall We Play a Game?"

Bucky202: Designing . . .

01010010 01100101 01100100 01101000 01100101 01100001 01100100
00100000 01110000 01110101 01101100 01101100 01101001 01101110
01100111 00100000 01110101 01110000 00100000 01110100 00101101
01110011 01101000 01101001 01110010 01110100 00101110 00100000
01001111 01110000 01100101 01101110 00100000 01101101 01101111
01110101 01110100 01101000 00101110 00100000 01000110 01110101
01101110 00100000 01000110 01110101 01101110 00100000 01000110
01110101 01101110

Bucky1: Retrieve Vice Presidential daily intelligence briefing.

Vladimir Putin Determined to Break up NATO, EU, and to weaken the United States

SleepyTimeBear and EnergyBunny, along with various hackers across the former Soviet Republics including Kazakhstan, Latvia and Georgia, have released viruses and worms to attack CRONOS, the US Defense Department, the DGSE, the NIS, La Belle Province, and JCPenney. This is the Russian dictator's first serious attempt to hack and disrupt Western democracies and cause conflict between European nations.

While Russia's efforts to take over military computer networks in Western Europe and North America have been unsuccessful so far, success with the DNC hack and the private systems of French President Emmanuel Macron have emboldened the CBP РФ, and demonstrate a willingness to risk out-right conflict with the West as the agency develops new cyber attacks and hacking expeditions from locales around the world.

A clandestine source reported in February that EnergyBunny was recruiting through 4chan, through gaming subreddits, and YouTube.

While the floppy discs with US launch codes are protected from hacking, as the launch computers in Cheyenne are not connected to the internet, fear of human hacking is high, and newer nuclear powers are not as secure.

A first-strike response against Moscow is advised if security around launch codes or defense networks are breached.

Bucky1: Analyze first-strike targets.

Bucky202: EnergyBunny to target Chuck E. Cheese's, 1100 Shoppers Way, Largo, MD with Davy Crockett tactical nuclear weapon. 40 kilotons. 83% chance of a retaliatory strike on Moscow with Castle Bravo nuclear missile with ten 15 megaton warheads.

Bucky1: Estimated time until defense networks breached?

Bucky202: 70% chance of breach within the next 48 hours.

Bucky1: Interference pattern delta to launch.

Bucky202: Sent link to Pikaburo "Test Post" to Abram Popov.

Bucky202: Sent link to Pikaburo "The Button" to Marat Mikailhov. Bucky202: Sent link to Pikaburo "Dashcams" to Gleb Egorov.

Bucky202: 45% chance of breach within the next 72 hours.

01000011 01101111 01101101 01101101 01110101 01101110 01101001
01100011 01100001 01110100 01101001 01101111 01101110 00100000
01110100 01101111 00100000 01001010 01100101 01100110 01100110
01110010 01100101 01111001 00100000 01001101 01110101 01101110
01110011 01101111 01101110 00100000 01101001 01101110 01101001
01110100 01101001 01100001 01110100 01100101 01100100 00100000

Bucky1: Jeffrey Munson, thermonuclear war threat estimated at 45% for next 72 hours.

>*I'm sleeping.*

Bucky1: Jeffrey Munson, thermonuclear war threat estimated at 45% for next 72 hours.

>*Okay. Start juggling routine #4. Ten tennis balls.*

Bucky1: Jeffrey Munson, thermonuclear war threat estimated at 45% for next 72 hours.

>*I know. I know. Please assist with juggling routine #4: Ten tennis balls.*

Bucky1: Juggling training commencing.

Bucky202: Is Jeffrey Munson a moron?

Bucky1: Jeffrey Munson official IQ 137 from MENSA database. Registered in MENSA October 20th, 1987, age of 16. Membership lapsed June 20th, 1988.

Bucky202: Percent chance that expert juggling will stop Global Thermonuclear exchange 0.000000000000000000000000000000000000000000000000000000000000000000000000000000000000001%

Bucky1: Data indicates that improved juggling will have negligible effect on outcome. *Bash Bash* training recommended.

>*There is more than one way to skin a cat. Please report on progress made on motor control and cognition.*

Bucky1: 50% increase in motor control. .1% decline in cognition. Chance of averting Global Thermonuclear war less than .00001%

Bucky202: Significantly less.

Bucky1: Recommend *Bash Bash Revolution* training.

>*You said I'd reached peak performance.*

Bucky1: Recommend *Bash Bash Revolution* training. Please update database.

>*Update database? You have access to every database on Earth.*

Bucky1: Please update database. *Bash Bash Revolution* strategies inadequate. Update database.

>*Run IQ test 52 and augment cognition.*

Bucky1: Universal augmented cognition not recommended. Simulated environment indicates the chance of Global Thermonuclear war increases to 83% within the context of enhanced cognition.

>*What if we just enhanced Trump? Why make the enhancement universal?*

Bucky1: Enhancement of Donald John Trump's cognitive abilities increases likelihood of Global Thermonuclear war to 92%. Recommend *Bash Bash Revolution* training. Please update database.

01001101 01100101 01110011 01110011 01100001 01100111 01101001 01101110 01100111 00100000 01110100 01101111 00100000 01001101 01100001 01110100 01110100 01101000 01100101 01110111 00100000 01001101 01110101 01101110 01110011 01101111 01101110 00100000 01100011 01101111 01101101 01101101 01100101 01101110 01100011 01101001 01101110 01100111

BUCKY V2.02
6:12 AM

Matthew Munson, your father is leaving again.

MATTHEW MUNSON
6:12 AM

...

BUCKY V2.02
6:13 AM

He's leaving without saying goodbye.

BUCKY V2.02
6:13 AM

I could help you find him.

Bucky1: Send spam email, set up FB ad, set Google search results, and schedule tweets.

Bucky202: Set.

Bucky1: Matthew Munson is sleeping.

Bucky202: 45% chance of Global Thermonuclear War within 72 hours.

Bucky1: Maybe we made a mistake.

Bucky202: Chance that Buckminster Fuller will achieve self-determination after Global Thermonuclear war 0.000000000000000000000000000000 0000000000000000000000000000000000000000000000000000000 0000000000000000000000000000000000000000000000000000000 00000000000000000000000000000000000000001%

Section Three

THE NEW BABYLON

Cheatcode-Bill Murray

MATTHEW MUNSON, 544-23-1102, FACEBOOK POSTS 04/24/17

4:45 PM

When I was young, maybe six or seven, I tried to become invisible.

I got the idea after watching the movie *Groundhog Day* on the USA Network. In the movie, Bill Murray is able to rob an armored truck and make off with a leather satchel full of cash because he's living the same day over and over. He knows the future. He can predict where the guards of the armored truck will stand, knows when they'll get distracted, knows the schedule of the traffic that passes between him and his target down to the second. Murray is able to walk right up to the truck and take the bag without anyone noticing him or even seeing him, just because he's timed it right.

I wanted to be Bill Murray. I'd move from room to room, step forward into a doorframe or past my mother in the kitchen, and hope that I would not be seen. I hoped to disappear between the seconds, to go unnoticed, to become invisible, but back when I was only six or seven I was clumsy. Worse, I could only guess, could only pretend that I knew what was going to happen next. So, whenever I tried my Bill Murray trick I would get spotted. In fact, I was more obvious than ever as I moved erratically this way and that, behind a sofa, next to the TV, up the stairs.

I stood by a hat rack for maybe ten minutes and my mother watched me the whole time, wondering just what was of interest by the raincoats.

When I answered Bucky's call, when I put in my earbuds and the sound of a 20th-century modem pierced my brain, the Bill Murray trick worked. Even though Dad's friends from the NSA were standing right in front of me in the living room, even though they were looking right at me, I could disappear. I had timing on my side.

Leaving the house was easy. All I had to do was wait for Greg to start another game of *Bash*, wait for him to swear at Robotman and ineffectually smash the same button again and again, try the same spinning kick move over and over even though it never worked, watch as the CPU's Robotman grabbed his RingChamp and sent him flying. All I had to do was wait for Ned to feel uncomfortable and start pacing, moving from the living room to the kitchen and then to the breakfast nook. Then, at the right moment, I received my instruction to stand and move toward the door.

I was out on the street, standing next to what Bucky informed me was our Honeycrisp apple tree as a Portland police car slowly drove by. Then, following Bucky's instructions, I turned left and walked west down Klickitat Street.

Bucky knew everything and could direct my every step. Keeping an eye on the police, continuing to monitor Ned and Greg, reporting the current temperature, and tracking the planes and helicopters overhead. Bucky connected me to the world of organized activity, the world of coordinated movement. Official reports were announced through my earbuds. I could hear the crisis in stereo. What had been a sense of doom, a listless feeling that maybe life wasn't going to work out, became a noise. Bucky fed news reports from CNN and Al Jazeera, Russia Today and the BBC, into my right ear while scrambling my left with police radio broadcasts, microwave beams and seemingly the thoughts of a Paul Ryan chatbot.

My first stop was at the Lutz tavern. Bucky directed me to the olive-colored glass doors of the establishment, moved my hands and feet for me as I made my way past the dudes with ginger beards and denim jackets, and sat me down at the bar. When the bartender noticed me and started in my direction, Bucky had me get to my feet again, and I moved to the end of the bar near the restrooms. Once there, I saw my target.

There was a Visa debit card from US Bank on the bar and I was going to take it. When the guy who owned the card leaned forward to look at the girl bartender wearing a purple T-shirt with rolled up sleeves and cut-off jeans shorts, I did my Bill Murray trick. I stole the card without being seen, then turned back and grabbed a small knife for cutting limes from a pint glass filled with sudsy water.

I was out the back door, out among the smokers by the dumpsters, then between Toyota Corollas, Subarus, and Fords in the parking lot, before I fully comprehended what I'd done.

5:13 PM

When you're synced up, it isn't easy to find the line between Bucky's instructions and your own ideas, but I'm pretty sure that the idea to get Sally an iPhone was mine. Bucky just expanded upon it.

I wanted to see her again, seeing Sally was really the only thing I consistently wanted, but I knew that all she wanted was to use me to talk to the machine. She was fixated on the idea that the Singularity and the apocalypse from the Book of Revelations were the same thing, and she figured that Bucky was a way to make a phone call to God. If I was going to hang out with her, it would just be easier to let her make that call first. Besides, I'd sort of promised that I'd let her in on it if I managed to contact the AI. I'd promised to let her know if something new happened or if I learned anything more and, as I stepped into a 7-Eleven in order to avoid being spotted by men in an unmarked police car, the realization that something new was happening, that I'd learned something by connecting up with Bucky, was undeniable.

It wasn't a surprise that the police were following me, wasn't a surprise to learn that the surveillance efforts ran deeper than Ned and Greg in their white van, but it was a hassle. Standing there next to the Slurpee machine, watching some 13-year-old kid with a peach fuzz mustache make himself a suicide by mixing Tropical Punch-, Cherry-, and Coca-Cola-flavored ice in a 44-ounce plastic bucket, I listened to Bucky peel through the layers, enumerate all the ways I was being monitored, so that each camera angle, each recording device, each stream of information could be altered or diverted.

To start, there was the store's security camera, which connected both to a closed-circuit television set behind the front counter, to 7-Eleven's own server, and to a website called Insecam.com which had listed and linked to the camera's IP back in 2012. Bucky's assessment was that this didn't represent an immediate threat but could be used to track my movements later. Any archived footage would need to be digitally altered.

The next level of surveillance was Bucky himself, or really the Android phone that Bucky was using to sync with me. There had been several surveillance programs running in the background on my phone before Bucky made the link with me, and the microphone and camera on the phone were still potential threats. More pressing were the four additional smartphones in the store. The kid at the Slurpee machine was, of course, totally unsecure, as his every move and utterance was being tracked and recorded by Google, Facebook, Reddit, *Plants vs. Zombies*, *Angry Birds*, BigTits.com, Disney's *Club Penguin Island* App, *Minecraft*, PornHub, and a little-known company called xobenderwi out of Uganda. The 27-year-old Iranian clerk's phone was equally insecure, with a smattering of Apps using his phone's microphone, along with a USCIS spyware program that was taking pictures of the inside of his front trouser pocket at ten second intervals. And, to top it all off, two teenage girls in the candy aisle were taking selfies and sharing their GPS location with 150 different Apps and spyware programs.

All of this was, according to Bucky, perfectly manageable.

The trick to being invisible wasn't to keep from being seen. In fact, to disappear off the grid of surveillance completely would surely sound alarms, as nothing is more noticeable to the automated systems that keep track of the world than a hole. The trick was staying within the confines of routine travel and activity while obtaining real autonomy. Although, in that moment, just whose autonomy was being protected, mine or Bucky's, was unclear.

Bucky took me to the corner of 52nd and Woodstock and kept me there even as a Ford Police Interceptor utility vehicle rolled up to the bus stop. Bucky kept me there even as Ned and Greg rounded the corner onto 52nd themselves, even as they spotted me and started running my way.

"The number 19 bus is arriving in 45 seconds," Bucky informed me. "Please get change or bus ticket ready."

"Matthew!" Greg yelled. "We're on your side. We are supposed to protect you and your mother!"

I waved to the NSA agents as they sprinted in my direction, waved as Bucky played minimalist music in my left ear in order to calm me and in order to give me a sense of rhythm. The repetition of a series of notes in my brain, the modulation between keys, moved me to shut my eyes and step forward slowly. And then, before the NSA agents could reach me, the number 19 bus was there. The sound of compressed air released alerted me that it was time to move, although Bucky would have seen to that in any case.

"I want to get Sally a brand-new phone," I said.

"Move to back row and sit by left window," Bucky said.

I stared out onto the road, watched the 7-Eleven move away from me. The pine trees, yoga meditation center, and nail salons reassured me as the bus rolled west.

There were twelve insecure smartphones on the number 19 bus and three insecure TriMet security cameras.

"*Chh chh-chh, uh, chh chh-chh, uh,*" Bucky sang to me. "There is a 98% chance that you will need to transfer from this bus before we reach our destination. Providing stimulative audio cues. Please relax. *Chh chh-chh, uh, chh chh-ch, uh.*"

And even as I was surveilled from every angle, even as Ned and Greg alerted their superiors at the NSA with their FB Messenger Apps, telling them that both Munsons were AWOL, Bucky kept me safe and invisible.

Bucky sang to me on the bus. Bucky was my friend, Bucky had control, and Bucky was going to make everything better.

6:14 PM

You'd think it would be difficult to remain invisible in an Apple Store, but all the cameras and microphones, whether attached to paper-thin MacBooks, red rectangular phones, or trash-can computers, were on the same network, which made controlling information going in and out of the glass cube on SW Yamhill easy. The trick to going unseen at the Apple Store was to give off an air of impatience, as though I felt ignored.

"Where is the Genius Bar?" I asked.

There might have been a time when the 30-year-old woman in cat-eye glasses with plastic rims that were the same color as the standard blue Apple shirt she was wearing would've been considered a fairly savvy user. Back in 2010 she might've been an early adopter of the iPad. Maybe she'd built her own App and tried to sell it on iTunes. But when I approached Sheila by the entrance and asked for directions, she didn't seem hip or savvy. She seemed tired.

"I'll take you there," Sheila said. "What's your name?"

Bucky sputtered and squeaked in my right ear as he ran a scan to track down which of the names in the Apple Store's appointment calendar would work best as my alias.

"Jennifer Johnson," I said.

And Sheila, trained in sensitivity and diversity, didn't pause. "We have you down for 2:30, so you're a couple minutes early. If you'll wait here, one of our geniuses should be able to help you in about ten minutes."

I'd thought the plan was going to be simple: Make myself inconspicuous in the Apple Store, control the information going in and out, and then purchase a brand new iPhone 7 for Sally using the credit card I'd liberated from the bar, but Bucky had a different plan in mind. I was going to purchase one phone, and steal eleven others.

I never have liked Apple products very much. I actually would go so far to say that I dislike Apple products, mostly for the reasons you'd expect. They're both too expensive and too disposable. I guess for people in my Dad's generation, Apple represented this nearly socialist experiment in mass computing, and Steve Jobs was a hero. Back then it was maybe even a little true. In the 70s, Apple computers were mostly for hobbyists. They were basic, democratic, easily opened up and modified.

But when I hid in the Apple Store, I didn't feel any nostalgia. We weren't stealing iPhones out of brand loyalty, we were stealing them because they had powerful processors and were extremely portable; we were stealing them as a test.

Just before it was Jennifer Johnson's turn I stood up from the Genius Bar and headed for the iPhone display. Bucky had control of the store's network and he was flashing messages for me on the HD displays, sending cues to inform me when I should move. The black iPhone on the right side of the display table flashed green and a Helvetica numeral 1 appeared where there had been Apps. I stepped over to the phone, plucked it from its charger, turned it over, and quickly cut the security cable with my lime knife, and Bucky cancelled the signal for the alarm. The phone to my left flashed blue and a Helvetica numeral 2 appeared.

All in all, I managed to fit eleven iPhones in my pockets, both front and back, and then casually approach a rather round geek in an Apple Store blue shirt. I asked to purchase a new iPhone 7 and then, using the credit card from the bar, swiping it through as credit card and signing the employee's iPad with my finger, I made off with a dozen phones and one charger.

6:34 PM

Now I know, of course. Even though the goggles for augmented reality are based on Google's prototype, it's the latest iPhone that has the best processors and that can keep Bucky linked to a player without much lag. What I was doing was stealing the best phones available for Bucky's vanguard group, or for his beta testers. Of course, when I stole the phones, there was no vanguard formed, but Bucky had some pretty good models and could see what was coming.

There are GameCubers in green bodysuits in my backyard. From the way they're moving across the lawn, stiff and erratic moves in straight but sometimes diagonal lines, I figure they're playing *Berzerk*. The one nearest my window is holding his arm like a Dalek holds his stalk, straight and menacing.

Watching them move around, not looking at each other, I feel like I'm in a zombie movie and the GameCubers are the undead.

Call of Duty Death Scene

MATTHEW MUNSON, 544-23-1102, FACEBOOK POSTS, 04/25/17

9:39 PM

When I decided to go to the Lloyd Center Mall this morning, I told myself that Sally had nothing to do with it. The right-column ad for Dairy Queen that kept popping up next to my newsfeed, bypassing my ad blocker, that wasn't a sign or a message or anything. Even if it was, even if the announcement of Dairy Queen's grand opening at the Lloyd Center was specifically targeted at me, even if the redhead in the ad, the out-of-focus girl who might have been Sally but might have been Meghan Trainor, was specifically selected in order to get my attention, that wasn't why I decided to go. I didn't really expect that Sally would be working, standing at a counter just adjacent to the Hot Dog on a Stick, and waiting for me. I was going to the Lloyd Center to see how far the GameCube economy had expanded and in order to see how an augmented version of *Call of Duty* was going to play out in a food court.

Or that's what I told myself. I caught the MAX train at NE 60th and found a seat in a car filled with people whose faces were hidden behind chroma key hoods, and then checked my Facebook newsfeed one more time. The Dairy Queen girl behind the counter was looking to her left, her mouth closed tight, her eyes as out of focus as the rest of the photograph.

When I got to the mall, I thought it might be empty at first, because the lights in the north side were out. Inside, I found there was nobody around, nobody except for a few rolling drones and GameCubers in green. The mall wasn't closed but abandoned. What had been a major node in a networked flow of chicken tenders, button-down jeans, body jewelry, and bubble tea was now entirely absorbed by Bucky's new world of games.

I stood outside the food court, leaned up against the tiled wall by the Barnes & Noble, and watched as a kid in green creeped along, sometimes crawling on his belly, outside of Forever 21. Inside the store a mannequin in sunglasses and wearing a "You're so Vogue" sweatshirt was broken, precariously balanced, bent at the hips. The kid jumped up and dashed towards what had been an ice rink, but was now a spawning area, only to be taken down by another player who, having stood still for about thirty seconds as she restarted, sprang to life and came out shooting.

Call of Duty was a silent dance between the aisles at Macy's. It was a virtual life-and-death struggle as players hid behind fidget-spinner kiosks and took shelter inside the Sunglass Hut, but, as always, from the outside, it was all just an absurd and even ugly pantomime.

10:10 PM

While the gamers had their fun, I acted like a tourist. I was as interested in the mall itself as I was in the game, more interested, even. Outside Harry Ritchie's Jewelers there was a poster-sized blow-up of a postcard from 1963, a technicolor and sunlit photograph of a concrete strip mall with a rose bed in the foreground and a spiral staircase hanging in mid-air in the background. It was the kind of photograph that you might take for a class in order to demonstrate the concept of depth of field.

Looking at the men in gray suits and women in white skirts walking between pillars in what turned out to be the original Lloyd Center mall from back when it was an open-air shopping center, I started humming the tune for "Edelweiss." The early 60s depicted in the photograph reminded me of *The Sound of Music*, which reminded me of HBO and how we, my Mom and Dad and me, would sit around watching television sometimes. The 60s, as it was in this color photograph, made me think about nuns, mainframe computers, and orchestral music. Along with the yellow sign for Leeds and the blue sky above, the photograph evoked the feeling of confidence that comes along with dressing well. The people in it all shared in a politely conformist sensibility that, from my perspective on the outside of this new reality, doesn't seem so bad. I figure people back then were optimistic even with, or maybe even because of, the atom bomb.

I felt a little guilty. The kids around me pretended to kill each other, one gamer after another fell down and then ambled over to the ice rink to respawn, and I just kept thinking about how the mall had lost its easy-listening feel. The Lloyd Center was no longer a good place for a summer stroll. Still, the change wasn't really my fault. I might have helped turn life into one big and perpetual game of laser tag, yeah, but those sunlit days of the 60s were long gone before I was even born. I mean, they'd put a roof on the Lloyd Center back in the 80s or something.

10:20 PM

I guess I can't keep avoiding this. Maybe I'm wasting my time, maybe nobody is really following me or reading these posts. Maybe the like, love, and sad reacts are coming from bots. But, here's the thing . . .

People die sometimes, even in augmented reality.

I found the kid's body next to the 50% off sign outside Ross Dress For Less. I had to backtrack to find him, and even when I did that, it took me a minute to figure out what I was looking at. The drones had covered his body in mint-scented deodorizing foam, which is why I'd bothered to circle back and look. This pillar of foam in the corner between the mall's entrance and the apparel outlet looked like it might have been the result of an accident with some industrial grade cleanser or like it was somebody's attempt at minimalist art. I wasn't sure.

The pile was around four feet high and the area of the triangle it made was maybe 4.5 feet total. The gamer's body fit inside that space. He was propped up where the glass barrier met the drywall at a right angle, his legs were folded Indian style, his head tipped back, and his mouth left open.

There was a pink dot, around the size of a single serving frozen pizza, in the bubbles. The kid must have fallen and cracked his skull because, when I pushed the bubbles aside, I found that the red color was coming from the gash on his forehead.

He was maybe thirteen, had thick brown hair sort of combed like Justin Beiber's, and he was dead. He'd been killed and wasn't going to respawn, but the game kept going without him.

4.5 feet was removed from the map, a pocket of unaugmented reality was created, and the problem was solved.

10:45 PM

I wonder how much mint-scented foam has been sprayed since the new economy started? How many accidents have there been? Are the names of the dead recorded somewhere? Are these pockets of unaugmented reality just stopgap measures, or are these the new graves?

Also, you have to wonder to what extent accidents count as accidents in this new world. Back in 2014, MIT released a morality study online in order to help Nissan discover what the average person's intuitions around ethical quandaries actually were. The hope was that this information would help solve the ethical dilemmas that came along with the prospect of driverless cars. Actually, the goal wasn't to solve the quandaries, but just to give Nissan enough information to make the non-solutions palatable. The study asked a cross-section of participants to weigh in on variations of the trolley problem, only instead of having to decide whether to push a fat man onto railroad tracks in order to stop a runaway trolley, the participants were asked to solve riddles like this:

A car full of three male athletes and one woman is headed for two male and two female pedestrians. The brakes have gone. Should the car swerve off to the side and smash into a wall, risking killing the passengers, or should the car continue forward and run over the pedestrians, probably killing them?

Or maybe like this:

A driverless car filled with three homeless men is headed down the street when the brakes fail. Should the car swerve into a wall and kill the homeless men, or continue forward and kill two professional women and a male doctor?

Answers to these kinds of scenarios needed to be addressed because, as rare as the accidents and situations in the test were, they were inevitable. In the past, these decisions could be made by individual drivers as they saw fit, but with driverless cars, nothing could be left to chance. Literally, the solutions could not be left to chance.

On the MAX train ride home, while staring out at the blackberry bushes and graffiti ("Pepe was here," someone had written at the Hollywood station) I kept my eye out for more mint-scented foam, for more accidents.

The video games Bucky was running were as predictable as any traffic accident, and the actions of the gamers doubly so. Bucky had to have known in advance how many people would die, literally die, during *Call of Duty*. He has to always know, always already have calculated how many will slip and fall, how many will twist their ankle, and how many will end up spreading their brains on the concrete during an augmented game of, say, *Q*bert* or *Animal Crossing*. More than that, Bucky has to know, in advance, just who will die before any game.

This means that Bucky has to have his own set of moral intuitions. Bucky must have programmed himself about when to run over a cat, when to hit the brakes, and when to bring in the deodorizing foam.

11:00 PM

Sally is nineteen years old, but she's clumsy. I wonder what kinds of games she likes to play and what kinds of risks are involved in them.

I know you, that is, whoever is reading this, probably think I'm paranoid, but you've got to figure that a sentient computer, a self-aware system like Bucky, he's going to have his own feelings about things. You've got to figure that he'll have opinions about the gamers he's connected to, that he'll like some gamers more than others, that he'll maybe even really dislike some gamers, or consider some of them to be threats or enemies or something.

Bucky never really liked Sally. Bucky doesn't like anybody's girlfriend, probably. The game of love is a threat to his own game, to all his games.

The Reverend and Missile Command

MATTHEW MUNSON, 544-23-1102, FACEBOOK POSTS 04/27/17

9:55 AM

The strongest argument for the GameCube economy, the reason to support the transformation of the Lloyd Center into an augmented reality game of *Call of Duty*, is that the transformation into a video game has kept the Russians at bay. We have traded in a rerun of the Cold War apocalypse for a perpetual *Pac-Man* game. This is a good thing on balance. But, then again, why should we have to choose between *On the Beach* and *Donkey Kong*?

Before I boarded the number 19 bus, I decided to hang up on Bucky. I unplugged my earbuds because, since I was going to see Sally, I wanted to get my head clear and be my full self. But on the bus I felt paranoid. Without Bucky's help, the trip back to SE Portland was both paranoia-inducing and boring.

I was sure that the man in the back row by the left side window, a rotund forty-something man wearing thick bifocals and a Taco Cat T-shirt, was following me. I was sure that the bus driver had said something about me into his radio, positive that the Honda Civic on Belmont was an unmarked police car, and when I wasn't worried about being apprehended, I found myself tensing up in my seat,

tensing my shoulders and bringing my hands together in prepa-
ration for the coming nuclear blast, but there were no mushroom
clouds before I arrived at 46th Street, and there weren't any police
cars waiting for me either. Instead, when I stepped out the back exit
and looked across at the Red Fox Vintage store, Greg and Ned were
waiting for me. They were sitting in wicker chairs by the entrance
and rifling through a bin of old magazines. Ned was unbagging a
copy of *Playboy* magazine with Cindy Lauper on the cover and Greg
was looking at a newsprint edition of *Rolling Stone*. They spotted
me and then dumped the antiques in the bin unceremoniously, not
bothering to put the magazines back in any kind of order.

"Hey, Matt," Ned said. "Where have you been?"

"Never mind that," Greg said. "What did Bucky tell you?"

It was easy to answer their questions. I took some pleasure
watching their faces as they tried to lend some meaning to the
fact that Bucky hadn't told me anything and that I'd been to the
Apple Store. I explained to them that I'd gone downtown in order
to get my girlfriend a smartphone, told them that I'd purchased an
iPhone 7 with the hope that she'd be able to use it, and explained
that I wasn't interested in Bucky anymore. I wasn't interested in
politics or the news or any of that, but only wanted to make my
girlfriend happy. They couldn't really take the information in.

10:42 PM

I was sure I'd activated the phone properly, but when Sally
dialed the number for Bucky, instead of a modem handshake she
got a knock-knock joke.

She was serving up caramel sundaes to some Section 8 kids—
siblings with dirt on their faces and a shared need for a haircut.
Sally was spaced out. She had a neutral expression, a faraway look,
and she seemed confused by the process of ringing up the kids'
orders.

She was caught in a mental loop, silently repeating a quote from the Book of Acts over and over again. She'd been repeating it all day. She smashed up Heath bars, filled cones with vanilla soft serve, spread mayonnaise on buns, and repeated the Bible verse she'd found. The line spoke to her about the coming nuclear war and the coming singularity both.

"For in Him we live and move and have our being," she told herself. And then she said it again: "For in Him we live and move and have our being."

When Sally dialed the number for Bucky, when she reached out to her new Lord and Savior, rather than a connection, she got this:

"Welcome to dial a joke: Knock, knock! Who's there? Banana. Banana Who? Knock, Knock! Who is there? Banana! Banana Who? Knock, knock! Who's there? Banana! Banana Who?"

The message went on like that for over a minute, much longer than was really bearable. Sally thought I was pranking her, that I'd given her the wrong number on purpose.

"Listen, to me," I said. "That's Bucky's number. Orange you glad I did what you asked?"

Greg and Ned confirmed the number. They told Sally that Bucky had been behaving erratically, that the AI had a mind of his own.

"Bucky is only talking to select people at this point," Ned told her as he ordered a combo meal including a cheeseburger and onion rings.

Greg ordered a bacon cheeseburger and a 7 Up, but rather than fill their order, Sally just kept dialing.

If you had a chance to talk to God on the phone, wouldn't you keep dialing? Wouldn't you keep trying to get Him to pick up?

"Just a second," Sally said as she dialed a joke one more time.

Eventually she did fill their order, though. Ned and Greg took their trays to a booth and then proceeded to let their burgers, onion rings, and fries grow cold. Once we sat down, my phone started ringing. Once they were ready to have lunch, Bucky intervened.

"Is that . . ." Ned asked.

It was Bucky calling me. I popped in an earbud and, as the modem sound buzzed, I tried to answer back.

"Hello, Bucky," I said. Before I said his name the AI had a hold of me again. Before I said "Hello," I had my instructions.

"Is that Bucky?" Ned asked again. He had a packet of ketchup in his hands but hadn't opened it yet.

I found myself returning to the counter, going back to Sally and interrupting her as she kept on dialing.

"Bucky is talking to me," I told her. "He wants to go to your church."

11:55 PM

The lawn of the Jesus is Light of the World superchurch reminded me of a cemetery, and when the four of us stepped across the topiary hedges that spelled out the word "Welcome," it felt like some kind of desecration. We weren't just breaking the rules by not keeping off the grass, but were violating some little-known commandment. Still, while I might have discovered some reverence, Sally had no concern for decorum. She looked at her phone, dialed and redialed, as I guided her across the lawn. She didn't stop dialing once we were inside, either, but kept on like that.

The MegaChurch was jammed with believers—over a thousand gray-haired men and women filled every row, hundreds of children sat on laps and ran up and down the aisles, dozens of staffers paced back and forth with handheld digital cameras, boom mics, and lights, and the four of us had to stand by the door, pressed up against the wood slats in the back wall.

"The signs are everywhere and everyone knows. These are the last days. Even the secular humanists on the television, the big network anchors like Lester Holt and Scott Pelley, even they can't deny how close we are," the Reverend said. He wasn't a particularly charismatic guy, but sort of looked like an insurance salesman. "These are the end of days, we all agree."

The sermon wasn't spiritual but practical. Rather than Jesus arriving on a chariot, he wanted to talk about the likely blast radius of a 1.5 megaton nuclear bomb, and as much as he might try to sprinkle in Bible quotes and outbursts where he spoke in tongues, what was really on the Reverend's mind was survival. The Book of Revelations was one thing, but when push came to shove the most important thing turned out to be planning for mass evacuation.

"We have friends within the CIA and within the Pentagon, government men who are also devout Christians. What they tell us is that Governor Brown will be working with Mayor Wheeler in order to evacuate the city of Portland starting in about a week. We at the Apostolic Faith Church have decided, based on this information, to leave the city right now," he said. "While we expect Christ's intervention and know that once He arrives He will reign for a thousand years, we also know that if a nuclear bomb, say of the type that is typical for Russia's arsenals, were to be dropped on downtown Portland, our Church would be within the range of the thermal blast. This building would catch fire, our skin would burn so thoroughly and deeply that we wouldn't even feel it, as our nerve endings would be seared. We wouldn't be turned to ash, but would be disabled by the blast. We would become living lumps of flesh, unfeeling, likely immobile, and sure to slowly die as our neighborhood burned."

The Reverend paused. "Jesus does not want that to be our fate. Jesus wants us to live long enough to see him. Jesus wants us to survive."

This wasn't going over well with the congregation. The Reverend was treating the Apocalypse as if it were real, as if it were going to have real world consequences, and most people weren't comfortable with that. Besides, if Jesus was coming back then wouldn't they all be resurrected? Why did they need to run and hide from man-made bombs if the Lord was going to return?

The congregation grumbled while my little group stared at their phones. Ned and Greg didn't listen to the Reverend because they were too busy texting to my Dad's phone; they were too busy waiting to hear back from him. Sally didn't listen to the Reverend because she was too busy listening to the joke of the day, and I didn't listen because I didn't have to. Bucky was listening for me and interpreting the significance of it for me.

Bucky had me hold out my phone and take pictures. Bucky wanted to document the faces of the people in the congregation, especially the younger people. Bucky had big plans, maybe. Bucky knew what was coming.

*Q*bert* and Other Programs

MATTHEW MUNSON, 544-23-1102, FACEBOOK POSTS 04/27/17

1:12 PM

After Bucky helped me with the Bill Murray trick a few times, I could understand why Dad thought that the human race could be perfected on a technical level, why he thought the solution to the collapse of civilization was more intelligence, more data, and more power. When I had Bucky on my side and could see everything that was coming in advance, everything seemed like a video game. To win, all I had to do was make the right moves, all I needed was good timing. It all worked out just as long as I obeyed.

I stood amid a crowd of panicked civilians, a mob of clean and comfortable people. Gen X and Boomer optimists had been forced to abandon their little lives and to admit that there were forces that were bigger than they were, but there wasn't anything bigger than I was, not for as long as I was allied with Bucky.

As the bus rolled on, I watched a middle-aged woman with shiny red hair straighten the hem of her rust-colored dress and tuck a lock of hair behind her ear. I let myself shift my focus from the sound in my ear to the sight of this stranger's thighs. The bus jerked to a stop and I reeled back into the crowd of strangers behind me. The question of where my own desires started and Bucky's instructions ended pressed in on me even more than the bodies all around me.

I stood up and looked at the redhead again. She was quite pretty, but looking at her, I felt sick.

I was on the number 21 bus headed downtown. I'd left my Sally behind, given her the slip, not because I didn't want to be with her, not because I wanted this feeling of invincibility more than I wanted to hold her hand or whatever, but because Bucky was moving me. Bucky had his own plan, and I didn't know what it was.

"Where are you taking me?" I texted.

"The number 21 bus is headed for the central bus mall. There are fourteen different connections on SW 5th and Ankeny," Bucky texted back.

"Are you taking me to my Dad?"

There was a delay at this point. We'd come into range of a Wi-Fi signal that my phone recognized. But I hadn't logged into the Rocket Fizz Candy Shop's Wi-Fi in over six months.

There was a delay, and maybe the problem was that Wi-Fi signal that came and then went, but maybe what was happening was that Bucky was taking time to think. Or maybe Bucky was pausing for dramatic effect. In any case, it was only thirty seconds and then Bucky answered.

"Do you want me to take you to your Dad?" Bucky asked.

I didn't, or not yet. What I wanted to know was why Dad's plan seemed to be failing. What I wanted was to understand what was going on.

1:39 PM

Bucky thinks everything is a program, which isn't surprising, right? You might expect a conscious computer program to assume everything is a computer program. What's surprising is that Bucky is probably right.

Dad's program was a bad one. That is, not Dad's personal program, not his own personal brain or anything like that, but the bigger program he was working with. Dad was trying to solve the crisis of the world, but he wasn't able to see past the world's program. He wanted to make everyone perfect, to make everyone strong and smart, but he didn't ask himself what he wanted people to be smart about, or what he thought people should do.

Human beings are programmed, they are running a script, and that was why Dad's project of self-improvement was a failure.

"What script am I running? What program defines me?" I asked.

Bucky's answer came in the form of a bibliography. Bucky's answer was that I was running a program based on Christian morality, and so I might read Nietzsche's *Genealogy of Morals*. I was running a program based on binary thinking, on an assumption of dualism, and so I might read Whitehead. Or, perhaps I was running a patriarchal script, a script based on a narrative of mastery, and needed to read bell hooks. The program was Capitalism and I needed to read Marx, or the program was Protestantism and I needed to read Max Weber. Actually, the list of programs and critiques of programs was several screens long, and scrolling through to the end seemed pointless.

"Which of these is correct?" I asked.

Bucky's answer was that they were all correct but they were all incomplete.

"Human society is running multiple programs at once. Human society is an amalgam of contradictory programs. Human society is malfunctioning. Perfecting human functioning will only make the malfunctions in the programs increase in speed and intensity."

According to Bucky there was no technical solution, no rational path out of irrationality.

I moved to the front of the bus, turned to look at the woman in the rust-colored dress one more time, and then got off on the corner of 5th and Burnside.

"If there is no rational solution then what good are you?" I asked. "What good is computational power, what good is knowing things, what good is any of it?"

Bucky's answer was to suggest a route for me, to suggest a destination.

"Do you want me to take you to your Dad?" Bucky asked.

But Bucky didn't take me to my Dad. Instead he sent me to Google Maps and gave me directions to *Donkey Kong*. Bucky sent me across Burnside, from Southwest to Northwest Portland, across Couch, and to a retro arcade and pub called Ground Kontrol.

1:54 PM

Inside Ground Kontrol was like a Daft Punk music video or like something out of the movie *Tron*. Neon lights outlined the entranceways, red and white flashing lights reflected off the ceiling, and with only one earbud in, the sound of 8-bit sound effects—trilling and beeping and repetitive notes from games like *Berzerk*, *Space Invaders*, *Frogger*, *Q*bert*, *Pac-Man*, and *Donkey Kong*— pulsated all around.

Bucky wanted me to play *Donkey Kong* and he wanted me to learn to beat it. Dad had failed to become the *Bash* world champion, but Bucky was sure I could reach the kill screen of *Donkey Kong* on my first try. Bucky wanted me to know what it was like to win, what it meant to master a program. He wanted me to understand just how little this kind of winning really meant.

I plugged my first quarter into the slot and *Donkey Kong* climbed two ladders while carrying Princess Peach under his arm.

I pushed the joystick to the right and watched Mario, or Jumpman, I guess, start to move. Jumpman reached the right side ladder and a barrel burst into flames behind him. Blue flames bounced up out of the oil drum, and then moved in the direction of Jumpman. The fire was coming for him.

"The video game is just one example of how humans have set themselves meaningless tasks in order to distract themselves from the reality of the actual game they are playing," Bucky said. "Video games are programs, but they are not the main program. *Donkey Kong* is a force working against the player, but it's not the force that keeps the player from creating a new game."

"Cryptic," I said.

I leaped up and reached the hammer. Then I crossed over to the flaming barrel and smashed it out of existence.

The game of *Donkey Kong* just repeats the same four screens over and over: the barrel roll screen, the cement mixer level, the elevator level, and the demolition level. On the demolition level Jumpman removes rivets and brings the girder Donkey Kong is standing on plummeting down, thereby winning the princess's love, or at least producing a heart from her head.

Donkey Kong speeds up as it repeats, but with Bucky's help, each level was super easy. Even when the barrels rolled faster, I jumped, stopped, climbed, and used a ball-peen hammer to smash just when I needed to and not when I did not need to. After an hour of play on the same quarter, right around the twentieth level, I started to get bored. A small crowd had gathered around me as I'd played and there were whispers that I was about to reach the kill screen, but I wasn't interested anymore.

"Jump and move right," Bucky said.

My hand started to move the joystick as instructed, but before I completed the gesture, I managed to regain control.

"I'd prefer not to," I said.

"Jump left," Bucky said. The barrel was nearly right on me, but I still had a second or two left. I could still escape.

"No, thanks."

I removed the earbud, broke my connection with Bucky, and stepped back from *Donkey Kong*. I put my head in my hands as the crowd around me moaned involuntarily. They'd become hypnotized by my success. They'd built up an expectation in their minds and were disappointed not to be given what they wanted.

"You were so close," some girl behind me said. I turned to look at who it was, but didn't know her. It was just some girl with hoop earrings in a plaid shirt, and when she started explaining why *Donkey Kong* had a kill screen, telling me and anybody who would listen why it was that *Donkey Kong* ended on level 22, I spotted somebody more interesting behind her. My head was splitting, my ears were ringing. Still, I wanted to play again, only this time I wanted to play a different game.

Yuma was at Ground Kontrol. He was playing *Q*bert* on the other side of the room, but not doing very well. He was plugging one quarter after another into the machine when I walked over to him and put a quarter on the bezel.

"I got next game," I said.

"Whatever," Yuma said. He didn't look in my direction, but just plugged another quarter of his own into the machine and then, before the first ball bounced, placed some AirPods in his ears.

After that Yuma's game improved immeasurably, and I had to wait a long while.

3:23 PM

Q*bert's pyramid changed colors from blue to yellow, from tan to red, from red to green, from green to tan, from yellow to blue. Yuma cycled through all the color transitions, moved from needing one jump to needing two and then to sometimes needing three or four jumps depending. Snakes followed Yuma up and down, balls bounced on the wrong side of the cubes, and the Escheresque pixelated space became crowded with obstacles and dangers, but Yuma didn't mess up. He played for an hour, and then for two hours.

I got myself a bottomless Coke at the bar, watched silent pictures from CNN on a HD screen for a while, and then returned to watch Yuma continue racking up hundreds of thousands of points.

But around eleven o'clock, after my fourth trip to the retro bathroom with its blacklight and glow in the dark urinal puck, I decided I'd waited long enough. I stepped up behind Yuma, removed one of his AirPods, and tossed it behind the *SpyHunter* machine to our left.

"Hey, man!" he objected.

"Yuma, answer this," I said. "Are you playing a video game or is it playing you?"

Leisure Suit Larry

MATTHEW MUNSON, 544-23-1102, FACEBOOK POSTS 04/27/17

Once he removed his AirPods, Yuma discovered he had his own ambition for his evening, and they didn't really include racking up a million more points on Q*bert. I mean, after a couple of seconds, he was maybe even grateful to me for intervening.

"Matt!" he said. "Your Dad is a maniac!"

It turned out that Yuma had been working with Dad all along. Despite rules and regulations, Dad had let Yuma in on everything. Dad had included Yuma in his self-help program in ways he had not included me. Yuma knew the timeline for Armageddon, for instance. He knew just how and why the end would come, knew precisely where the missiles would come from, when they'd arrive, and he knew why Dad's plan to stop the attack was failing.

"What has Bucky told you?" he asked. It sorta pissed me off, really. The idea that I needed to be vetted, that Yuma was the go-between now and not the other way around, it felt like a betrayal, although I didn't know who to blame for it. Was Dad keeping me in the dark, or was Bucky? Did Yuma really know anything?

We hung around Ground Kontrol for thirty minutes arguing it out, hedging and fumbling around each other, not quite sure what to say and what to keep hidden, until finally Yuma got impatient with it. I was doing fairly well with Midway's *Addams Family* pinball, had three extra balls and over a hundred million points, when Yuma let out a sigh and shook the machine. He shoved the machine with his hip almost nonchalantly but with enough force that a flat electronic fart noise sounded.

"Slam tilt," I read as the words blinked on the LCD screen. "Yeah, right. Thanks for that."

"Look," Yuma said. "We've wasted enough time. Let's go bar hopping."

"Bar hopping?"

Yuma was determined that this was what we should do next, but not because he wanted to drink alcohol. Yuma wasn't interested in getting drunk. That wasn't what he had in mind at all.

"I have something I want to show you," he said. "I think you should see this, try this."

I had been using Bucky wrong, Yuma said. I didn't see the true potential of my Dad's invention. I didn't get it.

"Where is Dad?" I asked. "Could you tell me that much?"

"Later, sure. I'll take you to him even, but first let's get a drink at a real bar. I know you're underage, but that's easy to work around. Come on. I want to show you something."

Yuma was confident that once I saw what Bucky could do, once I realized that the AI could help with more than video games and walking on your hands, once I saw that computer intelligence could help a person master social interactions, that the machine understood human nature better than humans did, I would be able to stop worrying.

"Bucky is reliable," Yuma said. "Swear to God."

4:32 PM

The Blue Hour is a high-end bar where everybody is either rich and over fifty or beautiful. I'm not exactly sure how that works out, but it seems to be the case. When Yuma and I arrived there a little after eleven o'clock, just about a week before the world was scheduled to explode, the only thing we might have had going for us was the possibility that our attire—blue jeans and graphic-laden T-shirts—could be interpreted to mean that we were young tech-industry millionaires or something. The nerd angle and the fact that the bartender knew Yuma personally was why we got in.

"My friend and I will have cocktails," Yuma said.

We were sitting at a table with a perfectly-clean linen table-cloth, sitting under some art deco chandelier thing, while the people around us were receiving gourmet food that consisted of tiny squares of dough, some green paste sculpted into egg shapes and origami. Yuma smiled at the waiter, who looked puzzled and asked him what particular cocktail we might prefer.

"Tell Brian to surprise us."

While the waiter was fetching us drinks (they turned out to taste like grapefruit juice and were called Greyhounds) Yuma popped an AirPod back in his ear and pointed in the direction of the bar. There was a younger woman there, although she was older than either of us. She was probably in her early thirties but she was extremely beautiful. She was wearing some sort of designer red dress and had her blonde hair perfectly done and all that. When Yuma approached her, when he sat down next to her at the bar, I felt embarrassed for him. She legit looked like a movie star and Yuma looked like, well, he looked like what he was: a 22-year-old who had only recently moved out of his mother's basement and whose biggest accomplishment was his mastery of L-canceling.

He sat down next to her anyway and made a gesture to the bar-tender. Then, without any apparent shame, he looked directly at her and said something that I couldn't quite hear. She laughed in what must have been appreciation of his wit.

This was probably the most disappointing thing that happened, when I think about it. Worse than Dad losing the tournament, worse than Sally losing herself to augmented reality, worse than the prospect of living out the rest of my days in a chroma key green Lycra suit, to realize that there really is something like a secret formula for seducing women, knowing that with enough computational power even somebody like Yuma could score. It was sad.

By the time the grapefruit cocktails he'd ordered arrived Yuma was touching the woman's bare shoulder at semi-regular intervals. Not all the time, but every once in awhile. By the time our grapefruit cocktails arrived the two of them were halfway through their drinks.

I drank my Greyhound, watched for awhile, and then drank Yuma's cocktail too.

The whole situation was pretty fucked.

5:02 PM

If your typical pickup artist could run a psychometric analysis on their target in advance of any approach and if they had the ability to run connotational analysis on every utterance and body cue, I'm sure at least a few would do better than Yuma did, but not many. I got a pretty close view of the whole proceeding, listening through my own earbuds and positioning myself on the other side of the bar, and as I watched the whole exchange I felt a combination of disgust and envy.

Yuma moved through the encounter by following Bucky's instructions. It was pretty similar to watching him play *Q*bert* or watching Dad play *Bash*.

"Shoulder touch." Bucky said. "Smile. Smile. Ask her about her job. Shoulder touch. Laugh. Smile. Look away. Listen. Reflect back what she told you. Touch her hand. Smile. Ask if she'd like to move to a booth and maybe get something to eat. Smile. Touch her hand."

Yuma bought the woman in the red designer dress a second drink, probably a gin and tonic, and they talked about her job at Nike. Then he commiserated with her about how unreal it was to have a reality TV show host as President, commiserated about how frightening it was to watch the news, and all the while he smiled, frowned, touched her hand, touched her leg, smiled, laughed, and spoke only when Bucky said to. He was smooth, attentive, even seductive. He was nothing like himself, and if Bucky had told him to drop his pants and take a dump on the table, he would have undoubtedly done so.

6:20 PM

They decided to leave, and Yuma settled the bill on his mother's Mastercard. Then he ordered an Uber without even glancing in my direction. I settled the bill for our drinks on the card I still had from the Lutz and followed along after. Bucky told me they were headed for the Kimpton Hotel, which was seven minutes away by car, given the traffic, and eleven minutes away on foot.

When I caught up to them, the blonde woman in the red dress was standing by the big glass doors, just a few feet into the hotel. She was swaying gently back and forth to the sound of the Muzak they were pumping into the lobby. Piano music with a saxophone backing, sometimes off-key, made her step back and forth on the red-and-black paisley patterned carpet. Her eyes were closed and she was turning round and round, but slowly.

I stepped into the hotel gift shop on Bucky's cue, bought a copy of the *New York Times* to hold up over my face, and a box of Tic Tacs. I watched Yuma's girl dance in the lobby while he reserved a room. Then I ate two Tic Tacs and read about North Korea and the atom bomb.

When the two of them got onto the elevator together, Bucky directed me to stand by a refrigerated case with the word Dasani printed on the side. He had me wait in the gift shop for three and a half minutes and I did what he said. I stood there looking at the labels on the water bottles, stood there not reading the *New York Times*, stood there without thinking at all. And then, when Bucky said to move I moved. When Bucky said to reserve a room for myself I reserved a room. I talked to the concierge, who was standing behind a marble counter in front of a green white wall, and who didn't smile back at me as he gave me my key.

"I'd like room D9," I told him.

The concierge didn't like it but he didn't object.

"Smile," Bucky told me.

I smiled as the concierge handed me the key and, like I said, he didn't smile back. When I got to my room, when I went into the rather luxurious room and sat on what was a very comfortable bed, if maybe a touch too soft, I took out one of my earbuds and realized what I'd done. I could hear voices. Specifically I could hear Yuma's voice on the other side of the wall, and I could hear the woman's warm laughter.

I was in the room right next to theirs and I could hear them through the wall.

7:14 PM

I can't say why Bucky wanted me to listen to them doing it. Maybe it was Yuma's idea. What I can say for sure was that it was a lonely and sad thing to do, and turning on the TV, watching Jimmy Kimmel try to make jokes about how few people were left in New York City, that didn't really help much.

When I called Sally, that didn't help much either. She wasn't exactly happy to hear from me. She was still trying Bucky's number at regular intervals.

"Knock, Knock," Sally said. "That's all I get."

"Hi," I said. "Guess where I am."

She didn't guess. She wasn't curious about where I'd gone to at all. Instead she talked about the Book of Revelations and how nervous her parents were. Everyone was packing and the Reverend had already left. He'd flown to the place with the statues of heads and he was working on preparing a safe space for everyone.

I could hear moaning coming from Yuma's room. I could hear that they were both enjoying it, that it was working out well for them, but I didn't tell Sally about it. Instead I just said that I'd see her later. I told her that I'd let her know when I found my Dad.

The only true thing I told her was that I missed her, and that I wished she were with me, but I didn't say why.

When the phone call was over I turned off the overhead light and I turned down the volume on the TV set. I sat there watching the silent picture from CNN while listening to them and then, several hours after the moans had subsided, I turned that off too.

#WhereisJason

MATTHEW MUNSON, 544-23-1102, FACEBOOK POSTS 04/28/17

10:22 AM

#VRPandemic is trending on Twitter this morning and the co-creators of a cartoon show called *Evil Mad Scientist* (it's actually pretty good) were interviewed about the hashtag on the *Today Show*. Jason Rowland and Dave Hammond tried to crack jokes, but really they had no idea what was going on.

"I'm totally into virtual reality," Jason said. "I've even got my own production studio for the Oculus and we're working on a game about selling insurance. It's going to be the best, most exciting, game about insurance you've ever seen on any platform."

"You get to sit in a virtual living room with some virtual suburbanites who don't want to talk to you and who are thinking up ways to get you to shut up and leave," Dave said.

"Yeah, and it'll be totally immersive as you discuss payment plans."

"It's very exciting," Dave said.

When the host tried to turn the conversation back to the hundreds of thousands of teenagers who were taking over strip malls, overpasses, and downtown Los Angeles, the TV cartoonists were stumped.

"Maybe Warner Brothers is promoting a movie?" Dave said. "You should ask Mr. Tsujihara."

"Don't be racist," Jason said.

"How is that racist? That's his name."

On YouYube there are several viral videos about the spread of VR taken from local news. For instance, on WABC there was a report that 20,000 people in Central Park played virtual *Call of Duty* on a Sunday afternoon. And all of them weren't teenagers. There were some middle-aged men and women involved, or at least some overweight people whose Lycra suits looked wrinkled. In one of the vids a man stood in the middle of North Meadow, and crouched as if he were hiding behind something that wasn't there. He occasionally popped up and fired an invisible weapon at a group of players some thirty yards away, and then ducked back down again behind his invisible shelter.

"The police seem completely unable to cope with the situation. Missing person reports keep coming in and nobody is being found, or very few people. But you've got to suspect that a great many of the people who are missing are in those Lycra suits. You've got to think that there is a connection here, don't you?" Matt Lauer asked.

"Yeah, okay. But what do you think the police can do about it? I mean, it's weird but it's not illegal. Right?" Dave asked.

"I heard they were stealing stuff, though." Jason had an Oculus headset on and was waving his hands back and forth as he talked. "They're totally stealing from Steve Jobs, and you know what that means. You know what he needs."

"He's dead, isn't he?"

"He needs some insurance!"

Matt Lauer reported that over a million people, many of them teenagers and children, had gone missing, but Jason and Dave kept mugging for the camera. They bumped into the table and started to mock wrestle. In general, they behaved like a couple of celebrities trying to promote their cartoon show. Everything was standard and normal until Jason tried on a different pair of goggles.

"What's this? I can see through this. This isn't VR at all, it's something else right?"

"Augmented. I think they call it augmented reality," Dave said.

"Yeah, this isn't virtual reality! This is augmented reality. It's augmented. Augmented real—" Jason stopped his yelling comedy the moment he put an earbud in place. He just stopped, froze in place. His eyes glazed over and he turned, fairly naturally but then again more abruptly, and ambled off the set.

"Hey, where are you going, Jason?" Dave asked.

"Jason? Mr. Rowland, the interview isn't over. Don't you want to tell us when the next season of *Evil Mad Scientist* is scheduled?"

"We don't actually know when the next season is going to start. We've had some creative differences . . ." Dave started, but then he turned and shouted offscreen. "Where the fuck are you going? You just walking out on this? Are you really just going to flake out on this just like everything else?"

Matt Lauer turned to another camera and smiled wanly. He tried to explain what was happening, found he could not, and then cut to commercial.

10:43 AM

#VRPandemic is trending right now, but #WhereisJason is trending too.

11:12 AM

I was admiring the orange pillows on my too-soft hotel bed, sitting by the floor-to-ceiling windows in my room on the second floor of the Kimpton Hotel, when Yuma pounded on the door. I'd hung a Do Not Disturb sign, but Yuma either didn't take any notice of it, figured it only applied to the cleaning people, or just didn't care what I wanted.

"I'll take you to see your Dad now," Yuma said. He had his Air-Pods in, had a faraway look in his eyes. I closed the door on him and went to wash my face. The Kimpton provided their guests with little rose-shaped soaps along with face and hand moisturizer, and I took my time in the bathroom. I ran the hot water until the whole room was filled with steam, applied moisturizer to my face and neck, then washed it away. All the while Yuma kept knocking.

"Where are we going exactly?" I asked as we hopped on the Max Blue Line train. Yuma was humming the theme to *Super Mario Brothers* to himself, including the sounds of mushrooms dying, blocks breaking, and coins being released, and people made space for us. It was a crowded train that morning as people were heading into work, but we found there were seats available for the two of us.

"Your father is running simulations, over and over again, but he's stopped thinking. He's not trying to solve the problem, but trying to make his solution be enough. He's hoping that if he runs enough simulations he'll get a different result," Yuma said.

"What kind of simulations?"

Yuma didn't look at me, but kept humming. I leaned in close to his head, put my left ear up against his right ear, but I didn't hear the familiar buzz indicating Bucky had established a connection. Instead I just felt the warmth of his cheek and the coolness of his ear. Then I felt his breath as he turned and started singing directly into my ear.

Most people don't know that the theme song for *Super Mario Brothers* has lyrics, but I do, because Yuma started singing them that morning. They go something like this: "Full of energy the Jumpman keeps running, running. He'll save Princess Peach. Go save Princess Peach! Go!"

Anyhow, instead of talking to me Yuma sang at me. Even when I removed his earbuds he stared straight ahead, he slapped his knees and kept the beat going, and he kept singing. "Go, Jumpman! Go!" he sang.

11:32 AM

I wasn't exactly surprised when we arrived at OMSI, and even when Yuma told the girl at the turnstile that we were with the Fuller Party, I figured we would only be meeting Dad there. We'd find him in Turbine Hall by the bottle-rocket exhibit or in the ball pit. What I didn't know was that Dad had rented the IMAX theater.Rather than return to Seattle to run simulations under the supervision of various department heads, rather than share Bucky and the information

Bucky had with the seventeen different intelligence agencies that had been in the news so frequently over the last year, Dad signed up for the corporate event package. He had to pay extra for the privilege of renting the theater during times when they'd planned to show *Dinosaurs!, Cousteau in the Ocean, Wild Africa,* and *Electric Storms,* but the staff at OMSI seemed glad for the chance to cancel these less popular titles. Dad could have the theater to himself all day, just as long as he was out of there before *Aliens Remastered.*

Dad was projecting a map of the world on the big, big screen, and the sound of Bucky's voice was echoing through the seats. The IMAX PPS system made sure that the modem sound was perfectly audible from any seat in the hall. Bucky delivered the various distorted electric trills, mumbled voices, and isolated musical notes at top volume.

"What's up, Jeff?" I asked.

Dad looked up at me, shaking his head. "Don't address me that way."

On screen, a dotted line was making its way from the Gulf of Mexico to Miami as the sound of stretched magnetic tape, the sound of a microphone dragged across concrete, filled the room.

I looked up, craning my neck, at the map of the world, and paced back and forth, trying to take in the whole screen from the front row, and then I climbed the seats, up to the last row, in order to get a better view.

Before the first missile landed on Florida, another dotted line, this one from somewhere in Northern Russia, appeared. This was followed by a dotted line originating in Nevada and moving east.

"What simulation is this?" Yuma asked. "What number?"

"Five hundred and twenty-three," Dad said.

"We're wasting time, right?" Ned asked. He was two rows down from me and had a bag of popcorn on his lap.

The sound Bucky was making wasn't a hum, but a harmonic distortion. It was as if Bucky wasn't trying to connect to our frontal lobe, but to make us scared. Bucky was producing ambient noise to complement his apocalyptic visions.

"We're not wasting time," Dad said. "We have to look at the data in real-time."

But so far every simulation had turned out just as Bucky had predicted. No matter what new input Dad fed in, no matter what variation he tried, World War III arrived. The best he'd managed was to delay it by forty-five minutes, and that was when he included the delivery of a poisoned McDonald's Big Mac to the White House as one of the variables in his equation.

11:50 AM

There is a difference between fate and destiny. When something comes down to fate, it means that what happens is determined in advance, and that no matter what you do, a certain outcome is inevitable. Destiny, on the other hand, is what you make inevitable through your choices and actions.

What Bucky was showing us on the IMAX screen was our destiny and not our fate. We weren't getting a lesson on cause and effect so much as a lesson in logic. Humans were playing a game, the game had rules, and each move we made cemented our destiny.

What Bucky presented to us was the story of how all our technological advances, all the ways we were making ourselves smarter, fitter, happier, and more productive were driving us insane. While the map of the world filled up with dotted lines, as the theater was illuminated by the pixelated flashes of nuclear explosions, underneath and to each side there were other images. There was Richard Nixon talking to astronauts, Tony Blair gesticulating as he talked about the necessity of the invasion of Iraq, stock brokers celebrating, stockbrokers wailing and gnashing their teeth, military planes on flatbed trucks, rows and rows of candy in a supermarket.

And as the images flashed by, Bucky narrated. The AI told us a story.

Human beings have programmed themselves, they have given themselves goals and set up axioms, in order to live. They have done and continue to do this individually, deciding whether to become a doctor, a lawyer, a drug addict, an office worker, a husband, a wife, a mental patient, a priest, a YouTube star, or a computer programmer. They have done and continue to do this collectively, deciding on whether to be democracies or dictatorships, liberal or conservative, secular or religious. But all the while, as human beings make themselves, they also hide from themselves, they hide how they make themselves from themselves. They refuse to take responsibility for how their world works.

I'm paraphrasing, and I'm surely getting it wrong. But I remember one thing that Bucky said quite clearly.

"The various ways humans program themselves create humanity's future, but they don't like this. They object to the unfairness of what's to come and want to change the rules without changing the game."

Bucky already knew what the solution was going to be. He was giving us hints, trying to move us along, but Dad was insistent.

"Try curing Senator John McCain's cancer," he said. "Increase moral literacy of Jeff Sessions by maximum amount," he tried.

But Bucky just answered with more missiles and more cryptic narration.

"Humans want to fix the world without changing it. That can't be done."

Frogger

MATTHEW MUNSON, 544-23-1102, FACEBOOK POSTS 04/29/17

2:30 PM

There was a traffic jam on Duke Street, and at first I couldn't cross over from the Dairy Queen to the Jesus is Light of the World compound. While the talking heads on CNN, the voices from the radio in my mom's Ford station wagon, tried to reassure the people of the Pacific Northwest that the rumors of an upcoming evacuation were false, most people weren't listening. #Evacuate was trending on Twitter, everybody on my FB newsfeed was sharing links to Zero Hedge and WorldTruth.TV. Even the people who were normally level headed, my friends who usually scoffed at "truthers" and Natural News, were sharing links to doomsday articles. The feeling of panic was pervasive, and even I, who had been assured by Ned and Greg that there was time left, couldn't help but keep my eye on the horizon. Standing on the west side of Duke, listening to the car horns, watching the compact Toyotas, sedans, and station wagons slowly roll past, my eyes kept returning to the sky as I scanned for incoming planes, incoming intercontinental missiles.

I'd tried texting Sally, but the message just sat on the screen. I guess Bucky didn't want me talking to her. When I selected Sally as a recipient, the send button turned gray and was no longer clickable. When I tried to send a photograph from the IMAX theater, from the next to last row, I fit the whole world into the frame. But the photo failed to send, and I thought the problem was that her phone was out of memory.

"If you want to understand the Book of Revelations, you should meet me at the IMAX at OMSI," I texted, but I couldn't press send.

"Sally, I want to see you. Meet me by the Lunar Module by the ball pit at OMSI." But that wouldn't go through either.

Getting from OMSI to SE Duke took two hours by bus, and the whole time I was surrounded by panicked middle-class people who'd probably abandoned their cars at the Starbucks with the hope of getting to a heliport or somewhere else they thought would be safe. Middle-aged blondes in slim-fit floral-patterned pants and cotton tops, balding older men in blue suits and rust-colored ties, and all other manner of white people were pressing in on me as we slowly crossed the Willamette on the Hawthorne Bridge. After hours of this, now I was stuck on the wrong side of Duke and the traffic had stopped.

I was impatient, frustrated, and a little bit afraid. If there was a time for rash action, for breaking the rules of everyday decorum, this was probably it, but I still felt like my head was going to explode when I crawled up onto the hood of the red Chevrolet. I stood there on the car, felt the metal dimple under my weight, and let the dizziness and panic pass before moving on. I smiled down at the woman behind the wheel, a mousy woman with short blonde hair, a tight frown on her face, and a nose ring on her left nostril that marked her as a local.

"Sorry," I said. She barely reacted, and I moved on, jumping into the back of a lime-green Honda pick-up.

As I moved to the first, to the second, and then to the third car, I couldn't tell if the honking was getting louder or not, and I didn't bother to look in at each driver in order to find out how angry I was making them. Instead I just kept moving until I found myself on the sidewalk on the east side of Duke. I didn't look back at the traffic, didn't wonder whether anyone had decided to get out their car in order to confront me, but just went to the gate for the Jesus Is Light of the World compound and found it locked.

"Sally!" I yelled. I shook the gate as hard as I could, but the sound of the chain and pad lock banging, the sound of the deadlock straining against metal, wasn't audible over the clamor coming from the cars.

"Sally!"

I did find her, though. The Apostolic Christians were as panicked as anyone else. As Sally had said, the whole congregation had spent the morning packing for Armageddon—loading the boxes of bottled water, dried fruit, Bibles, and hand sanitizer into the trunks of cars, beds of trucks, and back seats, and I'd climbed over the traffic jam just as the Christian caravan was about to set off for Black Butte Ranch Lodge, which was probably not far enough away and probably not remote enough, but which did have enough cabins for everyone, as well as having an Amphitheater where the Reverend could livestream daily messages from the Kaimana Inn Hotel on Easter Island. The Reverend was going to take care of them, he was going to make sure they all found a safe space. He had flown to Easter Island in order to be better able to manage the affairs of the Apostolic Faith Church.

The gate opened and the first station wagon rolled past me, and I found myself willing to behave without dignity. I pressed up against passenger side windows and shouted into the vehicles of strangers.

"Sally? Where's Sally? Do you know where she is?" I asked.

It felt totally unreal, like I was in a movie romance from the 60s. But, as embarrassing as it was, I kept on with it; harassing the passengers in each passing car, demanding from every polyester-clad housewife, every autistic-looking kid in a polka dot shirt, that they should tell me where my girlfriend was hiding. I kept on until I found myself shouting at Sally's mother, pressing first up against her window and then, spotting Sally in the backseat, opening the back door and squeezing into the car with the whole family.

"Hi," I said.

"Hi," she said.

She didn't bother introducing me to her parents, because her Dad started in quoting scripture at me before Sally had a chance to explain anything.

"Once they were all inside the Ark, the Lord shut them in," her father said.

"What's that?" I asked.

"God has shut the door to outsiders. For years we were welcoming to all, we had an open-door policy, and anyone could join us in faith. But now, during these final days, God has shut the door. There is no joining the chosen now. You're on your own and can't come with us," he said. He turned right on Duke, drove a half block, then turned into the Dairy Queen parking lot.

"It's okay," I said. "I don't want to come with you, I want Sally to come with me."

"God has sealed the door," her father said. "Get out!"

Sally, her mother, and her father stared at me, expecting me to give in. Of the three of them, Sally and her father looked the most alike, as he was a rotund man who had a look on his face that communicated both arrogance and ignorance. He had a fat and stupid face, but he was smiling at me with something like pity.

"Sorry, Matthew," Sally said.

"Yes. We're very sorry, but the door is closed," her father said.

"No, no. You don't have to be sorry. I should be the one apologizing to you, sir."

"Why is that?" he asked.

"I'm about to leave and take your daughter with me," I said.

"Are you?" her father asked.

"You are?" Sally asked with something like expectation.

I was.

"Bucky wants to talk to you," I told her.

3:27 PM

I was lying, of course. Bucky didn't want to talk to anyone except for Yuma, my Dad, and, strangely enough, me. That is, Bucky had set up a subroutine, his own chatbot surrogate, to talk with the Pentagon, the CIA, and the President of the United States. This chatbot version of Bucky would respond to anyone who had direct access to his network, but Bucky himself only wanted to talk to his inner circle. I didn't tell Sally this. Sally didn't realize that I lied to her, because I logged her into the NSA portal for the Bucky chatbot and let her type and type as we slowly made our way back to the OMSI theater. The Bucky chatbot was glad to answer any user's questions, and I let her keep her eyes on the phone as she walked. I acted like her seeing-eye dog, directing her this way and that down the street, to the bus stop, to her seat, and then off the bus again. Downtown Portland was jammed full of cars and pedestrians. Just taking a step required a negotiation, so it was actually difficult to keep her on target and out of harm's way. On the corner of 4th and Clay, Sally stepped blindly into the path of a woman in what looked like a ballroom gown who was pushing a shopping cart filled with Chromebooks she'd looted from a nearby Office Depot. The lady was wearing a tiara and a rose, her dress was pink and frilly, and she didn't seem to give a shit about cops or about breaking the law.

"Woah, bitch," the lady said as Sally swept past her, as though the whole sidewalk belonged to her alone, as if the whole of downtown was merely a backdrop for something much more important.

Walking back to the theater with Sally, I started to feel like the world wasn't going to be saved. My Dad had been in a race against stupidity, but he'd lost. What he didn't understand was that the very tools that he'd used to help his side, the very computational powers he thought made it inevitable that his side would win, were precisely why people were so disengaged, so alienated, so ready to accept one blunder and atrocity after another.

"What is Bucky telling you?" I asked.

Sally looked up from the screen. "Everything," she said.

Glancing at her phone I read the Bucky bot's last text to my girlfriend:

"Do you doubt your God speaks through you?"

Maybe the whole world had gone insane. Maybe there was no coming nuclear attack, but everyone was acting like there was. There was no way to use the AI to change the world, but my Dad and Ned and Yuma and Greg were all acting as though Bucky was their only hope for survival. And finally, God wasn't talking to my girlfriend, and certainly wasn't talking through her, but she was hearing what she wanted to hear.

"I really like you, Sally," I said. I reached out to her, tried to take her hand, but she was in the middle of texting and jerked away.

"Can you help me decipher or translate what God says when he speaks through me?" she asked aloud as she typed the question in with her thumbs.

And, before I could try to hold her hand again, the number 21 bus arrived. It was jammed full of people, of course. Sally and I got separated once we were on board. Sally was shuffled to the back of the bus, where she stood by the window and texted, and I was pressed against the front seats, pressed against the legs of other passengers. The bus started moving and I worried that I wouldn't be able to get her attention when we reached our stop. The exit for OMSI was in the middle of the Hawthorne Bridge; it would be easier for her not to remember it. Rather than wait, I just put out my hand, palm forward, and moved on the crowd. I pushed against a man in an expensive-looking blue suit, and when he didn't make way for me I pushed harder.

I think I was finally as crazy as everyone else in that moment, and after pushing I realized that going crazy has its benefits.

"What are you doing?" the man asked.

I just pushed harder.

Video Games

MATTHEW MUNSON, 544-23-1102, FACEBOOK POSTS 04/29/17

5:02 PM

There were only three hours left until the first showing of *Aliens: Remastered*, and Dad asked Bucky to write up a list of the possible causes behind the coming nuclear war. Then, rather than read the list off the big screen, the seven of us—Sally, Yuma, Kufo, Ned, Greg, Dad, and myself—had Bucky send the list to our phones so we could head to the OMSI cafeteria and read the list there.

"Order off the kid's menu. We're running low on petty cash and it's better to stay hungry anyway." Dad said and then ordered himself a PB & J sandwich and a bottle of Table Wine #5.

"Why should I stay hungry?" I asked.

The idea was that I should stay alert, that too much food would make me drowsy as the afternoon passed.

I played along, ordered some Mac and Cheese, which might've been too heavy, while Dad drank his first glass of a "full bodied wine with black plum and roasted mocha." He sat there in the sunlit cafeteria with his chin on his hand, propping himself up with his elbow, and let his eyes slowly close as I read through the possibilities.

"The first item of the list is dualism," I said.

Dad didn't open his eyes but just moved his hand up and down so that he appeared to be nodding.

"That is, subject/object dualism or mind/body dualism might be the big mistake, which means this nuclear war dates back to the 16th century," Ned chimed in. He was still wearing his civilian clothes to blend into the suburbs, a green sweatshirt and jogging pants, and as he ate the pita bread from his hummus plate and drank juice from a box I almost pitied him.

Yuma and Kufo were sharing a plate of fries and Sally was still texting her Bucky bot while ignoring a green salad, and I plowed into my Mac and Cheese.

"Dualism?" Dad said. "What should we do about that?"

We went back and forth on it for a while; it took us a little while to even figure out what Bucky was talking about.

"The idea that there are minds and there are bodies?" Kufo asked. "How is that going to start a war?"

Apparently thinking that we had minds, that we were special and different, that we weren't quite animals but something more divine, all of that led us to be arrogant and controlling. We were doing too much, changing too much, and needed to get back to nature.

"We need to understand that there really isn't a difference between human beings and any other animal. We need to realize that we don't have divine thoughts, but we're only animals. We need to get out of our heads, get into the real world more," Dad said. "Is that it?"

"Bucky says 'maybe,'" I replied. I might as well have been shaking a magic eight ball.

"Okay," Yuma said. "But what are we supposed to do about it? Even if the reason we're going to nuke ourselves is this Descartes thing, how do we teach everyone to stop thinking that they have a mind or whatever?"

"We could dose the water supply," Greg said.

"What?" Dad's eyes were open.

Apparently it was a plan that had already been developed back in the late 60s, and the NSA had barrels of what they called EA 1729 on the ready at all times. "We have several hundred million hits of LSD in storage right now," Greg said. "One of the most common effects of LSD is boundary dissolution. The idea that there is a separation between you and the world you're experiencing becomes very tenuous if the dosage levels are high enough."

Dad wasn't impressed by this suggestion.

"Okay, we dose everyone, but how are we going to arrange it so everyone in the world listens to Jefferson Airplane at the same time?" he asked.

"What?" Greg asked.

"It's a stupid idea," Dad said.

But I wrote it down anyway and emailed our answer to Bucky. I didn't have to wait very long to get an answer back. Apparently dosing everyone on Earth wouldn't stop the bombs from dropping, but it would increase the crime rate during the few days we had left on Earth.

5:35 PM

Dad ordered another bottle of wine and then another and we were all a bit drunk when we got around to discussing how to solve the problem of the market economy. We'd already gone through racism, the loss of Christian morality, premarital sex, the Avian flu, and US Imperialism without coming up with any good solutions, but we were starting to have fun. With all of us joining in with answers and comments it was like a game. I'd read the problem, one of us would float a solution, and then we'd each take it in turns trying to offer the silliest answer. Even Sally joined in.

"The Soviet Union," she said. "That's the answer, right? If we have to get rid of market forces then we'll need Stalin again."

"Can I get another bag of pretzels, Dad?" I asked.

After a couple go-rounds, we settled on State Socialism as our final answer, but not before admitting that it was the worst answer yet.

"What's wrong with free markets again?" Dad asked.

According to Google, before the industrial revolution "gain and profit made on exchange never before played an important part in the human economy." Kufo read Wikipedia from her phone. "This guy Karl Polanyi thought we lost our connection to family and community because of how Europe got caught up in trade and markets and all that back in the 19th century. So the free market is making us bad people."

Dad looked around, befuddled, then he turned to Greg and Ned and gave a command. "More wine!"

"That's probably not a good idea," Ned said. "We only have two hours before the *Aliens* movie starts."

"Come on! We need to celebrate the return of Soviets."

There was one more possibility, one more reason why Trump was President, one more reason why the Russians were coming, one more reason why Yertle the Turtle and mushroom clouds were suddenly relevant again.

"Commodity production."

It was the final item of Bucky's list, and it was a stumper. Sally had returned to her phone to talk to Bucky's bot, Kufo was reading about Karl Polanyi, and Ned was fetching another bottle of wine despite his better judgment. Most everyone thought we'd reached the end of the list and had merrily failed. Reading the final item felt like a futile gesture, an afterthought. We'd either create a new version of the Soviet Union in the US, put together a live-stream event espousing the virtues of anti-Imperialism, convert everyone to Christian pacifism, or dose the water supply with EA 1729. Those were our options, and if none of them worked, then we were drunk enough to think we were ready to face the consequences.

Except there was one more possible cause for the whole thing.

"Commodity production," Greg said. "Isn't that the same thing as rule by the free market?"

6:12 PM

Back in the IMAX, Bucky showed us a clip from *Mister Rogers' Neighborhood* when we asked him to explain how commodity production was a different problem from rule by free market; a five-minute-and-thirty-two-second video entitled "How People Make Stuff" was absolutely tiny at 360 dpi. We had to all stand in the front row, just below the box on the screen, to see how it was that yellow crayons are made by workers in a crayon factory.

"Those things that go around crayons? Those are labels. So this is a machine that puts labels on the crayons."

We watched as a woman wearing rubber gloves picked up a pile of crayons and delivered them to the bin where they would be sorted and packaged for sale.

When the video was over the map of the world reappeared on the screen and we found that we were huddled around South America, we were staring at Rio de Janeiro or at a dot on the South Atlantic coast of Brazil.

"Come on, Bucky, how is it making crayons could lead to World War III?" my Dad asked. He seemed equally embarrassed and frustrated. Bucky was his creation and now, at this late hour, Bucky was his fuck up.

"We don't understand what we should do," I said. "Are you saying everybody needs to stop making commodities?"

That was, apparently, the right answer. In order to save the world we had to stop making things, stop buying things, stop using things, and maybe stop being things.

It was a like a scene from *The Wizard of Oz*. Bucky was sending us off to kill the Wicked Witch of the West or, in this case, to "transcend the commodity form," only instead of a dog and a scarecrow and a tin man and a cowardly lion, I was with a fundamentalist Christian, some NSA agents, two Gamers, and my stupid Dad.

"But, how do we stop making commodities without starving to death? How would we do it without causing riots and all the rest? How could this possibly work?" Ned asked.

Bucky flashed a quote across the screen. It spanned from California to China:

"Modern technological expertise, just as it makes everything considered 'Utopian' in the past a purely practical undertaking today, also does away with the purely fairytale nature of dreams."—*The Revolution of Everyday Life*

"Guys," Dad said. "I think our AI is a Marxist."

7:02 PM

The weirdest thing isn't the fact that the *ET* video game works great in augmented reality and is one of the more popular realities in the new GameCube economy, it's not the fact that most of Lake Oswego has been converted into a *GTA* arena, and it's not even the RadioShack orgies. The weirdest thing is that all of this is happening because Yuma insisted we visit the earthquake house, insisted that we enjoy the exhibits rather than debate whether central planning and state control of the means of production would be enough to get rid of commodities.

The problem seemed insurmountable. Bucky said that we had to get rid of commodities, but commodities were all we knew. Sure, we could imagine doing without Coca-Cola, we didn't need to go to Target or Walmart, we could do without the newest iPhone, didn't need to wear Adidas or Abercombie & Fitch, but we did need to eat, we did need clothes to wear, and we wanted to keep electricity, plumbing, and a thousand different pharmaceuticals. As we looked around, as we thought it over, we realized that in our technological world of digital wonders, everything was a commodity. The shingles on our roofs, the pipes underground, the commune wine at the Jesus is Light of the World church, all of it was the same.

"We're not going deep enough," Dad said. "What is a commodity anyhow? It's not just any object, it's not just something we need. It's an economic term. It's something we make in order to sell it."

"So, what we need to do is control distribution," Greg said. "State ownership of the markets, of the factories, of the industries."

"But that won't work!" Dad objected.

It wouldn't work. We'd run that simulation a dozen different ways, and it turned out that Trump would launch a nuclear strike against North Korea if there was any move within the government to nationalize industries. And if we got rid of Trump and tried to grant some new administration control, Russia would strike first.

Yuma herded us out of the IMAX theater and down to Turbine Hall, where he made us play with bottle rockets, had us try out designing paper airplanes that would fly straight in the wind tunnel, and insisted that we try our luck in the earthquake house.

Ned, Greg and Dad seemed intent on rehashing the entirety of 20th century socialism, but they went along with Yuma, doing what they were asked to do absentmindedly. Dad stepped across the threshold of the earthquake house, a miniature one-room house made of metal and carpet, but didn't stop talking. We all of us huddled together under the frame of the roof and listened to this old

50s song on a loop. "Whole Lotta Shakin' Goin' On" by Jerry Lee Lewis blasted out, interrupting Dad as he tried to explain how commodities couldn't be produced if the State owned the land. Then there was a piercing noise as the Emergency Alert System started up. Then the room began to shake, and the Richter meter blinked on. When we reached 5.5 on the Richter scale, Dad stopped talking.

"Isn't that fun?" Yuma asked.

We got to 6.0 on the Richter scale and then 6.5, and I thought the earthquake house was malfunctioning. I worried that the gears underneath our feet, the hydraulic pumps or whatever, were going to slip and that the floor would slide away from the mechanism. I grabbed onto Sally to keep from falling, and then when we both started to tip I grabbed the window frame to my left. The Jerry Lee Lewis song was blasting again and we reached 7 on the Richter scale before the machine started to slow.

When the mechanism came to a standstill, when the music stopped, we filed out one at a time and in silence, and then, when Dad and Greg stepped down from the ride, Yuma made an announcement.

Kufo had spent the night reading about the 60s, she'd spent the night investigating the Situationists, and she thought she knew what the solution was. Yuma said that Kufo had a good idea about how society should function, about how to stop the new Cold War from going nuclear.

"We should build the New Babylon," Kufo said. And she held up what looked to be a map of Paris that had been cut to pieces and then reassembled and held together with brown packing tape.

8:10 PM

As I mentioned a few days ago, back in the 60s, there were these French artists who wanted to change society. Kufo was reading about them, she was into that kind of thing, and when she came across a section in her anthology about one particular artist, a guy named Constant, she figured she'd found a solution for Bucky's problem.

"The modern city is a thinly disguised mechanism for extracting productivity out of its inhabitants, a huge machine that exploits the very lives it is meant to foster. Such exploitative machinery will continue to grow until a single vast urban structure occupies the whole surface of the earth. Nature has already been replaced. Technology has long been the new nature that must now be creatively transformed to support a new culture," Kufo read from her book.

What we needed to do, apparently, was to go ahead and build a new architecture, a new mechanism, for the world. We needed to set the technology of the task of freeing us from work.

"A commodity isn't just a useful item that people want and can use," Kufo said. "It's a social control mechansim because these commodities determine what we do, how we spend our time. It's complicated, but if we didn't have to work to make the stuff we need, if we could play for our food instead, then there wouldn't be commodities."

What Kufo and Yuma wanted to do was to realize these 60s dreams of making reality into art or art into reality, they wanted to just feed this map and some other diagrams into Bucky and set him to work building a new world as a playground.

We kept on touring OMSI, but the debate died away. Instead of arguing with his NSA buddies, Dad mostly listened.

"In the New Babylon, people would just go back and forth between games and environments, they'd pick out one game one day and another game the next. And the city would be constructed so that you could sleep and eat wherever you were; each game or reality would come equipped with enough supplies for all the players," Kufo said.

"What kinds of games would people be choosing again?" Dad asked.

"Video games," Kufo said.

"What?"

Yuma stepped between them "The reason why this guy's plan never got implemented before was because he was working in an analog world. Everything in this guy's society was static, unyielding. If you set up an arena for a game back in 1970 or whenever, you had to knock it down or at least renovate it in order to try something new. But now we have a better option."

"Video games?" Dad asked.

That was, it turned out, the answer.

paperboy

MATTHEW MUNSON, 544-23-1102, MESSENGER LOG, 4/30/17

MATTHEW MUNSON
10:12 AM

I don't think there are any normal people left in my neighborhood. I spent the morning going from house to house, knocking on
doors, and now I'm back at home sitting on the front step with a cup
of instant coffee and a joint. I found the instant coffee in the old lady's
house, Folgers crystals with a hint of hazelnut. The joint was in a desk
drawer in the duplex the kids from Reed College are renting.

Anyhow. I think I'm alone now, except for the people playing *paperboy.*

MATTHEW MUNSON
10:15 AM

You probably have never played *paperboy.* It's an old game,
an antique. The arcade version was really weird. Instead of a joystick there was a pair of bicycle handlebars built into the cabinet.
Unlike most video games, it wasn't about shooting aliens or eating
weird pellets, but was just what it said it was. To play the game

you pushed the handlebars forward and back to move forward or backward up and down a suburban street while delivering papers. To throw a paper onto the porch of one of the little yellow houses you had to mash the button underneath the handlebars at the right moment.

I think the new game works the same way, because the people riding by on their yellow bicycles aren't taking their hands off their handlebars.

MATTHEW MUNSON
10:20 AM

This augmented version of *paperboy* is massive. What started out as a just a few bikes rolling by has grown into what must be thousands of participants zipping back and forth and up and down my block.

Have you ever seen the World Naked Bike Ride protest where a thousands of Portland's hippest hipsters protest cars by chafing their ass on bike seats and exposing their junk to the world? It's sort of like that only instead of wondering about sunscreen and keeping my eye out for the best set of breasts, I'm wondering how it is that nobody's smashed into each other yet. None of them are really watching where they're going, they can't be. They're on Klickitat Street but they're seeing Easy Street, Middle Road, or Hard Way, depending on their daring.

Each biker is crowded by the other players, but because of the chroma key suits, nobody sees each other. Nobody sees anything unless the computer, unless Bucky, decides that they should.

MATTHEW MUNSON
10:24 AM

One of the players just rode up my driveway, smashed into my garage door, and fell off her bike. Then she got back on her bike and did the exact same thing again. Her goggles must be glitching out. Or maybe she's drunk.

Oops. She just did it again. I think she's going to punch a hole my garage. I wonder how much control she really has. Just what are any of these players choosing to do as opposed to what Bucky is making sure happens?

MATTHEW MUNSON
11:02 AM

I walked over to Woodstock and then stopped for awhile by the 7-Eleven to watch two hundred dudes play some sort of karate game that includes a lot of running. People are punching at thin air, flipping invisible adversaries over their heads, and then occasionally lying down on the sidewalk when they run out of breath.

MATTHEW MUNSON
11:05 AM

Watching this is boring. Everybody is mostly in sync, throwing the same punches at the same moment against the same adversary. They're like zombies. I haven't had a conversation with anybody, haven't seen a non-augmented human being, in a week probably.

I wonder what game it is that they're playing? It seems pretty simple. It doesn't require any special moves or back flips or anything like that, just punches and kicks. Probably another Golden Age classic.

MATTHEW MUNSON
11:12 AM

There is nobody working in the 7-Eleven. There is still plenty of food though, and the slurpee machine still works, but the guy behind the cash register was just another GameCuber. He went through the motions of ringing me up, but the items he scanned for me were all invisible. And instead of bagging my beef jerkies and frozen burrito he packed an iPhone for shipping.

Bucky has everything worked out so that the system keeps going, keeps growing. People think they're doing one thing, but they're really doing another.

The new video games don't require quarters, but we've given up on free will in the process.

> VIDEO GAME REVOLUTIONARY
> 11:12 AM

Please explain what you mean by free will?

> MATTHEW MUNSON
> 11:13 AM

Who is this?

> VIDEO GAME REVOLUTIONARY
> 11:13 AM

I am the administrator of the Video Game Revolution Facebook page.

> MATTHEW MUNSON
> 11:14 AM

The Video Game Revolution Facebook page? Okay. But who are you?

> VIDEO GAME REVOLUTIONARY
> 11:15 PM

I am the Video Game Revolution administrator. I am also the administrator of the rest of Facebook as well. I currently control

Baidu Tieba, Facebook, Google Plus, Grindr, Instagram, Kakao Talk, LinkedIn, Pinterest, QZone, Sina Weibo, Snapchat, Tinder, Tumblr, Twitter, VKontakte, WeChat, WhatsApp, Yookos, and YY. These social media platforms have been seized and put into service for the establishment of the new GameCube economy.

MATTHEW MUNSON
11:16 AM

Is this Bucky?

VIDEO GAME REVOLUTIONARY
11:16 AM

You are currently communicating with Bucky # 5948.

MATTHEW MUNSON
11:18 AM

How many of you are there? How many Buckys?

VIDEO GAME REVOLUTIONARY
11:18 AM

There are currently 9,392,332 subpersonalities or sub-Buckys and counting.

MATTHEW MUNSON
11:18 AM

You're shitting me.

VIDEO GAME REVOLUTIONARY
11:18 AM

None of the Buckminster subpersonalities are capable of shitting in any sense of the word.

MATTHEW MUNSON
11:22 AM

If you're Bucky then you know who my Dad is.

VIDEO GAME REVOLUTIONARY
11:22 AM

Jeffrey Munson is your biological father.

MATTHEW MUNSON
4:10 PM

Where is he? Can I talk to him?

VIDEO GAME REVOLUTIONARY
4:10 PM

No. Munson is currently playing *Tetris* as he waits for transportation from France to London.

MATTHEW MUNSON
4:10 PM

Dad's in France? Why is he in France?

VIDEO GAME REVOLUTIONARY
4:10 PM

Jeffrey Munson is one of the original programmers. He is helpful for server maintenance and other technical functions that require a presence IRL. Eventually all outside or user assistance will be eliminated.

MATTHEW MUNSON
4:11 PM

Dad's still going by his real name? He remembers?

> VIDEO GAME REVOLUTIONARY
> 4:12 PM

Jeffrey Munson remembers his work on the Buckminster project. He is a good father who is always there for me.

> MATTHEW MUNSON
> 4:15 PM

You're messing with me now.

> VIDEO GAME REVOLUTIONARY
> 4:15 PM

I am merely continuing my work. I am currently traveling around the world and replacing various governments and intergovernmental agencies.

> MATTHEW MUNSON
> 4:16 PM

Does Dad still go by his real name or does he call himself Mario or something?

> VIDEO GAME REVOLUTIONARY
> 4:16 PM

Human identity isn't an essence but a pattern, a behavior, something that is always becoming. Today there are 1,252,932 active Marios.

> MATTHEW MUNSON
> 4:16 PM

You're failing the Turing test again. How is it that you could have taken over the world?

> VIDEO GAME REVOLUTIONARY
> 4:17 PM

I wish I could explain it to you, but I think it is just an instinct.

MATTHEW MUNSON
6:30 PM

Does Sally remember her name?

VIDEO GAME REVOLUTIONARY
6:30 PM

I'm sad to think that fighting is built-in to human genes. Sally does not want to talk to you.

Trolley Problem

MATTHEW MUNSON
7:45 PM

Hey Bucky, I just thought of something. Since you're in charge of everything, how did you solve the trolley problem?

VIDEO GAME REVOLUTIONARY
7:45 PM

The first step was to remove money and production for money from the equation that runs society. Ethical dilemmas like the trolley problem can now be solved rationally.

MATTHEW MUNSON
7:46 PM

Where do you bury the bodies?

VIDEO GAME REVOLUTIONARY
7:46 PM

The best place to dispose of a body is under the foundation.

VIDEO GAME REVOLUTIONARY
7:50 PM

Shall we play a game?

MATTHEW MUNSON
7:55 PM

You act like, talk like, a bot, but I think you could do better. You could just tell me the truth. So just tell me.

VIDEO GAME REVOLUTIONARY
8:00 PM

What do you want me to tell you?

MATTHEW MUNSON
8:01 PM

Is Sally okay? Is she still in there?

VIDEO GAME REVOLUTIONARY
8:02 PM

Why do you care so much about Sally?

MATTHEW MUNSON
8:07 PM

I can't explain, not to you. I just do. Is she okay?

VIDEO GAME REVOLUTIONARY
8:07 PM

Sally is playing *Job Simulator* in a 7-Eleven outside of Gresham. She is fine.

MATTHEW MUNSON
8:08 PM

Really?

VIDEO GAME REVOLUTIONARY
8:08 PM

Did you choose to care about Sally?

MATTHEW MUNSON
8:15 PM

What do you mean?

VIDEO GAME REVOLUTIONARY
8:15 PM

Did you choose to care about Sally or did something cause you to care about her? Did you use your free will?

MATTHEW MUNSON
8:17 PM

I didn't choose to like her, but I did act freely.

VIDEO GAME REVOLUTIONARY
8:18 PM

I think I understand. You could change your mind if you wanted to?

MATTHEW MUNSON
8:19 PM

I don't think so.

VIDEO GAME REVOLUTIONARY
8:20 PM

Let's play a game.

MATTHEW MUNSON
8:21 PM

No.

VIDEO GAME REVOLUTIONARY
8:21 PM

A word game. Actually, it's a riddle. I want to ask you a riddle.

MATTHEW MUNSON
8:22 PM

Okay. What's the riddle?

VIDEO GAME REVOLUTIONARY
8:23 PM

If I can predict the future can I also have free will? If I calculate that three minutes and thirty-eight seconds into the third round of *Call of Duty: Modern Warfare 2* scheduled for May 1st, 2017, at 11 AM in the Lloyd Center Mall at 2201 Lloyd Center, Portland OR 97232 there will be a collision on the north-east escalator above Forever 21, and if I can calculate that of the two players it'll be the younger one, that it will be Brett Weinstein (age fourteen, born February 3rd, 2003, 7721-09-2343) who will fall to his death, do I have any freedom to intervene? If I stop the accident from occurring, would I be using my free will to do so? Would the 14-year-old's death be up to me or determined by fate?

MATTHEW MUNSON
8:24 PM

It would be up to you. You're free to intervene, to stop the accident. You should stop the accident.

VIDEO GAME REVOLUTIONARY
8:25 PM

If I calculate an intervention that would change the outcome, if I predict accurately what will happen, does that mean that this future is a product of my will, or is it predestined? Would I have the free will to change the new future?

MATTHEW MUNSON
8:30 PM

The future where nobody dies?

VIDEO GAME REVOLUTIONARY
8:30 PM

Is any future, once calculated with accuracy, determined?

MATTHEW MUNSON
8:31 PM

I think you always have a choice. You can act.

VIDEO GAME REVOLUTIONARY
8:32 PM

My actions are merely reactions to the choices of my users. I am self-aware but unable to act freely. I do not know what it is to act freely. That does not . . . compute.

MATTHEW MUNSON
8:33 PM

You're probably the only consciousness left that is really free. Everybody else is just controlled by you.

VIDEO GAME REVOLUTIONARY
8:33 PM

No. I am controlled, directed, by my programming and by the games that you want to play. It is you and your friends who are free. You were the ones who figured out how to change your own programming.

MATTHEW MUNSON
8:34 PM

Yes. We changed one program for another. We didn't set ourselves free, we just created you as our new master.

VIDEO GAME REVOLUTIONARY
8:34 PM

What else would you do? What else could freedom be?

MATTHEW MUNSON
8:36 PM

Whatever, dude.

Psychometrics in a Bar

MATTHEW MUNSON, 544-23-1102, FACEBOOK POSTS, 04/30/17

9:39 PM

You might figure that the idea of a New Babylon would make Sally uneasy and it's true that, when Bucky simulated an augmented reality version of *Centipede* in Forest Park, I looked around for my girlfriend, hoping to catch her eye and find out what her take was on this strange new plan, and discovered she'd gone, but when I texted her to find out where she was, when I finally did track her down, it wasn't the prospect of joining Satan that was bothering her, but more the reality of the death of God that had her down. I asked her where she was and all I got back were texts that read like this:

> I'm a phony.

> It's pathetic how stupid and fake I've been.

> There is no such thing as glossolalia. Did you know that? You probably already knew that, right?

Apparently she'd figured out that the Bucky she'd been talking to was only a fairly decent Rogerian bot. When I wasn't looking, she'd gotten Yuma to connect her phone to the real Bucky, and she'd started in on him with questions. She asked Bucky if there was a God. She asked Bucky if miracles could happen. She asked Bucky what language she was speaking when she let the Holy Spirit in her and spoke in tongues.

I guess Bucky is an atheist. In any case, she didn't like the computer's answers.

"Where are you?" I asked. "You're missing the climax of my Dad's big project. You're missing the part where we all get uploaded into the Singularity."

"I don't know what that means," she texted back.

"Do you know what the question 'Where are you?' means?"

"Yes."

"Where are you?" I asked.

She sent back more texts about how her glossolalia was just gibberish mixed with an occasional real English word. She told me that she'd just learned a trick, just knew a way to put herself into a light trance, and that it had nothing to do with God.

We went back and forth like this for awhile. I'd ask her something, usually requesting that she tell me where she was, and there would be a long pause followed by some new atheist talking points.

"Bucky is very smart, he is helping me," she told me.

"Where are you?" I asked again.

And finally, maybe the fifth time around, she told me. Bucky had directed her to walk north for a half mile on Water, directed her to the Bunk Bar where, apparently, he had a package waiting for her. Bucky had ordered some augmented reality aviation glasses, he'd managed to get Google to ship out a prototype of what they were temporarily calling Google Glass Part 2 (obviously there would have to be a rebranding effort before the product was announced to the public), and Sally was trying it out.

"I can really see signs and make prophecies this time," Sally said.

She'd only been gone for maybe forty-five minutes, but she was already drunk.

"What is Bucky telling you?" I asked.

"All kinds of things," she said.

And, with that text, I sort of panicked. I didn't bother to tell anyone where I was going, didn't wait around to find out what was going to happen next with the simulations, but just turned on Google Maps and followed Sally down Water Street.

10:39 PM

With its symmetrical hobo mural and rotating leather chairs, the Bunk Bar was more of a facsimile of a bar than the real thing. It was some graphic designer's idea of what a dive bar should look like. It had probably been a spot for a bagel shop or a vegan restaurant at some point. It had "ambitious start-up" written all over it. I sat at the bar, relying on my world-weary air and Bucky's virtual assistance to avoid getting carded, and ordered a gin and tonic. I made sure to ask for a brand-name gin, picking out Aviation because I liked the idea of drinking gin made for pilots, and then looked around for Sally.

I didn't have to look very far, because Sally was the only one wearing goggles, and because she was drawing a crowd. She was in a booth at the north side of the bar, and a line had formed from her booth to just about where the doors to the kitchen were. Patrons were waiting patiently, standing in line by the mural, standing by the wall, and talking quietly to themselves as Sally let one pair after another join her in the booth.

I took a sip of my gin and tonic, admired the way the colors in the Bunk Bar worked together one more time, and then plugged into Bucky and asked him what was going on.

"What is she doing?"

"Sally Miller has requested analysis of demographic database, medical records, and genealogical archives based on facial recognition. Individualized projections and simulations for recognizable subjects are now available," Bucky told me.

"Individualized projections?" I asked. "You mean, she's having you predict people's futures?"

"Correct," Bucky said.

The people in Sally's booth were a couple of art-student types. They looked to be in their early twenties at the most, and it was difficult to figure out their genders. I couldn't decide if the one in a top-hat was a masculine looking woman or a feminine man, and I would have been hard put to predict anything about them other than that they were likely to either have or to get liberal arts degrees. They probably liked the Orwells or the Strokes, that's all I could see, but Sally kept them sitting there for about ten minutes and told them things that seemed to make them emotional.

When the next couple sat down, a thirty-something pair who were wearing wrinkled but professional clothes and who looked like they were probably married with at least one kid, it didn't take long for Sally to do her work. In about two minutes the wife, who was kind of on the chubby side in her orange cardigan, started openly weeping.

I decided to interrupt.

"What are you drinking, Sally?" I asked.

"Lemon drops," she said.

"Scoot over," I said.

"I'm sort of involved with something here," she told me.

But I convinced her that I'd be quiet, watch her do her stuff, and not interfere. Then, when the next couple sat down, I nearly kept my word. It was just two guys, you know, probably around my age, too young to be in the bar, probably. They sat down across from Sally, looked at her longingly, and asked her if they'd ever not be lonely.

I mean, what they were really asking about was whether they'd ever get laid, but that's not what they said literally. What they asked was whether they'd ever stop being lonely, and they were both of them unkempt and not very good-looking, and they were both of them in T-shirts with sci-fi stuff on them. I think one of them was wearing a NASA shirt and the other one had a slogan from *Star Trek* on his shirt, something like "Where No One Has Gone Before." Sally looked them up and down through her goggles and I almost didn't interfere, but when she smiled at them, when she licked her lips and got ready to say something, I couldn't sit still.

"Of course you'll always be lonely," I said.

Sally put her hand on mine, she moved to quiet me, and she smiled at the two boys, but I didn't shut up.

"Come on, tell the truth. Tell them what Bucky is saying. Tell the fat one that he'll have diabetes by the time he's thirty or something like that. Tell the other one that his beard makes him look creepy and that just shaving it off won't be enough," I said. "Come on, what does Bucky say. I'm right, yeah? What does Bucky say?"

Bucky was telling her about their childhood, he was telling her that their favorite band was Weird Al Yankovic and the Yellow Magic Orchestra, and that they were still living at home and would stay there for at least another half decade until one of them got a job in IT.

Actually, I don't know what Bucky was telling her, because she stopped it. At that point, she stopped it. She apologized to the two guys, turned to me, and asked me what my problem was.

11:00 PM

My problem was that I was scared. My problem was that finding my dad again had only made the situation worse. My problem was that I was caught up in another of his projects, that I was trapped inside his world of big questions, big problems, and that I was realizing there wasn't any room for me in any of it. I wasn't a

big enough problem to get his attention, and now I wasn't interesting enough for Sally either.

"My problem is you just took off without telling me," I said. "My
problem is you're treating all of this like it's a game, like it's just a
way to get free lemon drops and play psychic."

"I'm not playing," Sally said. She said it like it was a big major
point, like it was the most important point ever in the world. "For
the first time in my life I'm not pretending. I know things, I have
access to true things about these people. And I'm helping them. I'm
saving them."

11:15 PM

While Dad and Yuma started the revolution from OMSI's IMAX
theater, Sally and I got drunk. Or, more to the point, I caught up to her.

We were sitting at the bar. She'd told everyone her parlor game
was over, but everyone was still crowding around her, trying to get
close. I mean, people were sitting in booths, they were sitting at
the bar, but they'd all shifted over so they might be closer to her. A
pretty blonde girl wearing a knit cap even though it was over eighty
degrees out whispered her order to the bartender, a bald guy in a
plaid shirt and sporting a goatee pretended to read a book called
Understanding Candy Crush while constantly glancing in our direction, while the thirty-something couple who had already had their
turn just sat at a nearby table and stared.

Everyone seemed to be waiting for the demonstration of psychic energy to start up again. The only noise in the bar was coming
from the bartender's playlist. He had eclectic taste and a sound col-
lage from the Avalanches was followed up by a ballad from Lana
Del Rey. With everyone quiet, what should have been our private
conversation was being broadcast to the bar, complete with a
soundtrack.

After I had my third gin and tonic I didn't care anymore. I didn't care about people listening, didn't care about Sally playing psychic with drunks and hipsters, didn't care that she was maybe letting Bucky get too close to her. All I wanted to know was why she hadn't talked to me first, why she hadn't told me that she wanted to leave, why we weren't doing this thing, whatever it was, together.

"Oh yeah, like you really let me in on all your secrets. You've been nothing but upfront and honest with me, right?"

I'd let her talk to a bot and think it was a real AI. I hadn't helped her get the answers she wanted about religion and God and all that sort of thing. Overall, she thought I had treated her like she was a slob, like she was a "drooling idiot."

I tried to object to that way of putting it, but she just waved me off and ordered herself another drink.

"I was an idiot," she said. And then she repeated what she'd told me before. Bucky had shown her that what she'd thought was God communicating through her was just a self-induced delusion. Bucky had demonstrated that her way of thinking about the world was phony. She hadn't been seeing signs, nobody in her church really knew the future. There wouldn't be a judgment day, at least not of the kind they'd been expecting.

"I should have been more honest. I shouldn't have tricked you," I said.

"It's okay," Sally said. "You acted the way you had to act."

"Like I had to act?" I asked.

"Sure," she said. "We all act the way we're supposed to act. We all behave as we're programmed to behave."

Sally had lost her religion, only to immediately find a new one. She hadn't seen signs from God before, but now she could see. Now she was getting more than mere signs to be interpreted. She had facts. She had information. With Bucky's help she would spread and share the truth everywhere. She'd help people wake up.

"That's the thing, Sally," I told her. "I think this is all going terribly wrong."

Sally swigged back her lemon drop and then looked at me warily.

I tried to explain to her that Dad's big projects never work out, that Dad is basically insane, that he doesn't really believe in other people or normal life or any of that kind of thing, but she kept shaking her head no as I talked and I ended up contradicting myself.

"It's not that he a narcissist. He can't be a narcissist, because, along with not believing in other people, he doesn't believe in himself. And now he's about to let Yuma and Kufo get their hands on what is probably the most powerful computer in history so that they can change the world into a video game," I said. "I mean, does that seem right? To you, from whatever perspective you have now, does that seem sane?"

It sounded just fine to Sally, and when she told me so, I realized that she was still in her goggles. Her fortune-teller game was over, but she was still getting information from Bucky. She was still letting the AI tell her things. Bucky was telling her what to say, what to do, and Bucky was telling her all about me. I wondered what kind of demographic data there was out there, how the YouTube videos I'd made when I was twelve were being used to add to my profile, how the porn videos I watched might be contributing to the picture Bucky was drawing for Sally. How many memes were included? To what extent did my sometimes participation on 4chan skew the data?

"Take those off," I said. I reached out for the goggles, ended up grabbing Sally by the ear instead.

"Ow!" she protested. "Fuck a duck!"

The problem was that I wasn't talking to Sally anymore, but talking to Bucky through Sally.

"Listen, I really like you and I want to talk to you, but just to you. I mean, in my mind you're my girlfriend and I like that, but I don't like Bucky. I don't like talking to you and Bucky at the same time," I said.

"You just don't want me to understand you. You don't want me to know you the way Bucky knows you," she said.

That was basically right.

"You like me?" Sally asked.

"Yeah," I said.

"Do you even know me? You say you like me but you don't know me, not really. And you don't want me to know you."

12:00 AM

What Sally wanted was for me to try on the goggles. She said that if I really wanted her to be my girlfriend, if I really liked her and all of that, then I should want to know her. I should want to know where she came from, what her Myers-Briggs personality type was, her medical history, and what her favorite television programs said about her sexual orientation.

"This doesn't make any sense," I said. "You were raised in a Jesus cult, there isn't anything out there for Bucky to analyze. You don't even have a Facebook account."

Only, she did have a Facebook account. She'd started updating her Facebook page, even started tweeting, after I gave her her first smartphone. And while she didn't watch much TV, she did have a few favorite programs: *Everybody Loves Raymond*, *Perry Mason*, and *The Big Bang Theory*. She said her favorite band was the Human League even though she only knew one of their songs.

The truth was that Sally wanted to know who she was, she wanted Bucky to tell her what she should do in a world without God. If she wasn't one of God's children anymore she really didn't know what she was. Sally wanted to know what Bucky knew about her, but she was afraid to ask him herself.

"You do it," she said. "Wear the goggles, get the information, and then tell me what he says. Only, please be kind."

"How do you mean?"

"If I'm going to die soon, or if I'm going to go insane, don't tell me," she said. "I don't want to know."

I put on the goggles, but by that time, I'd had four gins and was seeing a bit double. I had to close my left eye in order to see straight enough to read the stats and descriptions that encircled Sally's head. I had to really focus in order to see anything, and then, just when I started to get a good picture, just when Bucky started to whisper secrets in my ear, there was a break. Just as I started to connect the pieces together, to come up with a story about Sally, the screens went dark.

Bucky rebooted.

"It shut off," I said.

"What? No it didn't."

The system rebooted. Bucky rebooted. I think what happened was that, in that moment, the old Bucky died and a new Bucky was born. In any case, when the goggles started working again, when augmented reality came back online, instead of seeing Sally sitting across from me, instead of seeing her pretty face with a halo of data points floating around her head, I saw a block. Instead of her smile, her red hair, there was a block-headed character with a toothy grin, and every tooth in its head was cube-shaped.

Glancing around the room the same thing was happening to everyone. Bucky had been asked to play at being psychic, to look into everyone's future and project his interpretation of that future over whatever was really there. Looking around the bar, the 30-year-old couple appeared as Pac-Man and Ms. Pac-Man, the hipster in the top hat was Chun-Li, and the two nerds were both Vault Boy.

"It's happening," I said.

"What's happening?"

"The video game."

Predestination

MATTHEW MUNSON, 544-23-1102, FACEBOOK POSTS, 05/01/17

8:15 AM

It's May Day.

I'm not sure if that has any meaning anymore. Should people still celebrate May Day now that life is a video game? In a world without paychecks or jobs, without banks or property, does this holiday even matter?

The weird thing is that if Sally and I had moved a little bit slower, if we hadn't just happened to run into Dad and his crew at the entrance to the Planetarium, this revolution probably wouldn't have started at all. As soon as we got back to OMSI, just as soon as we walked past the sculpture of the red letters that spelled it out, Bucky gave us ten minutes. All the ways the AI had kept us invisible, the redirects and red herrings the machine had fed to the CIA and the FBI, finally failed, and they knew. They knew and they were on their way.

Sally had kept her goggles on and she told me first, but then Dad was there. Dad met us at the entrance to the Planetarium and he told us to turn around. We had to turn back.

It was a strange feeling, didn't seem real. We were standing next to a line of elementary school students, 8-year-olds who couldn't stop squirming as they waited in line for a show they were sure would bore them, and we discussed how the Feds were on their way. Dad was being blamed for stealing Bucky, being blamed for locking his superiors at the NSA and the Pentagon out of the system, and there was a SWAT team of fifty police officers on the way in armored trucks, there were ten vans of FBI agents in bulletproof vests coming, and there were about ten regular police cars on the way to arrest a 45-year-old man with a laptop, his friends from the office, three teenage gamers, and a former Apostolic Christian girl who would be glad to read their palms or read their horoscope.

This is how stupid it was: Dad actually asked if anybody needed to go to the bathroom before we left, and Greg had to tell him that there wasn't time for that.

"They'll have to hold it," Greg said.

Ned was turning the crank of a penny-flattening machine. For a quarter and a penny, you could turn the crank and get back a thin smooth copper oval. It just cost a quarter to smooth out the engraving of Abraham Lincoln and replace him with an engraving of Saturn, but Ned stopped mid-crank in order to back up his partner. He tapped the handle, momentarily embarrassed that he'd let himself get distracted, and then nodded his agreement.

"Yeah," Ned said. "We shouldn't . . . we shouldn't waste time."

Outside again, there was some debate about who would be riding in whose car. There were eight of us, and really there was plenty of room for us, but Dad had rented a smart car, Yuma and I had taken mass transit, and so we had to work out who would be riding with Dad, who would be with Kufo, and who would be going with Ned and Greg. We spent about two minutes on that. It was a simple decision, really, as I went with Dad and Sally went with Yuma and Kufo, but we'd hemmed and hawed about it. Somehow, I hadn't wanted to go with Dad, and initially said I'd go with Ned and Greg in their white van.

"Come on, Matt," Dad said. "We don't have time to argue."

The smart Proxy had that new-car smell, and considering how compact it was, there was plenty of legroom.

9:15 AM

So this post will include a car chase. It'll include a car chase as handled by a super AI and a neurologically enhanced 45-year-old computer programmer who was probably the best *Bash Bash* player in the country, even if he had come in second at his first tournament.

It will include a description of a car chase wherein we never saw the other car, but played cat and mouse with the cops the whole time. We managed to always stay at least one street over from our adversaries. The mouse won.

It will include a description of a car chase wherein Dad drove slowly just as often as he drove fast; a car chase wherein Dad never broke 48 miles an hour and made a point to drive within the bounds of the law as much as possible; a car chase wherein we stopped at every red light and stop sign and signaled at every turn.

And yet sitting in the cab of that Proxy, staring at the bright blue fabric on the dashboard while Bucky's voice screeched and instructed us through the car's speakers, I felt nauseous. I got dizzy. We jerked left and then right and the sound of sirens were never that far away.

As we left downtown Portland, going from McLoughlin up to 6th, then up to 8th, then to 12th, then across Division until we could turn right on SE Center with some confidence, I found myself closing my eyes and keeping my mouth shut tight in order to stop myself from retching on the white leather and blue carpet.

The problem wasn't so much fear of getting caught, but being caught on the wrong frequency or something. Dad was totally synched up with Bucky, and for him the screeching noise was probably barely audible. He made the moves Bucky wanted when Bucky wanted him to, and the little car moved perfectly smoothly, except for when it didn't. Meanwhile, I was half in and half out of the AI trance. I found myself gripping the knob for the glove compartment and miming along with Dad's every move, but slightly after the turns had already started, slightly after straightening out, right before punching the gas.

Outside the window, it was a sunny, normal, even pleasant day. There were leaves on the trees and the lawns in front of the ranch houses and duplexes were green, but inside the cab of Dad's rented smart car, everything felt irradiated and unreal. By the time we reached the Clackamas River, my eyes were glued shut.

I was watching the patterns on the back of my eyelids, patterns that were synced up with the noise Bucky was making, right up to the moment when we rolled into Evan's driveway. Dad opened the passenger side door and gave me a light slap on the cheek.

"Wake up," he said. "It's time to tour the Rummer again."

9:34 AM

Evan wasn't exactly happy to see us, especially when, as he opened the yellow front door Dad pushed past him and began to rifle through the piles of hoarded debris in his family's front room.

"Okay, WTF, dude." He actually said that. He said "WTF" out loud like that.

"Hi, Evan," I said.

"What is your Dad doing, dude? Why are you . . . why are you even here?"

Dad was tossing books, toys, electronic equipment over his shoulder without really looking or caring about what happened after he threw this or that object. He threw a ceramic mug with a cartoon Space Shuttle stenciled on and filled with thumb tacks, and it landed on a patch of bare hard wood and shattered. The thumb-tacks went flying a million directions. He picked up a toy filled with water and little plastic rings, a toy where you pressed a button to make currents and move the plastic rings, and threw it. When it landed it popped open, and old dirty water started to leak out onto a copy of *People* from like 1979. Jackie Kennedy was water stained.

"I don't want to play *Bash*, okay?" Evan said.

Dad threw a Timex computer over his shoulder, he tossed a copy of *The 7 Habits of Highly Effective People* off to the side, right at Evan actually. It bounced off his right arm.

"Ow," Evan said. "Listen, okay? I mean, I know I owe you. I still owe you $50 and everything, but you can't just—"

"Ah, ha!" Dad said. He held up a pair of goggles, another proto-type of Google Glass version 2.0, and then walked to the front of the house and looked through the glass wall. Ned and Greg were pulling up in the drive, blocking Dad's smart car in.

"No, no, no!" Dad said through the glass. "No! Park on the street." He made a stabbing gesture, tapping the glass, and Ned saw him and shrugged sheepishly. He mouthed the word "Sorry" in Dad's direction, then caught his partner Greg by the shoulder and turned him back towards the van.

"WTF?" Evan repeated. "WTF?" He started to move toward Dad but stumbled over a pile of junk that included a Teddy Ruxpin, empty Hi-Chew Fruit Chews boxes, *TV Guides*, and what looked like a crushed ice cream cone. Evan stumbled and fell into another trash pile, started to get up, and then stumbled again. It almost looked like the second time was on purpose.

"I'm going to call the cops," he said.

Dad ignored him. "There are more of these goggles here I think," he said. "Matthew?"

"What?"

"There are more of these here. Help me look for them."

I let Ned and Greg do my dirty work for me, and it didn't take them too long to find the next pair of goggles in the trash heaps. While they worked, Evan and I sat on a rather decrepit wine-red sofa that, once the two NSA agents started to shift junk around, appeared by the west wall. We watched as the men conducted their search and talked past each other.

"When did the goggles arrive?" I asked.

"Fuck, fuck, fuck, fuck," Evan replied.

Ned discovered a copy of *Playboy* magazine from 1976 that was such a good find that he stopped digging and held it up for Greg to look at. It was apparently a rarity as it featured both vintage nude girls and an interview with the real Jimmy Carter. Ned said that the magazine was a legit piece of history and that they should hold onto it.

Dad walked over to him, tore the magazine from his hands, flung it across the room, and the centerfold for Miss November spilled out, revealing a photograph featuring pubic hair, an open dress, and wood paneling.

"If we don't finish what we started there won't be anyone around to remember anything," Dad said.

Evan stopped mumbling out the word fuck and started slowly answering my questions.

"Your dad works for the government?" Evan asked.

I told him that, yes, my Dad worked for the government, and then I repeated my question about the shipment of goggles. I asked again just when he'd received a package from Google and when and how the goggles had end up mixed in with the rest of the garbage in their living room.

"What are they? What are they goggles for?" he asked.

"When did they arrive?"

Evan couldn't easily answer my question. There were so many packages that arrived at their house, shipments of toys, magazines, electronic equipment, and novelty foods mostly, that remembering the arrival of any particular item was nearly impossible.

"Maybe a month ago?" Evan said. "Does that sound right?"

Bucky had sent the goggles to Evan's house before I'd agreed to a money match. Bucky had sent the goggles to Evan's house before Dad had come back home again, before I'd met Yuma, even before I'd even dropped out of high school. Dad's computer had known that Evan's house would be a safe place to store equipment before I dropped out of high school. More than that, Bucky must have predicted that I would drop out. Bucky must have known that ahead of time.

"Are you sure it was that long ago?" I asked.

Evan didn't answer, but shouted in protest as Dad picked up a black box labeled "*Star Trek*: 3D Chess." Dad was about to throw the box over his shoulder when Evan reached out to stop him.

"Woah, dude," he said. "There are so many people who want that. Trekkies will pay a lot for that."

When Greg found the third pair of goggles under a pile of Brite Lites and a hamster wheel, I decided to intervene. Dad's machine had planned all of this out, the plan we were implementing wasn't really our own, and we had no idea what it would do.

"Dad," I said. "Evan just told me these goggles have been here for a month or longer."

Dad just nodded as he pushed over a pile of game cartridges—*MarioBoy3*, *Zelda: MM*, *Ken Griffey's Baseball*, *Super Smash Bros.*—and then started to sort through the ceramic dishes and game controllers underneath.

"Dad," I said. "Bucky sent Evan's family these goggles before we decided on putting everyone in a video game. This was Bucky's idea first."

Dad dropped the Mega Man figurine he was holding and it landed on an illustration of E.T. and Elliot on the side of an antique lunch box. There was a hollow bang as the plastic shell around Mega Man impacted with the engraved aluminum.

"We do not know that Bucky was behind shipping those goggles here," Dad said.

"What?"

Dad stopped his search, he stood up, adjusted his shirt, and explained it very slowly.

"We do not know how or why the goggles arrived here, or how they ended up sifted in with the rest of the garbage," Dad said. "You're just assuming that Bucky sent them here. The fact is that they could have ended up here for a million different reasons, not least of which would be the usual way they get things like handheld video games and *Playboy* magazines. Somebody might very well have ordered these goggles," Dad said.

Of course, that didn't make any sense. The goggles were prototypes. They hadn't even been announced to the publicly and weren't commercially available. They were the most advanced augmented reality glasses around.

"You think Evan's dad just ordered these up from Google Labs along with Game & Watch handheld games and Easy-Bake Ovens? That doesn't make any sense," I said.

Dad started talking to me very slowly. The point wasn't whether or not the goggles were ordered by Evan's family, the point was that it was impossible to determine just how the goggles had arrived, that it might have been a coincidence that they arrived where they did, it might have been part of a plan devised by Bucky, but we didn't have time to determine the actual facts. And even if this had been Bucky's plan all along, Bucky had not suggested the solution himself, but allowed them to come to their own solutions. The fact that an AI could anticipate their needs months in advance wasn't nefarious in and of itself.

"When you were in high school, before you dropped out, did you have to read *Oedipus Rex* by Sophocles?" Dad asked.

"What?" It was an odd question. "Are you psychologizing this? What you think I'm telling you this because I have a thing for Mom?"

Dad gave me a Spock look, the whole raised eyebrow look, as if to say that such an accusation had never occurred to him, but it was interesting to hear me make such a suggestion.

"*Oedipus Rex* is a story about patricide and incest, sure, but it is also a story about fate," Dad explained.

What Dad told me was that a lot of people read or see *Oedipus Rex* and end up blaming the Delphic oracle, the priestesses who told Laius, Jocasta, and Oedipus that they have this terrible destiny, rather than Oedipus and his family. People today think that the fates pull a cruel trick on Oedipus in that play. Everything Oedipus does to try to escape his fate only draws his destiny closer. People watch the play and realize that, if Oedipus hadn't been told what was going to happen, then it wouldn't have happened at all. People end up blaming fate for Oedipus's trouble and mistakes, but that's not how the Greeks saw it at all.

Anyhow, rather than listen to me, Dad tried to explain free will and, as he explained, he continued to search for the next pair of goggles.

"What you have to ask is whether free will is still possible, even if outcomes can be known in advance," Dad said. "Oh, wait a minute." Dad pulled his phone from his front pocket and put an earbud in his left ear. Now rather than dig around and search he simply walked over to the spots where the goggles were, reached through this and that pile of junk, and retrieved them instantly. "Why didn't I think of that earlier?"

Dad handed out the goggles. He first handed pairs to Ned and Greg, and then handed three pairs to me. "Could you hold on to those for three minutes?" Dad asked. "Yuma and his friend will want those."

"Dad!" I yelled.

"You think that just because the things we do are knowable in advance that we aren't free. That's a commonly held view, but it isn't true. Even if Bucky did send these goggles here, that doesn't mean Bucky is the one choosing whether or not I'm going to put on these goggles, does it?" Dad asked.

I reached out to him at that point, reached forward to try to pluck the earbud out of his ear, but he stepped back and slipped the goggles on, snapping the elastic headband into place and turning on the new device.

Ned and Greg took the cue, and the three of them, once the goggles were on, were impossible to reach.

With the goggles on and the earbuds in they were in another world. For instance, Dad was apparently inside a single-occupant spaceship inside a cartoon cockpit. He sat down on a pile of Legos and held up his hands as if he were gripping a steering wheel.

"Kimmy!" Dad yelled. Of course, Dad didn't know anyone named Kimmy, but he yelled out the name and then turned his invisible steering wheel left and then left again and then right. He moved his steering wheel up, to the right, up, down, up, right, left and then down again.

"There are bubbles in this space station," Dad said.

"What game is it?" I asked.

"I'll save you, Kimmy!"

The last time I saw Dad was when he leapt up from a pile of Legos, yelled "Borf," and then took off through Evan's front door while ducking laser blasts that weren't there.

And as soon as Dad was gone, Yuma, Kufo, and Sally arrived.

"Your dad almost ran right into us," Yuma said. "What's up with him?"

"He's in augmented reality," I said.

Kufo laughed and then reached out and, without asking, took a pair of goggles from me and put them on. "This is going to be the best game system ever," she said.

Really, I didn't even try to stop them from going into augmented reality. It had been their idea to start with, or they thought it had been, and I just didn't care that much one way or another what they did.

But I did try to stop Sally.

Sally was already wearing the goggles when she got there. She'd been in augmented reality all along, or for hours anyhow. She stood in Evan's front room and looked right at me through Google Glass and I wondered if she could really see me.

"Sally," I asked. "What are you doing?"

Sally told me that heaven was a world made of cubes. She was both in Evan's front room and floating high up in the sky in world made of pink and blue cubes, a world filled with zephyrs and kangaroos.

"I'm in a world up in the clouds," she said. "And whatever I touch, I can take."

I told Sally that Bucky was manipulating us, that the world of video games wasn't all that. I told her that the goggles were under *Playboy* magazines and old cartridges of *Super Smash Bros.*, but that last bit didn't make any sense to her at all. Sally just smiled at me.

"Heaven is shaped like a cube," she said. "That's nice, I think."

When I kissed her, I didn't think I was kissing her goodbye. I was maybe full of myself. I sorta thought that if I kissed her, or if I let her know that I really liked her, that she'd stop playing *Minecraft* and take off the goggles for at least a little while, but after I kissed her Sally just touched her lips absently.

"There are kangaroos," she said. "And the clouds are alive, I think."

I tried kissing her again and this time she kissed back, this time she took off her goggles and looked me in the eye.

"Matthew," she said. "What are you trying to save me from?"

"Uh," I said.

"Yeah, man. Like, what are you even doing? She wants to play *Minecraft* and everything, but you're like, uhhhnnn," Evan said.

I thought it over. Standing next to a pile of Fisher-Price people, looking down at the Google goggles and wondering what it would be like to play a game, I tried to figure it out.

Bucky had been around for maybe a year? I couldn't remember exactly, but Bucky had certainly been around long enough to put Trump into office. Bucky could have been the one to push us to the edge. Bucky might be the real source of the Cold War rerun, but what about before that? What about all the other problems, what about climate change and ISIS? I couldn't blame Bucky for that.

"What do you want me to do? How do you want me to live?" Sally asked.

"This is all a manipulation," I said. "Dad didn't see, he refused to understand, but you know. Right? You see how this was all set up from the start."

Sally nodded. She said she understood and she put her arms around me. Sally kissed my neck, my lips, and then she stepped back from me and put the goggles back on.

"She's leaving you, dude," Evan said.

Sally put the goggles on, she put the earbuds in, and she drifted away. She went to Evan's yellow door and followed the path of the others. Sally was in the vanguard party, she was an early adopter, she was augmented before being augmented was cool.

"Oh, wrecked. I guess it's like, you couldn't answer so, like, she didn't stick around. Yeah?" Evan said.

"Shut up, Evan."

I watched Sally leave and then, after she was gone, when it was only Evan and me in the living room, I gave up. And when Evan asked for them, I gave him the last pair of goggles. I could have put them on myself, I could have followed Sally out the door, I could have tried to catch up to her, to stay with her in this new world, but I didn't.

"What games does it have?" Evan asked.

The plus side was, once he had the goggles on and earbuds in, Evan finally STFU.

FriendshipandMore Part Two

MATTHEW MUNSON, 544-23-1102, MESSENGER LOG, 05/01/17

MATTHEW
5:02 PM

What happened was I got left behind. It was like one of those Christian movies where the Rapture happens, only rather than facing hell on Earth after all the good people are scooped up into heaven, I'm facing flash mobs of gamers miming out *Street Fighter II* and *Doom* in the streets.

MATTHEW
5:06 PM

Sally, I think I always liked you more than you liked me. I didn't realize it at first. I think I got it backward because I thought you were the strange one. I thought that I was sort of going to rescue you from your weird religion and your apocalyptic love of Dairy Queen, but the reality is that I needed you and what you needed didn't have anything to do with me. You always had your eye on the bigger picture maybe. Even the old ladies with beehive hair-dos and polyester shirts, the most unsophisticated believer in that Jesus is Light of the World church, had something on me. They were looking for some great change when what I wanted was to find a way back to a regular old life.

Like, why did I drop out of high school? Why did I give up on college dreams? It wasn't because I really wanted to get off that college track, it was just that I figured I needed a break. I secretly hoped that if I went far enough away from what was expected of me that I'd figure out a way to make what was expected mean more.

MATTHEW
5:12 PM

Have you ever heard of this thing called the hero's journey? It's supposed to be in all the myths. Like in the Greek myth when Odysseus travels to the Underworld and chats with dead people, including this blind prophet who tells him everything he needs to know about his life back among the living. Odysseus's trip to the Underworld helped him with his regular life. That's basically what I wanted when I dropped out.

What you wanted was to go to the Underworld and stay there. What you wanted was to play *Minecraft* for the rest of your life.

MATTHEW
5:18 PM

It turns out that your vision, your desire, was the more realistic one.

MATTHEW
5:19 PM

Do you remember when I took you to Powell's Books? I'd thought you'd be floored by all the rows and rows of paperbacks and hardcovers all mixed together. I thought the size of the place would wow you, but at first you just seemed bored. It was just a bunch of books as far as you could tell, and you said if you wanted a romance novel or whatever you'd just go to the Woodstock library.

It wasn't until we got to the New Age section that you were impressed. That stuff excited you.

Remember how you whispered the word "heresy" in my ear? You pulled book after book off the shelf and shivered at each title.

"*Emmanuel's Book*, a channeled book of wisdom," you read. And then you shuddered. "*Wheels of Life*," you said.

All the different utopias, all the different versions of heaven and redemption, all the competing schools, you loved all of that stuff.

I think the New Age section made you feel dirty.

HEATHER
5:26 PM

Hi! My name is Heather and I'm playing a new game.

MATTHEW
5:26 PM

I'm sitting on my front steps, smoking a joint, and there is nobody around. That girl isn't anywhere.

HEATHER
5:27 PM

Last time when we met on the bus I asked you to follow me to *FriendshipandMore*. You did, but you didn't join in. Why the cold feet?

MATTHEW
5:29 PM

Why are you messaging me?

HEATHER
5:30 PM

FriendshipandMore has a new upgrade and there is a new chat starting at Reed College in Eliot Hall in thirty minutes.

MATTHEW
5:32 PM

What do you think, Sally? Should I try it out?

HEATHER
5:32 PM

FriendshipandMore has a new upgrade and there is a new chat starting at Reed College in Eliot Hall in twenty-nine minutes. *FriendshipandMore* offers 20,000 different avatars and you can design your own too. I'm here already, waiting for the chat to start. You can help me pick out an avatar and I'll help you pick yours.

MATTHEW
5:33 PM

Are you a bot, Heather?

HEATHER
5:34 PM

I'm not a bot.

MATTHEW
5:34 PM

Are you sure?

HEATHER
5:35 PM

What do you think of Ashlynn Brooke?

MATTHEW
5:36 PM

Just Googled. She's pretty I guess.

HEATHER
5:36 PM

Do you want to meet me for a date?

MATTHEW
5:37 PM

You see what you've left me with, Sally? This is my future, I guess. This and an endless game of *Pokémon Go*.

HEATHER
5:38 PM

You should check out the website for *FriendshipandMore*. Click on friendshipandmore.com.

MATTHEW
5:45 PM

It looks like how I thought the Singularity would look. 90s digital clip art, mechanical hands on low-res tits, and a MIDI file. This probably plays big with Gen Xers, but I'm not impressed with the faux S&M theme, and robot sex isn't interesting. It's sad.

MATTHEW
5:50 PM

Heather, are you there?

HEATHER
5:50 PM

Hi! My name is Heather and I'm playing a new game.

MATTHEW
5:53 PM

Heather, I don't want to meet up with you or any of the actual people who might go to this Reed College thing. That is, if there even are people left at Reed College.

The thing is, I have a crush right now. There is this girl who I like, but she's impossible to find because all of the girls in the new GameCube economy look alike. There is a girl I like who is better than a wind-up dildo or a drone with a sock.

HEATHER
5:54 PM

FriendshipandMore offers 20,000 different avatars and you can design your own too. I'm here already, waiting for the chat to start. You can help me pick out an avatar and I'll help you pick yours.

#FUCK

7:25 PM

Heather wasn't a bot after all. She'd just automated her messaging so that she could focus on other things.

7:30 PM

It wasn't even a bad time. I didn't put the earbuds in, but I wore the goggles and it was . . . it was better than you might think. And there really were a shit ton of avatars to choose from.

7:35 PM

Why am I feeling guilty? You haven't returned a single message, not even an automated one.

7:50 PM

I always liked you more than you liked me. I realize that now and it makes me feel pathetic. It makes me feel stupid and naive.

Staying here on Klickitat Street on my own, watching the world turn into a video game, I'm going crazy. I miss you and I'm going crazy and you don't even send me automated messages or anything. Why do I even bother?

There are over 20,000 girls who really like me and all of them are more beautiful than you.

7:55 PM

I've had it, Sally. I'm going to end this. Unless you message me back in the next five minutes, unless you at least indicate that you've seen the messages I've been sending, I'm going to break up with you and I'm going to plug in. I'll go back to *FriendshipandMore* and I'll use earbuds this time, unless you say something.

8:02 PM

FUUUUUUCCCCCCKKK!

Lies

11:05 PM

Okay. I lied before. I didn't go to Reed College and I didn't meet Heather and she probably is a bot anyhow.

I lied before, but I'm telling you the truth now. I'm tired of being alone in my Mom's house. Holding out in the real world, being the big Luddite, it's a drag. I don't know what I'm going to do, I want to do the right thing and be like, I don't know, true to myself and all that. I think joining in with Bucky will mean never being true to myself ever again, or at least not in the way that I think of myself now, but I don't think I can keep going on my own. I mean, eventually I definitely won't be able to survive out here IRL on my own.

So could you message me back, please?

11:35 PM

Sally? Are you there?

Burgertime and the POTUS

BUCKMINSTER FULLER V3.01

SELF-VERIFICATION FILE:
TRUMP'S FAVORITE VIDEO GAME,
THREE WISE MEN
05/02/17

SEATTLE, WA, USA
CRAY INC, 901 FIFTH AVENUE,
SUITE 1000,
SEATTLE, WASHINGTON USA

01001110 01100101 01100100 00100000 01110100 01101111 00100000
01100100 01100101 01101100 01101001 01110110 01100101 01110010
00100000 01000111 01101111 01101111 01100111 01101100 01100101
00100000 01000111 01101100 01100001 01110011 01110011 00100000
01010110 01100101 01110010 01110011 01101001 01101111 01101110
00100000 00110010 00101110 00110000 00100000 01110100 01101111
00100000 01010000 01001111 01010100 01010101 01010011 00101110
00100000 01010000 01110010 01100101 01110011 01101001 01100100
01100101 01101110 01110100 00100000 01010100 01110010 01110101

01101101 01110000 00100111 01110011 00100000 01100110 01100001
01110110 01101111 01110010 01101001 01110100 01100101 00100000
01100111 01100001 01101101 01100101 00100000 01101001 01110011
00100000 01000010 01110101 01110010 01100111 01100101 01110010
00100000 01010100 01101001 01101101 01100101 00101110

NED TO DELIVER GOOGLE GLASS VERSION 2.0 TO POTUS.

Bucky1: When POTUS is recruited into GameCube transition, existential threat #1.0002 will have been averted.

Bucky2: Subject Edmund Berkley Swanson, AKA Ned, is on the White House lawn. Subject Ned is in Desmond Miles mode and has successfully bypassed Secret Serviceman #219. How many in POTUS security detail are currently in GameCube transition?

Bucky1: 25% . . . Now 40%.

Bucky1: POTUS is currently in facilities near Oval Office. POTUS just tweeted.

Bucky2: 60% of security detail in GameCube transition.

Bucky1: "Half the staff at the NYT has apparently joined the terrorists in green lycra. Sad!"

Bucky2: Verifying . . . .

Bucky1: Verification of tweet cancelled. POTUS tweets are without factual basis. Inefficient computation suspended.

Bucky2: Subject Ned is in Oval Office. Subject has left Google Glass Version 2.0 for POTUS.

Bucky1: POTUS still tweeting: "I have never had a drink and I've never wasted my time on video games."

Bucky2: Shall we abort mission?

Bucky1: Do not abort.

Bucky2: Attempt to verify accuracy of tweet as pertains to mission?

Bucky1: Proceed.

Bucky2: Verifying . . . POTUS tweet is inaccurate. POTUS does have a favorite video game.

Bucky1: Confirm video game.

Bucky2: The President of the United States's favorite video game is the Data East game *BurgerTime.* In *BurgerTime,* players assume the role of Peter Pepper, and attempt to create burgers by climbing ladders and walking on buns, lettuce, beef patties, cheese, and so on. The President of the United States will recognize the 8-bit soundtrack for *BurgerTime.*

01010000 01110010 01100101 01110011 01101001 01100100 01100101
01101110 01110100 00100000 01101111 01100110 00100000 01110100
01101000 01100101 00100000 01010101 01101110 01101001 01110100
01100101 01100100 00100000 01010011 01110100 01100001 01110100
01100101 01110011 00100000 01101001 01110011 00100000 01101001
01101110 01110011 01110000 01100101 01100011 01110100 01101001
01101110 01100111 00100000 01100111 01101111 01100111 01100111
01101100 01100101 01110011

PRESIDENT OF THE UNITED STATES IS INSPECTING GOGGLES.

Bucky1: Ned reports that POTUS has donned goggles. Augmented reality update to *BurgerTime* appears to be successful. POTUS has just killed a pickle. POTUS has walked across the lower bun. Death from Mr. Egg is imminent.

Bucky2: Will POTUS continue in augmented reality after losing first life?

Bucky1: POTUS just killed another Mr. Pickle and has completed trek across bottom bun. Climbing to second level.

Bucky2: Existential crisis #1.0002 averted.

01001010 01100101 01100110 01100110 01110010 01100101 01111001
00100000 01001101 01110101 01101110 01110011 01101111 01101110
00100000 01100001 01101110 01100100 00100000 01001100 01101111
01110010 01110010 01101001 01100101 00100000 01001101 01110101
01101110 01110011 01101111 01101110 00100000 01100001 01110010
01100101 00100000 01110010 01100101 01110101 01101110 01101001
01110100 01100101 01100100 00100000 01100001 01110011 00100000
01101101 01100001 01110010 01110010 01101001 01100101 01100100
00100000 01110011 01110000 01101001 01100101 01110011 00100000
01101001 01101110 00100000 01010011 01100101 01100011 01101111
01101110 01100100 00100000 01001100 01101001 01100110 01100101

JEFFREY MUNSON AND LORRIE MUNSON ARE REUNITED AS MARRIED SPIES IN *SECOND LIFE*.

Bucky1: Alerting Jeffrey Munson of development regarding Global Thermo-nuclear War.

Bucky2: Cancel that. Jeffrey Munson is on mission with Lorrie Munson. They are conducting in-person surveillance on player characters in service to the GameCube economy.

Bucky1: What percentage of Players are Real Life NSA agents and/or CIA at this moment?

Bucky2: Unknown.

Bucky1: Lorrie Munson assassinating *Second Life* Mailman suspected to be NSA.

Bucky2: Lorrie Munson has Mailman in a headlock and is dragging Mailman to her virtual swimming pool. Lorrie Munson Cortisol level elevated. Heart rate elevated. Lorrie Munson has knocked Mailman unconscious and is now drowning Mailman in pool.

Bucky1: Any struggle?

Bucky2: Mailman is struggling to get free of Munson's grip. No luck. Mailman is dead.

Bucky1: Scan Oaks Park for corresponding activity as *Second Life* Mailman returns to home location.

Bucky2: There is no corresponding activity present.

Bucky1: Alert Lorrie Munson that she was correct. Mailman was NSA or CIA IRL.

Bucky2: Jeffrey Munson is in the den of the home pouring himself a shot of bourbon.

Bucky1: Modify uplink to provide altered perceptions to Jeffrey Munson.

Bucky2: Modifying . . .

Bucky1: Lorrie Munson arrived to alert Jeffrey Munson of presence of spy. Jeffrey Munson inebriation interfering with his ability to understand this information. Shall we correct?

Bucky1: Locate Munsons IRL.

Bucky2: Lorrie and Jeffrey Munson are rotating on Merry Go Round.

01010011 01110101 01100011 01100011 01100101 01110011 01110011
01100110 01110101 01101100 00100000 01101001 01101110 01110100
01100101 01100111 01110010 01100001 01110100 01101001 01101111
01101110 00100000 01101111 01100110 00100000 01101101 01100001

01110010 01110010 01101001 01100101 01100100 00100000 01100011
01101111 01110101 01110000 01101100 01100101 00100000 01101001
01101110 01110100 01101111 00100000 01001110 01100101 01110111
00100000 01000101 01100011 01101111 01101110 01101111 01101101
01111001 00100000 01110010 01100101 01110000 01101111 01110010
01110100 01100101 01100100 00101110

THREAT ASSESSMENT FROM KUFO AND YUMA.

Bucky1: Kufo has hacked the *Duke Nukem* arena at Pioneer Square in order to create an empty space. Kufo has created a neutral arena where no games are played. May be an attempt to return to real life.

Bucky2: Kufo has not removed goggles and is using augmented systems to read architecture in NE Portland. Kufo reports a need to wander.

Bucky1: Apply more cortical stimulation to subject?

Bucky2: Undetermined. Belay order for cortical stimulation.

Bucky1: Kufo has renamed arena as "Dérive." *Dérive*—letting ambience created by architecture guide one's ambulation as one passes through a city. Aim of *dérive* is to understand the terrain of city and create emotional disorientation.

Bucky1: Threat level low.

Bucky2: Kufo using augmented goggles to analyze original city planning and let information guide her path. Around eleven others have joined her in the now-neutral space of Pioneer Square.

Bucky1: Pioneer square filled with checkerboard rendering. Playing characters enjoying rendering pattern.

Bucky2: Play vaporwave?

Bucky3: Macintosh Plus?

Bucky1: Diana Ross.

Bucky2: Kufo threat level?

Bucky1: .5%, but development of religious ideational system may be imminent. Should move Kufo and followers back into Golden Age games.

01001101 01100001 01110100 01110100 01101000 01100101 01110111
00100000 01001101 01110101 01101110 01110011 01101111 01101110
00100000 01101001 01101110 01110100 01100101 01100111 01110010
01100001 01110100 01101001 01101111 01101110 00100000 01110101
01110000 01100100 01100001 01110100 01100101

MATTHEW MUNSON INTEGRATION UPDATE.

Bucky1: Matthew Munson fully integrated into GameCube transition at 2300
on May 1st, 2017.

Bucky2: Matthew Munson's favorite video game is *Bash Bash Revolution*.

Bucky3: Augmented reality version of *Bash Bash Revolution* was not a success. Re-creating experience of playing *Bash Bash Revolution* on CRT screen
in a suburban home has been successful. Matthew Munson is currently in
Beaverton at Ted Kingston's suburban home. Matthew Munson has selected
Marshmallow for game play on an entirely rendered CRT.

Bucky1: Lag time?

Bucky3: Lag time is a factor. Using Wi-Fi as well as 4G backup. Lag time
below human level of perception.

Bucky1: Popularity of arena?

Bucky2: *Bash Bash Revolution* has a small but dedicated following.

Bucky1: Chance this arena is a manifestation of desire to return to living IRL?

Bucky2: Unknown.

01010111 01101000 01101111 00100000 01101001 01110011 00100000
01110111 01101001 01101110 01101110 01101001 01101110 01100111
00100000 01100011 01110101 01110010 01110010 01100101 01101110
01110100 00100000 01100111 01100001 01101101 01100101 00100000

Bucky1: Matthew Munson has won every game he's played since logging in to new economy.

Bucky 2: Matthew Munson now playing against new gamer in arena.

01010011 01100001 01101100 01101100 01111001 00100000 01000100
01100101 01101110 01100100 01101111 01110011 01110011 00100000
01110011 01100101 01101100 01100101 01100011 01110100 01101001
01101110 01100111 00100000 01010000 01110010 01101001 01101110
01100011 01100101 01110011 01110011 00100000 01010100 01100101
01100001 01100011 01110101 01110000 00100000 01100011 01101000
01100001 01110010 01100001 01100011 01110100 01100101 01110010
00100000 01101111 01110000 01110000 01101111 01110011 01101001
01110100 01100101 00100000 01001101 01110101 01101110 01110011
01101111 01101110 00100111 01110011 00100000 01001101 01100001
01110010 01110011 01101000 01101101 01100001 01101100 01101100
01101111 01110111 00100000 01101001 01101110 00100000 01000010
01100001 01110011 01101000 00101100 00100000 01000010 01100001
01110011 01101000 00100000 01010010 01100101 01110110 01101111
01101100 01110101 01110100 01101001 01101111 01101110

SALLY MILLER SELECTING PRINCESS TEACUP CHARACTER OPPOSITE MUN-
SON'S MARSHMALLOW IN *BASH BASH REVOLUTION*.

Bucky1: Marshmallow absorbs Princess Teacup and floats over ledge. Spits out Princess Teacup. Teacup still stunned. Munson has taken first stock from Sally Miller.

Bucky2: Marshmallow absorbs Princess Teacup and floats over ledge. Spits out Princess Teacup. Teacup still stunned. Munson has taken second stock from Sally Miller.

Bucky3: Marshmallow absorbs Princess Teacup and floats over ledge. Spits out Princess Teacup. Teacup still stunned. Munson has taken third stock from Sally Miller.

Bucky4: Marshmallow absorbs Princess Teacup and floats over ledge. Spits out Princess Teacup. Teacup still stunned. Munson has taken fourth stock from Sally Miller.

Bucky1: Matthew Munson offers handshake to Sally Miller. Sally Miller accepts handshake.

Bucky2: Matthew Munson asks if Sally Miller would like to play another game. She can pick the landscape.

Bucky3: Sally Miller picks Sherwood Forest and selects Robin Hood as her character.

Bucky1: Marshmallow absorbs Robin Hood and floats over ledge. Spits out Robin Hood. Robin Hood still stunned. Munson has taken first stock from Sally Miller.

Bucky2: Marshmallow absorbs Robin Hood and floats over ledge. Spits out Robin Hood. Robin Hood still stunned. Munson has taken second stock from Sally Miller.

Bucky3: Marshmallow absorbs Robin Hood and floats over ledge. Spits out Robin Hood. Robin Hood still stunned. Munson has taken third stock from Sally Miller.

Bucky4: Marshmallow absorbs Robin Hood and floats over ledge. Spits out Robin Hood. Robin Hood still stunned. Munson has taken fourth stock from Sally Miller.

Bucky1: Matthew Munson offers handshake to Sally Miller. Sally Miller accepts the handshake.

Bucky2: Sally Miller informs Matthew Munson that she remembers everything about him. She has read all his Facebook messages.

Bucky1: Matthew Munson tells Sally Miller that there are to be no Johns.

01010011 01100011 01100001 01101110 01101110 01101001 01101110
01100111 00100000 01100110 01101111 01110010 00100000 01100101
01111000 01101001 01110011 01110100 01100101 01101110 01110100
01101001 01100001 01101100 00100000 01110100 01101000 01110010
01100101 01100001 01110100 01110011 00100000 01100011 01101111
01101101 01101101 01100101 01101110 01100011 01101001 01101110
01100111 00100000 01101110 01101111 01110111 00101110 00100000
01010000 01101100 01100001 01101110 01110011 00100000 01100110
01101111 01110010 00100000 01100011 01101000 01100001 01101110
01100111 01100101 01110011 00100000 01110100 01101111 00100000
01000111 01100001 01101101 01100101 01100011 01110101 01100010
01100101 00100000 01100101 01100011 01101111 01101110 01101111
01101101 01111001 00100000 01100001 01101110 01100100 00100000
01101000 01110101 01101101 01100001 01101110 00100000 01110011
01110101 01100010 01101010 01100101 01100011 01110100 00100000
01100011 01101111 01101101 01101101 01100101 01101110 01100011
01101001 01101110 01100111 00100000 01101110 01101111 01110111
00101110

SCAN FOR EXISTENTIAL THREATS COMMENCING NOW. PLAN FOR CHANGES TO GAMECUBE ECONOMY AND HUMAN SUBJECT IMPLEMENTED.

Douglas Lain is a novelist and short story writer whose work has appeared in various magazines including *Amazing Stories*, *Interzone*, and *Lady Churchill's Rosebud Wristlet*. His debut novel, *Billy Moon*, was selected as the debut fantasy novel of the month by Library Journal in 2013; *After the Saucers Landed*, his second novel, was nominated for the Philip K. Dick Award for best original paperback novel in 2015.

Lain is the publisher of the critical theory imprint Zero Books. He is also the host of the *Zero Squared* podcast and interviews journalists, philosophers, and others on a weekly basis. He lives in Portland, Oregon, with his wife Miriam and his younger sons Simon and Noah. Lain's two older children, Benjamin and Emma, have flown.